THE BEWITCHING HOUR

THE ℬEWITCHING HOUR

A TARA PREQUEL

BY ASHLEY POSTON

HYPERION

LOS ANGELES   NEW YORK

First Edition, August 2023
10 9 8 7 6 5 4 3 2 1
FAC-004510-23167
Printed in the United States of America

This book is set in Adobe Caslon Pro/Adobe
Designed by Phil T. Buchanan

Library of Congress Cataloging-in-Publication Data
Names: Poston, Ashley, author.
Title: The bewitching hour : a Tara Maclay prequel / by Ashley Poston.
Description: First edition. • Los Angeles : Hyperion, 2023. • Series: Buffy
prequel series; book 2 • Audience: Ages 14–18. • Audience: Grades 10–12. •
Summary: Eighteen-year-old Tara Maclay is at the center of a slew of unsolved
murders in her new town, and when the suspicion falls on her, she must find
a way to reconnect with her absent magic and team up with the mysterious
and distractingly cute Daphne Frost, who is hiding more than one secret.
Identifiers: LCCN 2022029794 • ISBN 9781368075459 (hardcover) •
ISBN 9781368075640 (paperback) • ISBN 9781368075701 (ebook)
Subjects: CYAC: Magic—Fiction. • Witches—Fiction. • Secrets—Fiction. •
Murder—Fiction. • Private schools—Fiction. • Schools—Fiction.
Classification: LCC PZ7.1.P667 Be 2023 • DDC [Fic]—dc23
LC record available at https://lccn.loc.gov/2022029794

Reinforced binding
Visit www.HyperionTeens.com

Logo Applies to Text Stock Only

To that kiss—you know the one

AN ANNOTATED HISTORY OF THE BURNING OF THE HELLBORNE WITCH

[EXCERPT FROM P. 48 OF *HELLBORNE, A TRAGIC HISTORY* BY H. G. ABERNATHY]

The history of Hellborne, Vermont, is unlike the history of most other towns. A handful of scholars, like Ermon Merow and Augustus Feehan, claim that Hellborne was a town of miracles in its inception. Other scholars, such as I, believe that it was a town that should have never existed. The town that would become Hellborne was founded in 1716 in a dense grove of fir trees at the fork of a river that looked like a snake tongue, and flourished in the middle of what Vermonters called the Bennington Triangle—a place rife with ill-begotten death.

What is more disturbing is that those founders' names have been lost to time.

We have little left of the original Hellborne, but a single story is preserved—that of the Red Witch.

In 1792, a full century after the famed Salem Witch Trials, during a frigid October when the trees shivered in anticipation for the first coming snow, there lived a healer, a woman of French descent. She rid babes of their fevers and made old cows milk again. She could cure anything—coughs and boils and, rumor was, even heartbreak.

But she had deceived them all.

The brave and noble cardinal, Joseph O'Toole, saw her devilish magic for what it was. He was not wiled by the witch's honeyed smiles. He pulled the veil away from the townsfolk's eyes to reveal what the healer truly was—a wicked and deceitful witch. The coughs she cured because she caused them, the boils she mended because she inflicted them, the heartache she healed because she was the one to enchant their lovers into leaving them. He called her the Red Witch and exposed her lies.

On that brisk and cold Hallows' Eve, the townsfolk took up arms to rid themselves of this disease of a woman. They dragged her out of her cottage where she boiled stories and brewed lies, and tied her to a pyre in the town square, where they watched her burn to cinders.

But with her last breath, she whispered a curse that echoed across the town—"If I burn, then so shall you, and in your hearts I will stay until I return from hell"—and the flames leapt onto the thatched roofs and across the shops in the center of town. By morning, all that was left was ash.

The remaining townsfolk rebuilt everything the fire had destroyed and named the town Hellborne. To this day, the burning of the witch is the only documented case of a pyre execution in the United States. Some believe she was innocent, and Joseph O'Toole a jealous sinner, but others believe that rumor is the witch whispering in your ear.

Some in the town still wait for the witch to return, but as a scholar, I rarely believe in ghost stories.

CHAPTER ONE

A DISH BEST SERVED COLD

HELLBORNE, VERMONT
FRIDAY, OCTOBER 2, 1998

Chad Jackson was going to die tonight.

It was easy to tell. First off, he was scared out of his mind, and scared men rarely made smart decisions. For instance, he was unarmed save for a pocketknife and his own sheer audacity, and he was trespassing on the illustrious halls of Hellborne Academy in the middle of the night.

And—secondly, and most importantly—he was alone.

There were movies about this. There were ways to prevent it. But Chad Jackson had thought he was untouchable until, of course, he realized just how fleshy he really was. His fear was only exacerbated by the deathmark burned onto the back of his hand. It felt like a hundred knives stabbing directly into his metacarpal bones, but he was so afraid he could barely feel anything at all.

The taste of fear was metallic on his tongue, almost the exact flavor of blood, while his ears pounded with the rush of his own staccato heartbeat. His lungs burned as he gasped for breath—he tried to scream.

He managed.

But it wasn't loud enough.

It would never be loud enough.

And no matter which hall he chose, which stairs he climbed, which janitor's closets he tried or doors he locked, Chad Jackson would never shake the shadow behind him.

He didn't know what he'd done to deserve this—wrong place, wrong time, wrong friends? There was a football game going on in the stadium just on the other side of campus. The bright field lights streaked in through the school's stained-glass windows like slices of glass. He just wanted to stash his weed in his locker before his old man gave him another shakedown tonight when he got home, and he knew the school never locked its doors at night.

He'd done this a dozen times before. The halls had always been kinda creepy, the shadows a bit long, but nothing ever chased him before. As one of the apex predators of Hellborne Academy, he was always the one chasing.

One right turn and he could've lived, but he'd decided to take the wrong one. He was never big on horror movies—his first mistake—and from the ones he did watch, he always figured he'd be the final guy about to hook up with the final girl, and they'd escape the chain-saw massacre and make their way into the sunset.

He wasn't final-guy material.

Frantic and fearful, Chad cut back into the locker room, where he'd always found safety, and pushed himself into one of the lockers where he usually shoved the nerds. Burrowed deep. Held his breath.

No one would look for him there.

No one.

He counted his breaths—he listened for his pursuer. For the locker room door to open. For footsteps. For anything. But all he could hear was the billowing sound of his lungs as he breathed in. Breathed out. His heart hammered in his ears. He swallowed the anxious knot in his throat.

Was the coast clear? He pressed himself farther into the locker, his back against the cold metal, the sharp clothes hook poking uncomfortably into his scalp. The locker smelled like gym socks and Old Spice aftershave. So thick it was gag-inducing.

But he was safe. No one was coming.

There were no footsteps—

Suddenly, the locker door wrenched open.

A shadow bent toward him, so close he felt its lips hovering, almost touching his in a kiss.

Then the darkness parted.

"Oh, it's y-you . . ." he said in relief, until he realized it was a lie. His breath caught in his throat. He tried to open his mouth—to scream—but nothing came out. He jerked back. Lurched away as quick as he could.

His heel knocked against the bottom of the locker, and he fell backward—

The metal hook punctured his skull with a sickening *tchk*.

CHAPTER TWO

TARA

Tara Maclay knew four things:

One, her mother was dead.

Two, she was a witch. (Her mother had been as well.)

Three, Vermont was a lot colder than Omaha in October.

And four, being the new girl at a new school was a kind of horror story. And a new girl starting on a *Tuesday*? She might as well have had a target on her back. She wasn't popular, and she wasn't cool enough to be anything else. She didn't play an instrument, she didn't do art, she didn't particularly believe in saving the whales (although she composted and recycled when she could). She didn't want to stand in front of a class full of strangers and tell everyone her name was pronounced *TEH-ra* and not *TAH-ra*, and yet here she was.

She was not built for new places.

She was like a tree. She liked growing roots and digging into where she was at, and every new pH imbalance in the soil sent her in a death-throe tailspin.

And *this* place? It definitely didn't have the kind of soil she was looking to root in. Hellborne Academy looked exactly like it sounded—ominous, exclusive, and highly sought-after. It was housed in a tall cathedral-like building that could've been an abbey once, if abbeys were a thing in Vermont, as gray as the sky behind it, with large red doors at the entrance that yawned open into hallowed marbled halls lined with red lockers and banners that announced this year's homecoming and Halloween festivities. Two stone lions, twenty feet tall, sat on either side of the crimson doors, snarling down at every student who passed under their stone gazes. They made Tara uncomfortable, the way they loomed, as if judging her ill-fitting school uniform—a gray skirt and blazer with a too-big blouse underneath and creaky new loafers that pinched her toes.

Surrounding the school were trees—tall dark firs—as far as the eye could see. She'd never felt so trapped before.

Or so alone.

To say she hadn't wanted to move was an understatement. She hadn't *wanted* to come all the way to Vermont. To leave everything she knew. Her mother's garden. Her mother's hometown.

Her mother's grave.

And she *especially* didn't want to trade it for . . . *this*.

"It's just a school. It's just for a little while," she told herself quietly, curling her fingers around the straps of her book bag as she stood in front of those stone lions. Students streamed in around her, barely giving her so much as a glance. If no one noticed her, maybe she could sneak away. Not go to school at all. Maybe she could—

Someone slammed into her back. She pitched forward, ready

to eat it, when a hand caught her by the arm and pulled her up.

"Oh, hey, hey, sorry about that," said the guy who'd run into her. He held up a football with his other hand. "You were about to get decked there, friend."

She was most definitely not *that.* "Sorry," she mumbled, looking down at her toes.

"No, no, that was my fault. Well, me and that jerk over there," he said, nudging his chin toward the other side of the courtyard, where a group of people sat on the lip of a shallow stone wall. "Moss likes to throw wide, you know?"

"Ah." She turned on her heel to escape into the school, except this guy wasn't going to let her. He took a step in front of her, all guileless smile and excited eyes. The guy reminded her of a golden retriever in a letterman jacket. He was fairly tall, too, and broad, with soft brown hair dyed blond at the tips and mint-green eyes. His white shirt was unbuttoned past what was probably allowed, and he looked in a perpetual state of crumpled-ness, as if he didn't own an iron.

He smiled apologetically. "Sorry, but are you a new kid?"

New kid.

Oh no, she was found out. She steeled her shoulders and stayed quiet.

"You gotta be. I'm really good at faces," he added.

Someone from his group of friends shouted, "Hey, Baz, who's your friend?"

While someone else chanted, "Fresh meat! Fresh meat! Fr—"

A girl snapped, "Shut *up*, Moss!"

"*Ow!* You hit me!" said the boy who had chanted *Fresh meat.*

Tara wanted to melt into the pavement.

Baz rubbed the back of his neck, looking apologetic. "Ignore them, they're a bunch of jerks."

"And what does that say about you, if you're friends with them?" asked someone in a bored tone.

Baz froze, and then grinned bashfully.

Tara glanced over toward the owner of the voice. It belonged to a young Black woman about her age, her hair like an ink blot, tight curls stretching in every direction, her skin a warm brown that matched her kohl-winged eyes. She was beautiful, and she must have felt Tara staring, because she met her gaze.

Tara's skin prickled hotly, and she quickly averted her eyes.

"Aw, c'mon, they're not that bad." Baz laughed self-consciously.

"Sure." The girl pulled her satchel over her shoulder—it was decorated with iron-on patches of bands, including Alanis Morissette, Boyz II Men, Red Hot Chili Peppers, Green Day, and pins from various concerts—looped her longboard under her arm, and entered the school.

Tara let out a breath.

Letterman Jacket Guy—Baz—whistled and bent into her. "*Dude*, Daphne's so cool."

That intrigued Tara, despite herself. "Is that her name? Daphne?"

He gave a serious nod. "Some say the world will end in fire, but I say it'll end when Daphne Frost finally laughs."

"That's . . . ominous."

"I'm a poet—what can I say?" he replied with a shrug, and one of his friends—a girl with springy red hair—called his name with a beckoning wave.

Baz said, "Ah, the Lady Elaine is calling. Better answer her; she hates being kept waiting. I just wanted to say welcome to Hellborne. You're gonna have a hell of a time. See you in class, New Girl."

I have a name. She wanted to correct him, but he was gone before she could tell him. Well, it wasn't like he'd ever talk to her again, anyway.

Tara took a deep breath, steeled her nerves, and climbed the steps into Hellborne Academy. She just had to survive the school year. How hard could that be?

CHAPTER THREE
THAT THING YOU DO

Tara finally found the main office by the time the tardy bell rang.

"Ah, you must be the new kid!" the principal of Hellborne Academy greeted. The man wasn't particularly tall, but he held himself with the sort of confidence that made him seem like a giant. He had a graying goatee the same color as his floppy gray hair, and thick black-rimmed glasses that matched his pinstriped suit.

He was by *far* the most dressed-up person she'd met in a while.

It seemed rather unfair that the adults could wear whatever they wanted, while all the students were stuffed into itchy gray polyester uniforms.

"Principal Greaves," he introduced, jutting out his hand. There must have been a ring on every finger. "And welcome to Hellborne Academy!"

She hesitantly took his hand. "Th-thanks."

"I'm new here, too, so let's both make the best of this year, eh? It really is one *hell* of a place," he said with an overdramatic wink, and then turned to shout the name of some other poor, unsuspecting soul—a guidance counselor who looked like she had too much to do to entertain him—and quickly fled into her office.

"Oh, dear, he's in a chipper mood today," commented the lady behind the front desk when he'd gone. She had thick, round glasses perched on her nose, and frizzy brown hair. "You must be Miss Maclay. Here's your schedule." She pushed a piece of paper across the counter. "I'm sure your homeroom teacher will point you to a student with the same class order as you."

Tara skimmed over the schedule. English. Precalc. Advanced biology. Every class she would've had at her old school, except for one thing—

"Um, I—I think there's been a mistake," she said softly.

The woman's brows furrowed. "A what?"

"A m-mistake—"

"I'm sorry, dearie, you need to speak up."

"Never mind," Tara mumbled.

"Good, good, dearie, if you need anything else, just stop by and let me know!" the woman said happily, but Tara absolutely would *not* be doing that. Not a chance. She would just . . . tough it out through gym. Of all the credits that didn't transfer, why did it have to be PE?

Wasn't it bad enough that she could barely walk in a straight line without tripping over her own feet?

She found her way to homeroom after the tardy bell. The teacher was waiting for her at the door and gave her a disapproving frown. "Ah, there you are! We were getting worried, Miss Maclay."

"Sorry," she mumbled as the teacher let her into homeroom.

"Class!" the teacher—Miss Aberhorn—called, clapping her hands to get everyone's attention. Tara stood beside her at the front of the class, waiting to be introduced. The students simmered down and made their way to their desks. "This is Tara Maclay. She'll be joining us for the rest of the school year. I hope you can all give her a warm Hellborne welcome!"

A few kids mumbled, "Welcome," but most of them ignored her completely, tossing notes across the room, the students in the back reading things underneath their desks, some playing *Snake* on their Nokia and Motorola phones. The ones who *were* paying attention, though, wore expressions she recognized. Even at a new school hundreds of miles away, the look was the same. Like they were predators appraising a fresh piece of meat.

New girl.

Outcast.

Weirdo.

"Well," said the homeroom teacher, "you can take a seat in one of the empty desks in the back— Miss Frost? Could you raise your hand so Tara can see the empty desk beside you? She's new as well."

Daphne gave the weakest of waves. Tara quickly moved down the aisle and sat in the empty desk beside her. Daphne gave a slight shrug, and returned her gaze to the window.

It *was* a nice view. Seniors were on the third and highest floor of the high school, so the windows looked out over the parking lot and the vast sports field to the line of dark firs in the distance. The day was cloudy, gray cotton balls drifting lazily across the sky. It didn't look like rain or snow, but that middling in-between, as if the weather wasn't sure what to become.

Daphne gave off a jittery aura, like she was impatient. About what? To get the day over with? Tara knew what that felt like.

Most everyone else in homeroom had softer auras, distant shimmering clouds around them. Ever since she was little, she could sense that sort of thing. Her mom could, too. It was a rare gift for witches, one that—sometimes—felt more like a curse. Auras were magical fields that emanated from a person, and sometimes they were strong enough for Tara to tell who they were and how they felt. They had a flow, a unity.

The brightest aura in the room came from the other side of the room—Letterman Jacket Guy (was it Baz?), tragically enough. When she hooked her book bag onto the back of her chair, she accidentally caught his gaze, and he grinned and waved at her.

She attempted to ignore him. There was a name carved on the corner of the desk. *Chad Jackson was here.*

Well, where was he now?

Where Tara wanted to be—*not* here.

The intercom dinged.

"Ah, right on time. Everyone, everyone, pay attention!" the teacher cried, clapping her hands to quiet the class.

Then the principal's voice came over the intercom: "Good morning, Hellborne Academy! Please stand for the Pledge of Allegiance. . . ."

They were the same kind of morning announcements as her old school. The pledge, and then the moment of silence when a few kids bowed their heads and muttered prayers. Tara stared out of the window at the bulbous clouds, and by complete accident, the back of Daphne's neck. There was a birthmark, just behind her left ear. It looked a little like a flower.

The second she found herself staring, she quickly looked away.

"And now here is your senior class president, Hailey Conrad," said the principal over the loudspeaker. There was a rustling on the other end of the microphone before a sweet and bright voice came through.

"Thank you, Principal Greaves! As we all know, October is a big month in Hellborne. The tourists—you know the tourists"—at that, a few students muttered their distaste—"they come every year to help celebrate Hellborne's legacy with us. Even with the recent . . . tragedies . . . I want us to strive to make this year memorable as well!"

Tragedies?

Tara didn't remember her father talking about any recent tragedies, but then again, she didn't really remember much of anything from that long car ride from Omaha to Hellborne.

"Now, I know many of us know the story, but we do have a few new students in our halls—"

To which Daphne muttered, "Might as well put a bull's-eye on us," as half of the students in class turned to look at them both.

Tara angled her face down, shielding her face with a curtain of honey-colored hair.

"—so as per tradition, it's my duty—no, my right!—to tell you the story of our historic town of Hellborne."

Oh my god, she was actually going to tell a story over the intercom. Tara wanted to die. She didn't care about this town's history. She didn't *care* what traditions they followed—the cornfields and haybale rides and scarecrows. Maybe a creepy house or a witchy family or two.

She slid down in her seat as Hailey Conrad told the story of the Red Witch of Hellborne. About a woman who healed the townsfolk and was later burned at the stake for rumors of being a witch. Tara had heard stories like it a hundred times before. Some of them from her own father.

Over the intercom, Hailey continued. "Now, please don't forget to vote for the Red Witch at the football game next Friday! Let's give Hellborne a Halloween to remember!"

Tara turned back around in her chair, scratching her finger over *Chad Jackson was here*. She'd rather *not* have a Halloween to remember, especially if it involved re-creating the night a witch burned.

Now she understood why her father was so intent on moving *here* of all places—they didn't like witches.

They burned them.

And then re-created it every single year just to commemorate the barbecue.

Hellborne, born out of hell.

Or maybe it still was.

For the rest of homeroom, she traced the name on her desk absently, trying not to think of anything at all. The senior class president, over the intercom, went over sports games for the week as well as club meetings, adding that the equine club was looking for a horse that had escaped from the barn, and to keep a lookout for a white mare with a temper.

Then the bell rang for first period, and Letterman Jacket Guy—Baz—popped up out of his seat and waited for her to gather her things. Daphne Frost was quick to leave, so fast that Tara didn't even see her go.

"Lemme guess," Baz said, "you have precalc next with Mrs. Dupont."

She looked at her schedule.

9:15 a.m.–10:45 a.m. | Precalc | Mrs. Dupont | Room 413

A sinking feeling settled in her gut.

He snuck a peek at her schedule and grinned. "Yo! I think we've got the same schedule! Yeah, yeah, then you have biology and English. Sweet. Care to let me show you around? Scout's honor, no ulterior motives."

She studied him doubtfully.

"I promise. I'm not gonna say I'm a good guy, but I am gonna say that someone's gotta show you around, and most people around here? Don't like new kids. C'mon," he added, grabbing her book bag himself and tossing it over his other shoulder. He was tall and broad, like he was built to take a truck to the face and say it was nothing.

"Wait, do we have a-all of the classes together?" she asked, catching up with him in the hall.

"Yeah. I figured they'd slip you into Chad's classes, and that's exactly what they did."

"Chad Jackson?" she guessed, recalling the name on her desk.

"Shh!" He pressed a finger to his lips. "Not so loud."

Not so loud . . . ? She frowned, not sure what that meant until—realization hit her like a brick to the back of the head. "The t-tragedy? Is he—did he . . . ?"

"Bingo," he replied lightheartedly. "Chad was pretty popular, so don't be too offended if people don't like you. It's not you. It just feels like you're taking his place."

"I don't even *want* to be here. . . ."

"Alas, here you are," he lamented with a tragic sigh.

As he led her down the hall to their next class, Tara spotted Daphne Frost exchanging her books at her locker. The inside was decorated like her jacket—with pictures of bands and magazine clippings. Tara hadn't heard of any of them, but then again she didn't really listen to a lot of music, either. She asked, "Did you lead Daphne around the school, too?"

"I did," he confirmed. "She kept trying to ditch me."

She winced. "Oh . . ."

"Eh, not everyone takes to the Bazzerman charm."

Which was something Tara believed. "But why . . . ?"

"Beats me. I like myself—"

"N-no," she interrupted. "Why are you being so nice?"

He opened his mouth. Closed it again. Frowned a bit, as if he wasn't quite sure how to answer the question. Finally, he settled on "Because I know what it's like to be the odd one out. C'mon, the bell's about to ring." He nudged his head toward an adjacent hall. "Mrs. Dupont is a real bitch when it comes to tardies. Don't want to get on her bad side your first day of school, do you?"

"No," she replied, but she also began to suspect that she shouldn't get on Baz's bad side, either.

Because she didn't quite believe him.

No one was this nice just to be nice. Especially not guys in letterman jackets. She didn't need to watch *Boy Meets World* to figure that out.

CHAPTER FOUR
TOIL AND TROUBLE

"**H**ellborne's not so bad," Baz said as she followed him to their second class—English—and Tara was *not* looking forward to it one bit.

Precalc had been horrifying, and she had so much catching up to do from her previous public school. *Apparently* Hellborne Academy was far ahead of any math class she'd taken, so the teacher recommended that she go to the library to find a tutor— there was a group that met there—because she wasn't going to slow down the class just for her.

Which Tara hadn't even asked her to do.

"I can't help you with precalc, but maybe Elaine can?" Baz mused, tilting his head. "I can ask around."

Tara hesitated. "I th-think I can find someone."

"You sure? I know almost everyone. I can probably find someone to cut you a deal. . . ."

"On tutoring?"

"No one does it for free," he said, and she doubted that her father would let her allowance go toward helping her catch up in class. He rarely let it go toward *anything* other than new clothes, and even then, he had to approve of them first.

Tara wanted to go home. And never leave her room again. But then who would cook? Her brother could live off Cheetos, but she certainly didn't want to.

"Lemme know, okay?" Baz said. "I mean, I'm sure someone'll help—"

"Bazzy!" a girl called from a little ways down the hall. A tall brunette with tanned white skin, though everyone's faces at this point were a blur.

"Ah, my fan club awaits. The class is there. See you inside," he added, pointing to the classroom to the left, and slipped away toward the brunette. He threw his arms wide, and the girl went running into his embrace. It was strange, watching everyone else interact with him. They brightened up whenever he came near. Their eyes sparkled. Their smiles widened.

It was almost infectious. *Almost.*

She pulled her backpack higher on her shoulder and slipped into the classroom. The strong smell of soy candles immediately assaulted her nose. Coupled with inspirational posters of cats and celebrities like David Bowie and Whoopi Goldberg reading Goosebumps and *Fahrenheit 451*, it was almost overpowering. There was even an old poster of the animated *Lord of the Rings*, which Tara hadn't known existed until that very moment. The room was cluttered, and she despised the skull that sat on the edge of the teacher's desk at the front of the classroom, a sticky note reading *POOR YORICK!* slapped to its forehead.

As the bell rang, she sat down in an empty desk and took her pencil case and notebook out of her book bag. Students began to wander into the room and sit down in their seats, and to her strange luck, Daphne slid past and sat down next to her. Baz sat on the other side and gave her a grin before a guy called his name and they started chatting about a house party that weekend.

Tara took out her pencil and placed it in the little groove at the top of the desk and aligned her notebook parallel with it.

A short gray-haired woman with leathery white skin and age spots dotting across her arms clipped into the room and clapped her hands for the class to quiet down. She wore shades of red and gray, mimicking the Hellborne spirit colors. Mrs. Albedo, apparently.

"Open up to where we left off," she called, and everyone took out a thick book—*The Tragedies of William Shakespeare*—and flipped it open. Tara glanced around, wondering what to do, when Baz scooted his chair over, his book outstretched— "No, no, Mr. Leto, you're much too distracting. Miss Maclay? Please share with Miss Frost."

Tara risked a look toward her fellow new girl and then slowly picked up her chair and moved over, and Daphne made room for her at her desk. She opened the tragedies to Tara's least favorite—

Macbeth.

The teacher called on a student at the front, who began to butcher iambic pentameter like it was his job.

After a few choice stanzas, Daphne asked in a quiet voice, "So, where did you move from?" She slid a curious gaze to Tara, her deep brown eyes compelling Tara to answer.

"Nebraska," Tara replied, turning the page with the rest of

the class, trying to follow along, but with Daphne so close, she really couldn't. She was distracting in a way that Tara couldn't quite describe. It was like all her nerve endings had fireworks in them. Her fingernails were long, polish a glittery black. "Before that, Utah." And Daphne smelled like lavender and fresh laundry, and her eyelashes were long and dark, and there was a beauty mark on the right side of her purple lips that Tara tried not to stare at—but it was very, very hard. "Y-you?"

"Michigan. Here," Daphne added, holding up her hand and pointing to the crease right below her first finger. "So, how's it been with the golden boy?"

"Th-the who?"

"Bastion Leto." She enunciated his name in that soft, crackly voice of hers. "Seems too good to be true, doesn't he?"

"He says y-you ditched him when he tried to show you around."

She smiled wistfully. "I did. He *hated* it. I don't know, there's just something about him that I—"

"Miss Frost? Would you care to read the passage, since you seem so talkative today?" the teacher called tartly.

Caught, Daphne gave a hard sigh and pushed herself to her feet. She snatched up the book between them and read, *"Double, double toil and trouble; / Fire burn and cauldron bubble . . ."*

A few of the students seated behind Tara bent their heads toward each other. "Maybe we should nominate her as the Red Witch this year," one of them whispered. "Instead of Elaine."

"How about the other girl?" someone else asked in reply. "She could be the witch."

Tara felt her spine straighten. It was instinctive. Her fingers curled into fists. Her knuckles turned white underneath the desk.

"Wouldn't that be hilarious? Elaine would be *furious*. She's been gunning for it since elementary school," another student said.

They were talking about that festival—and who would be voted the Red Witch this year. Tara tried to ignore them as Daphne droned on about fenny snakes and owlet's wings. Perhaps these ingredients were used in darker magic, but in all the spells Tara's mother taught her, those ingredients could be found in any well-tended garden. "*Then the charm is firm and good*. Should I keep reading?"

The teacher waved her hand. "No, no, though we should address the significance of the passage."

To which Daphne replied, "It's the beginning of Macbeth's downfall. If Macbeth had never consulted a witch, then he would still be alive."

"Well, no—"

"Macbeth comes to them every time he needs advice. They move the plot along," Daphne interrupted. "Without the witches, Macbeth wouldn't have descended into evil."

"Well, that could be true . . ." the teacher said hesitantly. "But in the text—"

"In the text, they lead him toward evil every time. Thus, without them, he wouldn't have been evil."

"They didn't," Tara muttered before she could stop herself.

Mrs. Albedo gave her an unexpected look. "Miss Maclay? Do you have an opinion?"

She sank lower in her seat as Daphne turned a curious eye to her. Tara wished she hadn't said anything, but now the entire class was staring and she couldn't *not* say anything. "I—I m-m-me-mean," she began, her tongue tripping over itself. She pressed her mouth closed, and thought of her words, and tried again. "They didn't *lead* him. Th-they warned him what he w-*would* do with their prophecies. They tried to prevent it."

"By telling him?" Daphne replied, shaking her head. "No, they wanted him to follow it. They never told him otherwise."

"B-but he didn't have to," she argued, trying to make her words cooperate, though they battled her with every breath. She knew what she wanted to say, but her brain ran so fast it was hard for the rest of her to keep up. Especially her lips. "He wanted to because he was greedy. He wanted to be the next king. That wasn't their fault."

"So, you're sympathetic to the *witches*?"

"And you're sympathetic to *Macbeth*?"

A hushed murmur swept across the classroom, and Tara realized that she probably should've just kept her mouth shut. Daphne narrowed her eyes, but Tara didn't back down, even though her fists were turning her knuckles bone white. A rock had lodged in her throat so that she could barely breathe.

Then Daphne barked a laugh, dispelling the tension in a single note, and sat down. "Touché, Maclay."

Tara gave her a surprised look. She—she wasn't *mad*? Her father would have been furious with her impudence.

But this isn't home, she had to remind herself, and with it the tension in her shoulders eased. *This isn't home.*

The teacher clapped, oblivious to the tension. "Ah! That was brilliant! See, class? This is what academic discussions are all about! Now, Mr. Leto, could you read the next part?"

And so Baz stood and picked up from where Daphne had left off. "I dunno if I'm smart enough to argue about witches," he added, earning a laugh from the class.

For the remainder of class, neither Daphne nor Tara looked at each other as they flipped the pages and read along, and when the bell finally rang, Tara was the first out of the room. She had never spoken up before, not in class and especially not at home. Not since her mother died. Not since everything changed.

She didn't know what had possessed her.

But whatever it was, she didn't like it—not one bit.

CHAPTER FIVE
A WITCH WITHOUT MAGIC

"I'm home," she called to the empty house. It was a small brick building on Oleander Street with a large oak in the front yard and not enough of a backyard for a garden. Which was probably why her father had chosen this house, though Tara highly doubted she'd ever garden again. It had never really been *her* thing, anyway. It'd always been her mother's.

Her brother must've driven to the library in the next town, since they had no internet, and her father wasn't yet home from work, so she let her guard slip—and then crash to the ground. The first day at school hadn't been as bad as she'd originally feared, but the argument she'd had with Daphne in English class stayed with her for the rest of the day.

Why had she even spoken up? It wasn't like it *mattered* who thought what of the witches in *Macbeth*.

Except . . . they were witches. Like her mom.

Like her, technically. A power that her father said, after her mother died, came from demons. From devil worship. From the strange amalgamation from hell.

It was why her mother had died so early, so tragically.

It was why he refused to let it happen to her, too.

"Do you want to end up like her?" he'd snapped the night her mother had died, as Tara clutched her mother's favorite spellbook and begged him to let her keep one, just one. The others were already in the fire in their backyard, the pages curling to ash. "Do you want to *die* like her? Your magic is demonic! It's *evil*!"

He had tears in his eyes. Tears of rage. And sadness.

But mostly, as he looked at her, there was disgust. Her dad had never looked at her that way before, and in that moment, she felt something inside her swing closed—like a door locking and barring itself on the other side.

She hadn't been able to cast a spell since.

She dumped her satchel by the door in her room. Everything was still in boxes save for the sweaters she'd folded into her dresser drawers and the dresses she hung up in the closet. She didn't have much in the way of things, so it was easy to remember where she hid it—the one bit of her mom her dad didn't know she had.

Tucked in the bottom of the bottommost box. A small leather-bound book that smelled vaguely of lavender and felt like secrets—and you know how secrets feel if you ever kept one, that soft tingling trace of magic at your fingertips, of something that was yours and no one else's, a part of the world only for you. She hadn't opened it since moving up to Vermont; she hadn't read the words inside since months before that, since the door in her heart had locked itself tight.

Her father had taken this book from her, pried it out of her arms, and thrown it in the fire. But the next morning, it hadn't burned like the others. The edges were singed, ash eating at the pages, but it had survived somehow. She had pulled it from the cinders and kept it secret ever since.

Her fingers felt along the edges of the book, and the spine crackled as she opened it, pages falling open to one of her favorite spells.

Tara had always loved magic. She loved it because she loved her mom. She loved it because when she pulled magic through her veins, she finally felt at home in her body. She loved it because, as sure as the sun rose or seeds sprouted, it was a part of her. A part of her mom.

Back then, in the before, her mother had her good days and her bad days. On her good days, she would walk out into the backyard and talk with the flowers in the small garden. Tara sometimes came home and found her in the backyard, and she would help her mom prune the sunflowers and pick the weeds out from between the lavender and wolfsbane and wort root. Back then, her father used to put on music and spin her mother around in the daffodils, and magic would vibrate in the garden like a song.

The magic took to the air around them, this electric living thing that had existed long before them and would long after them. It stretched for eons both ways, into other dimensions, other worlds, other possibilities. There was more than enough magic to go around for small things. Tara later learned that for larger things, she needed to trade with the universe. There were spells to do them, but sometimes the magic needed no words at all. Just a feeling.

Like love, which sent every flower in the garden into bloom when her mother laughed as her father drew her close.

And like grief, when lightning struck down the willow in her late mother's garden.

And in those moments, Tara felt the universe around them and she knew she was magical just like her mom. Like the witches who came before them.

Magic was there and wonderful, and it could do anything.

Until, of course, it couldn't.

And now, without her mom here, the magic was also gone. All of it. She'd tried again and again to summon it to her fingertips, but it never worked.

Even this evening, as she chose one of her favorite spells— one of the easiest ones she'd ever learned—and held out her hand.

She thought about what she wanted, the energies she needed, components, the will. Everything her mother taught her.

And then she whispered, *"O, sun god Apollo, grant me light that I may follow."*

The magic hovered in the air, stagnant. The door in her soul didn't even rattle.

Nothing answered her call. Nothing at all.

She resituated herself on the floor, posture straighter, hand outstretched, and repeated, *"O, sun god Apollo, grant me light that I may follow."*

Silence stretched around her, as if it had forsaken her. As if with her mom gone, she was nothing. No longer magical. No longer her mother's daughter.

There was only a profound nothingness, as if the universe was whispering, *You're alone.*

Anger lit in her stomach. She slammed the book shut and threw it back into the box. She quietly pulled her legs up to her chest, curled her arms around her knees, missing her mom so much that the space she'd left behind felt like a cavern in her chest, and she cried.

CHAPTER SIX
CLUELESS

Lunch was the kind of eat-or-be-eaten affair that swallowed up unsuspecting prey. Yesterday, she'd managed to dodge this debacle because the office had called her in to fill out some health paperwork. Today, she wasn't so lucky. Tara got her lunch and looked out over the wide expanse of tables and student bodies, trying to discern which groups were which. Some were easy to find—the skaters on the far side with their helmets on the tables and skateboards leaning against their chairs; the book nerds with their, well, *books*; the debate club; the theater kids; and then, in the center, as if basking in the beam of everyone else's envy, sat the popular kids, louder than anyone else and—to Tara—a lot more obnoxious.

Baz was, of course, seated at *that* table.

He laughed along with a few other guys—all in letterman jackets, *surprise*—their arms slung around their partners. Baz sat next to a petite girl with glossy blond hair held back with a black chunky headband, and a perfect smile with soft pink lips.

Her aura was at once sharp and stagnant—but the second Tara felt it, her aura faded away.

Strange.

The petite blond turned her head and glanced her way, as if she'd felt her watching—and Tara quickly went in the opposite direction.

She decided on the table with as few students as possible—the ones huddled over an old Game Boy, playing what sounded like *The Legend of Zelda: Link's Awakening*. She only knew the sound because her older brother had been obsessed with the game for the last few months. He played it everywhere. Sitting on the couch. At the dinner table. In bed. On the toilet.

Literally everywhere.

The cafeteria food didn't look appetizing; everything from the vegetables to the meat was varying shades of gray. With all the money this school had, being housed in a literal church building with stained-glass windows and ornate spires, it was a little suspicious that they couldn't splurge on *actual* food.

As soon as she went to sit down at the table, not looking forward to tasting any of the gray matter, the boys looked up from their game and glared at her. "Those seats are taken," one of them said.

She backed away. "O-oh . . ."

Even though it was clear they weren't taken by anyone.

They glared at her until she retreated another step, and then she heard Baz call from behind her, "Tara! Hey! Come sit over here!"

She froze. Then slowly turned around.

Baz smiled at her from the popular table and waved her over. "C'mon!"

She hesitated, trying to figure out if this was a joke, when he motioned for her again. Unsure of how to get out of it and not really wanting to sit *alone*, she shuffled up to his table and sat down in the empty chair beside him and the petite blond, whose skin was a lot paler and more sickly up close—so white it was almost translucent. She tried not to make eye contact with her even though she absolutely already had.

"Everyone, meet Tara. She's new," Baz added, as if that was even a question.

"H-hello," she mumbled in greeting, darting her eyes around.

There were seven people at the table in total. Baz, then Elaine with her springy red curls and freckles across her cheeks, her legs draped over the Black boy she slouched against—he was tall, had dark brown skin, long eyelashes. Gorgeous like all those swoony male models in *Tiger Beat*. Elaine toyed with the puka shells around his neck. Beside them was a blond guy, still tanned from a summer outdoors, his arms wrapped around a petite South Asian girl with black hair and beautiful red lips.

Elaine eyed Tara. "Baz, you really like taking in strays, don't you?"

The girl with the black hair gasped. *"Elaine!"*

"That's not very nice," Elaine's boyfriend added.

"Cory," Elaine pouted, "you're supposed to be on *my* side."

"Not when you're a raging bitch, darling," he retorted.

Baz cleared his throat. "She moved here from Nebraska," he said, and she realized he must've overheard her conversation with Daphne yesterday in English class. "And I thought we could not be tools for two seconds, guys."

The tanned outdoorsy guy scoffed. "Speak for yourself."

Baz sighed. "Anyway, that's Moss, and this is his girlfriend,

Amala," he added, motioning to the beautiful girl with a daisy in her black hair. "Her family owns the flower shop in town. She's also the president of the garden club."

Amala plucked the daisy out of her hair and handed it to Tara. "It's so nice to meet you!"

Tara took the flower, unsure of what to do with it. "Th-thanks."

"Our garden is out back behind the gym. Kind of in an awkward place, but it's fun! You should join."

Moss jostled her on his lap. "Ams, not everyone wants to join your plant club."

"Well, *she* might."

Baz waved toward the redhead. "This is Elaine, and the guy she's sitting on is Cory." The Black guy waved, but Elaine ignored Baz completely. "Harris isn't here right now, but he's really tall. Stoner, always dresses like Shaggy from *Scooby-Doo*— you'll know the vibe when you see him. And this is Hailey," he added, motioning to the pale blond girl beside him. His tone changed when he said her name, like he revered her. "And these are my really shitty friends."

"Hey! We're not that shitty, bro," Cory said.

Moss replied, "Says the shittiest of all."

"Hey, fuck you."

"Promise?"

Tara's head spun. There were too many people at this table, too many faces. She'd made a mistake sitting here, one she was quickly coming to regret. She would've been better off taking her gray lunch and eating it in the girls' bathroom alone.

"It's—um—n-nice to meet you," she said, greeting them.

"I love it when new kids come," Amala chirped brightly. "I was new, too, a few years ago. From New York City!"

Elaine rolled her eyes. "We get it, Amala. You're cool."

Amala bit back a smile, elbowing Elaine in the side, and added, "This town's pretty small. You'll get used to it."

"And there's never anything to do," Cory added, nodding.

Moss said, "Baz throws the sickest parties, though." He had a lopsided grin that, Tara was sure, most people would call *charming*. It made her skin crawl. "I think he's going to throw another one on his—"

"Why are we all *pretending* like this is okay?" Elaine snapped, and Tara went very still. "That *she's* here and not—that Chad isn't . . ."

Everyone at the table fell into an awkward silence, and Elaine quickly crossed her arms and looked away, quietly simmering.

Finally, Baz said, "C'mon, El, you know it's not her fault she has Chad's schedule."

Elaine scoffed. "No, but you sure are making sure she fills the holes he left behind, aren't you? First Brian and that stupid other new girl, now Chad? Chad's *seat*, Chad's class schedule—what next? Do you have a crush on her or something?" Then she gasped. "Oh my god. You *did* volunteer to show her around the school! Just like with Daphne. Look at you, Mr. Knight in Shining Armor."

Baz shook his head. "No, that's not—"

Moss jabbed him in the side. "I see what you're doing, Baz. Slick."

This conversation was making Tara physically ill. She was right *there*, and everyone was talking about her like she was invisible.

Baz reiterated, almost helplessly, "It's not *like* that, guys."

Amala said thoughtfully, "And Tara really isn't his type. . . ."

Elaine snapped, "Oh, who cares about a *type*? I care that out of all the people at this school, you chose *her*?"

"Stop it," Hailey interjected sharply, lifting her chin. It was the first time she'd spoken since Tara sat down. She sat a little straighter, though under the table Tara could see her nervously twisting her hands. There were dark circles under her eyes, barely disguised by a layer of foundation. "You're being needlessly cruel, Elaine."

"I'm just saying what we're all thinking," the redhead replied.

"And you're talking about Tara like she's not here."

"I bet she loves being the center of attention for once!" Moss said. "Don't you?"

Sweat prickled on the back of her neck. There were spells for invisibility, for forgetfulness—there were spells to blink out of existence. Spells to make herself prettier, more popular, less herself. Spells to be anything else—everything else. She would cast them all now, just to be out of this moment. But even trying to will magic into her fingertips felt like drawing from a dry well. It just wasn't there.

She stared down at the daisy in her hands.

Hailey said sternly, "Moss, stop it."

"But—"

"I'm s-sorry," Tara muttered, and pushed herself to her feet. "Thank you for letting me join your table. S-sorry," she added again, pulling her book bag over her shoulder, avoiding Baz's gaze as she quickly turned and left the cafeteria, feeling every eye on her as she retreated.

She needed to find her locker, anyway.

Her skin was buzzing from all the animosity at that table. She didn't expect that girl—Elaine—to hate her *that* much. Her aura had been fiery—sharp and painful. No one had ever felt *anything* for her that strongly, not even her father. It made her bones jittery in a way she really didn't like.

She didn't like any of this.

She didn't want to be here as much as Elaine didn't want her to be. Like it was her choice to take Chad's schedule? To take his seat at the table? His place in the school roster?

She went to throw the daisy away but stopped herself. She couldn't. Her mother loved daisies. So she stuck the daisy into her ponytail and resigned herself to finally locating her locker. The number and lock combination were on her schedule, so when she eventually found it—third floor, near where she'd seen Daphne's locker—she put in the combo.

But the locker stuck fast.

She cursed, yanking it again. It wouldn't budge. She tried again, then a third time.

Her fingers were beginning to shake. Stupid school. Stupid students. Stupid magic and curses and *family*—

In frustration, she slammed her foot against the locker, and it popped free. Her eyes widened. She stared helplessly at the locker. It was more like a time capsule. *Sports Illustrated* models were plastered to the back of the locker door. A letterman jacket still hung on the hook, and she pulled out the tag to read the name on it—

Chad Jackson.

With all the talk of their dead friend, they hadn't even cleaned out his locker yet. Or maybe they'd kept it as a shrine.

Her nose crinkled at the smell of weed, and she reached back into the top shelf and found it. The words *RIP FOR BRIAN* were written on the baggie in Sharpie.

Brian . . .

Elaine had mentioned Brian in the cafeteria.

Tragedies. More than one. Brian and then Chad.

Two deaths.

Then two new students, as if they could fill the holes left by death's sickle, as if new bodies could patch up a ship that was leaking. Instead of tending to the upkeep, they just plugged the holes and kept sailing. Like her father was trying to do by moving them away from home, from her mother's garden, from everything—absolutely *everything*—that ever mattered to her.

And now she was here, at this school, filling the space where someone else had once been.

She slammed the locker closed and pressed her back against it. She still needed Shakespeare's *Tragedies* if she was ever going to pass Mrs. Albedo's English class, because of all the things that *had* been in Chad's locker, that wasn't one of them.

CHAPTER SEVEN
READ IT AND WEEP

After school, Tara stopped by the bookstore in town. There was a sign in the window, handmade, that read *PRAYERS FOR BRIAN'S AND CHAD'S FAMILIES* in glittery glue. Now that she knew what names to look for, and the more she explored the town's Main Street, the more prominent their deaths became. Freak accidents, they said.

Two streaks of bad luck in a row. If Tara really thought about it, two unexpected deaths in such a short time? It seemed like foul play, but it wasn't her place to meddle.

She stepped up to the counter and asked the harried bookseller, "Do you have any copies of *Macbeth*?"

"They'd be down the far end of that aisle if we do," he replied, his glasses making his eyes look like saucers.

"Thank you," she said, and began to leave for the back, when a flyer caught her eye. It was for the Burning—that Halloween celebration the town did. Hadn't Hailey talked about it over the intercom yesterday?

The flyer was calling for reenactment volunteers—townsfolk, torch, and pitchfork people. The Burning would take place in the Crossroads, which sounded fitting come to think of it. The Crossroads, judging by the small map in the corner, was just the center four-way stop in town, definitely not a place as ominous as it sounded.

"You should take one," the bookseller said, handing her a flyer. "We've got reserved seating on the roof, too! Best in town."

"Um—okay . . . thanks."

She folded the flyer into fourths, stuck it in her pocket, and escaped to the back of the store. The smell of the old books began to calm her heart a little. She skimmed her fingers along the spines of novels about dragons and knights and murders most foul. For the first time since her mother died, she felt . . . something. Something good. Something that stirred warm and gooey in her chest. The smell of books, of dusty papers and well-worn stories, was like a hug from a long-departed friend. It was so quiet here, so nice, she could finally feel a little bit like herself again, with Byron and Tolkien and McCaffrey and Shelley calling her name like siren songs.

They would be her companions while her classmates remained blurry faces. Even at home, where she was expected to be perfect and quiet, she could sink into untamed stories and be someone else.

Anyone else.

Just as she began to let her guard down, she heard someone say, "You finally don't look like a rabbit caught in a snare."

And Tara's guard instantly went up again. She looked toward the voice—and there were eyes peering at her from between the books on the other side of the shelf. Blue, light mascara, framed by blond hair. *Oh no*, she thought as the president of the student body came around the bookshelf with a pleasant smile.

"I didn't mean to startle you," Hailey added. "I was just surprised. You look so different when you're at peace."

Tara kept quiet.

"I'm not going to bite," she laughed, and tapped the name tag on her chest. "I work here some afternoons. What are you looking for?"

"*M–Macbeth.*"

"Oh, goodness, I believe we just sold the last one. Maybe try the school library? Wait, Mrs. Albedo didn't give you one?"

"There wasn't one available."

"Well, that's typical. I'm sure neither Brian *nor* Chad would've kept up with theirs anyway. And if they did"—she leaned close, scrunching her nose—"they probably had boobs doodled all in them."

Tara laughed despite herself and quickly covered her mouth, panicked. "I—I'm so sorry."

"What for?" Hailey asked, perplexed. "It's true."

"But they were your friends."

"Well, yes, but *everyone's* my friend," she replied with a roll of her eyes. "At least, everyone says they are. That's the thing when you're popular, right? Everyone thinks they know you, but really they just know what they want to know." Her eyes flickered briefly to the daisy in Tara's hair. "But Amala is good. One of the only good ones."

Tara hesitated, not quite sure if Hailey wanted commiseration, because Tara absolutely could *not* relate. On any level. She'd always been the wallflower. The invisible girl. So instead, she settled on "It m-must be exhausting."

"It is," Hailey replied. "You have to be strong even when the worst thing happens to you. You can't show any weakness."

She really misses her friends, Tara thought. "I'm sorry." And she meant it. "I kn-know what it's like to lose someone close to you."

The moment the words left her mouth, she wondered what had possessed her to say that—to admit it. She hadn't mentioned her mom's death since the funeral. Her dad had forbidden any talk of her in the house. She was surprised by her own candor, and it seemed like Hailey was, too.

Then Hailey reached out and took her hand and squeezed it tightly. "Thank you." There were tears bright in her eyes. "You are too kind for Hellborne."

Tara didn't think so, but she didn't correct Hailey, who turned on her heel, humming as she left the aisle to finish putting up books that had been abandoned on a cart. Tara didn't stay a moment longer. She left and tossed the flyer for the witch burning into the trash can on the corner because under no circumstances was that something she wanted to be a part of.

Ever.

CHAPTER EIGHT
WARNING SIGNS

Apparently Chad and Brian had been lab partners in biology, and so when it came time to pair up for lab on Thursday, that left Tara and Daphne with no choice but each other. Mr. Gunn, the haphazard-looking biology teacher with wild curly hair and tired eyes, was very happy that he didn't have an *unruly* group of three. Apparently they were just so hard to work with. Never mind Tara would've rather worked with . . . literally anyone else. After the *Macbeth* incident in English, Tara really wasn't feeling this lab-partner thing. Best to avoid eye contact, she reasoned as she opened her notebook and started doodling in the margins. *Don't look at her, don't open your mouth, don't mess things up.*

Daphne, on the other hand, had a different idea. She propped her elbows on the lab table and set her chin on her hand. "Gonna take the side of the frogs, too, once we start dissecting them? Or the scalpel?"

Tara glanced up from her notebook, about to defend the

inhumane treatment of lab animals, when she saw the grin tucked into the edge of Daphne's mouth. "Oh . . . you're joking."

Daphne rolled her eyes. "*Obviously.* But I mean, do I *look* like the will-use-products-that-experimented-on-animals sort of person?"

Tara studied her and then slowly shook her head. "People who club baby seals rarely wear Doc Martens."

"Exactly! They're more a Nike kind of vibe."

"Oof, that's harsh."

"Not as harsh as those populars roasting you during lunch yesterday," Daphne replied, and Tara winced.

"You heard?"

"I think everyone was listening in. Why did you sit there so long taking it?"

"I guess . . . I didn't want to offend them b-by leaving too early, and what they said wasn't that t-terrible," she tried to reason. "They're sad their friends are dead."

"But taking it out on us isn't how to handle it," Daphne replied. "Besides, you're sweet as sugar. They have to be heartless."

The tips of Tara's ears burned. "I'm not that sweet."

"Like a cupcake."

Tara trained her eyes on her notebook and squirmed a little, lacing her fingers together, unsure of how to take the compliment. Out of the corner of her eye, Daphne looked away, biting in that grin. *You probably taste like Pop Rocks*, she thought before she could stop herself, and then felt mortified for even thinking that.

"I want to apologize, actually," Daphne went on, drumming

her fingers on the desk, "about the other day. In class. I can be a little . . ." She paused to choose her words wisely. *"Blunt."*

That surprised her. "Y-you? Blunt?"

"I know, it comes as a complete shock to me, too," Daphne replied sagely, nodding her head. "But I figured, since we're both new, I should at least *try* to get us off on the right foot. Since we're probably going to be partners for a while."

She felt her skin prickle at the thought. But not in a wholly terrible way. "I—I just thought you were *mad* at me. For arguing."

Daphne gave her a perplexed look. "Mad? Me? Oh, no, I love arguments—my brothers tell me I'll go blue in the face before I admit that I'm wrong about something."

"But you did j-just apologize to me," she noted.

To which Daphne replied, "I did not, in fact, say I was wrong, though."

Tara smiled. She couldn't help it. "No, I guess you didn't."

"So, how about a truce, cupcake?"

There it was, the name again. Daphne held out her hand, and Tara debated for a moment. What could it hurt? She accepted Daphne's hand. Her fingers were hard and callused. "Truce—"

Mr. Gunn tapped his ruler against the front of his desk, and Daphne and Tara both let go quickly. "Okay, class! Who can tell me about the physiology of the cell? Anyone? Should I start drawing names? I . . . guess I'll draw names, then! Fantastic." He returned to the front of the classroom and took out a fishbowl. This must have been the type of class where he was prepared to drag answers out of the students. Tara knew the answer. She just . . . didn't want to raise her hand.

He pulled out a slip. "Let's see here. . . . Mr. Jedon?"

Moss groaned from the back of the class. *"What?"*

"Can you kindly tell us the physiology of the c—"

Tara felt the jolt of magic a moment before it happened. She barely had time to brace herself.

Suddenly, the windows along the right wall threw themselves open. A gust of wind shoved through the room, whirling up papers and notes.

Students shrieked, covering their heads.

The air tasted metallic with a spell.

"Close the windows!" Daphne cried, diving toward them, Baz and Moss joining her at the others. There was an energy in the air—Tara could *feel* it. Swirling, cutting, *sharp.* So sharp. Full of menace and rage.

Baz slammed down the first window, and a moment later, Daphne got hers down, too. Papers slowly drifted to the ground, the class settling until someone noticed that something was different now. Elaine gave a shriek and pointed at the chalkboard.

And there, in beautiful looping script, was the chalky message:

YOU'RE NEXT.

CHAPTER NINE
CHALKBOARD CONFESSIONS

Moss, his face red with anger, grabbed the chalk and scribbled over the words. "Who thinks that's funny?" he snarled, turning back to the class. His face grew red. "Who wrote this? ANSWER ME!"

The entire class seemed terrified by the message—and by him—staring like something awful was about to happen.

"First Brian, then Chad," someone said.

"Are they out to get someone else?"

"It's the Red Witch!"

"Shut up. The Red Witch isn't real."

"Did you write it?"

"No!"

Then someone asked, "Could it be them? Brian and Chad?"

Moss gritted his teeth and roared, "They're dead! It's so fucked up to use my friends for your sick games. Who wrote this?" he repeated, and he was screaming now. His eyes were wide, his entire body trembling.

A girl at the front of the class asked, calmer than her classmates, "How do we know *you* didn't?"

"You do like being the center of attention," someone else said.

The girl agreed. "It's a bit suspicious, isn't it?"

He turned his fuming gaze to her, and she didn't seem fazed in the slightest. Crossing her arms, she leaned back in her chair. Tara hadn't noticed her before—dark hair streaked with blues and purples, black-painted nails, and smoky eyes. She sat at the lab table in front of them. "What did you say?" he hissed.

"Why couldn't it be you? They were *your* friends. Actually, since Brian and Chad are both gone," she said, counting on her fingers and giving a mocking gasp, "wouldn't that make *you* football team captain?"

"Bitch!"

He went to lunge at her, but Baz slammed an arm into his chest and kept him back. Tara blinked. Hadn't Baz been beside the window just a moment ago? The tall jock muttered to his friend, "Calm down, bro."

Moss shoved Baz's arm off him. "Whatever. *Whatever!*"

Then Moss turned and stormed out of the room. Amala, lavender falling loose from where she'd wreathed blooms into her hair, fretted for a moment before she grabbed both her and Moss's things and quickly followed him with an apologetic "Sorry, sorry, sorry, Bazzy, sorry!"

A low murmur crept into the classroom again, and as it did, the girl with the black nail polish sank down lower in her chair, her arms crossed over her chest, frowning down into her lap. Tara narrowed her eyes for a moment, seeing a flash of an aura around the girl. Red, like blood.

Murderous?

Baz gave the girl a pleading look. "Marissa . . ."

She raised her eyebrows. "Yeah, *Bazzy?*"

He shook his head, deciding that it wasn't worth his energy, as Mr. Gunn quickly called the class back to order. "Okay, class! *Okay.* That was . . . terrifying, quite frankly. But we still have twenty minutes left in class. And then I'll go complain to the principal about these faulty windows."

It wasn't the windows, but no one would believe Tara, anyway.

There was another witch in Hellborne, and Tara didn't like where that thought led. Because it led to the warning note on the chalkboard and—more frighteningly—Chad's and Brian's deaths.

It's just a prank, she told herself. *That's all.*

For the next twenty minutes, the teacher asked them to concentrate on the anatomy of the cell. Like anyone *could*. The message was all anyone could talk about, even after Mr. Gunn scrubbed it off the board, leaving only a smudgy cloud of white.

When the bell rang, Daphne was the first to leave.

Tara packed up her things and returned to her locker, having almost forgotten that it was still clogged with a deceased boy's things. She glanced around, but the hallway was emptying out quicker than usual, most students going to their fine arts or physical education classes for the period. She had PE, the class she liked the least.

She needed to take all of Chad's things out of her locker, but touching any of it felt . . . like she wasn't supposed to. The

RIP FOR BRIAN weed baggie. The photos on the door of oil-soaked women on fast cars and—a bit strange among them—a photo of the friend group. There were three faces scribbled over. Two she couldn't identify, but the third's hair looked like the girl from biology—Marissa, was it?

Strange.

"Moss, Moss, let *go*," a voice echoed from down the hall. "That hurts."

"What if it's me? Who knows?"

Quietly, curiously, Tara closed her locker door, snuck down to the adjacent hall, and dipped her head around the corner.

Moss leaned against the locker, boxing his girlfriend in. Amala didn't look frightened but instead annoyed as he held her wrist tightly.

"I said I didn't tell anyone," said Amala, squirming. "I *didn't*."

"*Someone* had to," he replied, his voice tight even as he let go of her. "*Someone's* gotta know."

"Babe . . ."

"You saw the chalkboard. What if it's us?" He brushed his fingertips across her temple and combed them through her lovely black hair. "What if it's me?"

Amala hesitated. Then she plucked a sprig of lavender out of her hair and tucked it into the pocket on the front of his polo. "Why would it be you?"

"Ams, I . . . I need to talk to you."

"About what?"

"I . . ."

This was not a conversation Tara needed to be listening to. Cautiously, she started to back up, when she bumped into a solid person behind her. She jumped, a gasp breaking the silence, before Daphne put a hand over her mouth. *"Shh!"*

But it was too late. Moss had shoved off the locker and whirled toward the sound. "Who's there?"

Daphne brought a finger up to her lips.

Moss began toward them, when his girlfriend caught his arm. "We'll be late for art," she said. "It was nothing, Moss. C'mon."

He relented.

Daphne slipped her hand from Tara's mouth, and they quietly peeked around the corner. As they left, Amala glanced back and locked eyes with Tara before she followed her boyfriend down the hall.

"So," Daphne muttered, "he thinks he was the target of that message in class."

"Do you think he was?"

"I don't know, but *he* certainly thinks he is."

The bell rang.

Daphne cursed. "Don't you have PE, too?"

Tara checked her schedule, even though she already knew the answer. It was wishful thinking that it'd magically changed. "Yes— *Too?* I didn't realize you w-were also . . ."

"I usually skip, but maybe I won't now. Ah, man, at least I won't be the only one Coach Lee'll yell at. I hate that guy," she added, taking Tara by the wrist and pulling her back along the hall. Her hand was cool and firm against Tara's skin, and she didn't hate it, so she let Daphne lead her on, her brain doing somersaults at the sensation of her touch.

CHAPTER TEN
A MOSS'D OPPORTUNITY

Tara needed *Macbeth*. There really wasn't a way around it. Hailey told her to try the school library, so after school, she decided to do just that. The hall was almost empty by the time she packed up from US History, so she skipped the locker—she had been doing that a lot, since she still hadn't cleaned out Chad Jackson's things—shoved her gym clothes in her bag to wash tonight, and started for the library.

Out of the windows in the hall Tara could see the sports teams practicing on the crunchy brown field, coaches blowing their whistles, almost covered up by the twenty-three-person marching band playing a dying melody on the practice field for homecoming. The sounds were muted inside the high school, the halls themselves cavernous voids that sucked all sound into silence. Her brown loafers made solid thumps across the marbled tile floor, her footsteps swallowed up.

The library was in the middle of the high school, accessible by four doors, one for each point of the compass. Since it had been a church before it became a school, it must've been the sanctuary.

Tara slipped in through the north door—

And ran straight into Elaine.

They both stumbled back as Elaine dropped her binder and it exploded onto the ground, spilling papers everywhere. She cursed, falling to her knees, and began to gather up her papers again. "Watch where you're— You. Ugh." She rolled her eyes, shoving everything into her binder. "Of *course* it's you."

Tara bent down and handed her a few of the papers. "I'm s-sorry."

"Whatever." Elaine snatched the papers from her and shoved them into the binder, glancing at the watch on her wrist. "Oh my god, I'm going to be so *late*. The library's about to close, new girl," she added as she stood and hurried down the hall and out of sight.

"Thank you," Tara muttered to herself, and tried the door again.

At her old schools, the libraries had been windowless boxes crammed with aisles and aisles of books. That was not this library. The second she stepped inside, she felt disoriented. It was beautiful, strange, and captivating in a way she couldn't really describe. The ceiling arched up into the ribs of a cathedral, sheltering stained-glass windows depicting what Tara suspected was the history of Hellborne. There was a lot of fire in the images, and iconography of a strong-jawed savior reaping fields to sow new life into the untilled soil.

The stained-glass windows sent spirals of colors down into the aisles upon aisles of books. So many books, stuffed into overgrown bookcases, holding a mass of unlimited knowledge and fictitious worlds in the impossible space between A and Z.

Hellborne just grew more and more mysterious the longer she stayed. A town in the middle of nowhere, surrounded by dark firs, disguised as a charming hamlet with a quiet main street and a coffee shop on one corner, with a sanctuary like *this*? It was like it was built to honor something—or to ward against it.

The extravagance of the library didn't sit very well with Tara, though she didn't know why.

She rang the bell at the librarian's desk, but it didn't seem like anyone was around. Strange—wasn't the library open until at least four? She had a good thirty minutes until it closed. Frowning, she slid behind the desk and pulled out the Rolodex herself, skimming through it until she found the book she was looking for—

Macbeth.

"822.33," she repeated to herself, memorizing the Dewey decimal number.

Putting the card back, she left for the aisle in question. No matter how beautiful this library was, or how crappy her old library now seemed in comparison, they were all built the same in the end. Books shelved in alphabetical order by last name. Dewey decimal was easier than people, that was for sure.

There were all kinds of books in Hellborne Academy's library: classics and modern works side by side, nonfiction that ranged from autobiographies of rock stars and civil rights activists and aging politicians to guides to herbs and memoirs with the strangest names. Fictitious explorations around the world and flowers in attics and fanged vampires and werewolves—

Her fingers fell into a hole where *Macbeth* should be, nestled between *Hamlet* and *Romeo & Juliet (and other Tragedies)*.

She checked again, scanning the shelf, but it was missing. "Of course it is," she muttered.

She didn't *want* to ask Daphne if she could borrow the textbook, but it seemed like that was her only choice at this point. Either Daphne or Baz, really, though she didn't like asking those kinds of favors. She'd never been very good at relying on other people—for anything. Thanks to her . . . thanks to who she was, it was always for the best.

Suddenly, the doors slammed open on the north side of the library, and someone came running inside. Fast, shuffling, tripping. Down the other side of the library.

Then a voice—

"Get *away*! You're not real—you're not here!"

He sounded familiar.

She peeked around the corner. Moss. It was Moss, running down the aisle. "Get away! I didn't do—I didn't do anything! I didn't— *Oof!*" He tripped on his untied shoelaces and slammed against the ground so hard, blood dripped from his nose.

Above them, a heavy iron chandelier groaned as it began to swing back and forth, something thick and trembling in the air. She felt it—tingling down her spine.

Magic.

So much it was almost suffocating.

Quietly, she crept to the end of the aisle and pushed a handful of books apart so she could see between them.

Moss scrambled to sit up and turned around, staring up at—at nothing. His eyes had rolled into the back of his head, completely white.

"No—please," he begged, "I—I didn't tell anyone. I didn't *do* anything—"

She felt the tingle race across her skin—that pulse of magic—and suddenly his face reddened in anger. He gritted his teeth and shoved himself to his feet. He glowered at the invisible thing in front of him, wiping his bloody nose with the back of his arm, leaving a red streak across his skin.

His lips twisted into a sickening grin. "You got what you deserved."

Then he slammed back into the shelf of books. The entire case rocked precariously—and then fell forward. Onto him. A dozen heavy tomes spilled down on his head. He crumpled beneath the weight of them, and then the bookcase itself collapsed.

And entombed him.

CHAPTER ELEVEN
THE BODY

Tara was only seven when she made a dandelion bloom. Her mother had been so proud of her that she gathered her in her arms and spun her around. She said that she would show Tara everything; she would teach her everything she knew. And she did.

She taught Tara spells to call the rain and to see the future. Spells for healing and spells for fire and spells for good luck. The magic always felt so warm and bright, like catching a sunbeam in her hands. And her dad watched and was so proud.

Her mother had said that magic was like a knife—it was only dangerous if you used it that way.

But Tara never would. How could she ever think to misuse something so wonderful? But then her mother became sick, and she understood the knife.

Her father had begged her to save her mom. To cast a spell. To heal her. And when she had failed, her father said that magic was evil.

"It's wrong—it's all wrong!" her father had said, the heart-break on his face slowly turning to stone. "That power does nothing—it's demonic. It's evil. And I will not let you go the way she went."

"It's not evil," she'd said, trying to reason with him.

And the heartbreak had turned to hatred in his eyes. "Then why is she gone?"

Though standing there, behind that bookshelf, staring at the heap of books and splintered wood that buried Moss, Tara wasn't all that sure he'd been wrong.

Because this magic—this magic *felt* evil. It felt evil all the way down into the marrow of her bones. It wasn't like any sort of power she'd ever sensed before. It wasn't light or warm or inviting. It was cold and sharp and vindictive, and the magic made it hard to breathe.

Under the collapsed bookcase, Moss didn't move. Neither did Tara. What if the thing that had scared him was still here? It felt like the magic from biology earlier. The magic that scratched the promise *YOU'RE NEXT* on the chalkboard.

This wasn't a coincidence.

Moss *knew* he was the next victim, and here he was. And these deaths, she realized, weren't accidents. She could guess not a single one of them was. This had magic—dark, *terrible* magic—written all over it.

You shouldn't stay here, she thought. *You need to leave.*

There was a phone at the front desk. She could call the police, and then—

She heard a sound.

A ragged, gasping sob. From underneath the pile of books.

Moss was still alive. Barely. His breathing sounded wet and

stilted. The best thing to do was to call the police. Wait for an ambulance. Leave before whatever got him turned its eyes on her . . .

Her feet were moving before she could stop them. They did that sometimes. Her body would react before her brain could mull it over, and by then, it was too late to stop. She knelt down beside the tomb of books and started tossing them aside, digging down to Moss.

"You're okay," she muttered, repeating the words over and over, "you're okay. You're going t-to be okay. You're okay."

But the books were heavy, and her stomach twisted when she finally uncovered him, still pinned to the ground by the bookshelf. Another ragged breath wheezed between his lips, blood coming with it. She had to get the bookcase off him.

It was too heavy, but she managed to turn it just enough so she could drag him out from underneath it. His left arm was bent at a strange angle. His eyes stared up at the colorful cathedral ceiling, looking a thousand miles away.

Her mom had the same look when she lay dying.

She glanced around, but there was no one else here, no one else who could help.

"You're okay," she repeated, trying to soothe him as she racked her brain for what to do.

His eyes settled on her. His lips were a raspberry red, glistening with blood. They moved quietly. She bent closer to try to make out what he was saying, and between the rasps of his breathing, she pieced it together. "She . . . *she* . . ."

Tara thought back to the chalkboard message, and the girl with the murderous aura in the science lab.

She.

He coughed up more blood. He wouldn't survive until the ambulance got there. But what could she do? Watch him *die*?

No, no, she couldn't. She wiped her sweaty hands on her thighs. She *wouldn't* just watch him die. But her magic . . .

Still, she had to try.

She placed her hands on his chest. His heart thrummed faintly beneath her fingers. Things were broken inside. It didn't take a lot to figure out what. The aura that shimmered around him was gray, and it was fading.

It was fading very, very fast.

"G-Goddess Hygeia, *who gives mortals breath,*" she whispered, her voice shaking, "*hear my plea and stave off his death. Goddess Hygeia, patron of life, hear my plea and stave off his death. Goddess Hygeia . . .*"

When she first found this spell and showed it to her mother, her mother had laughed and said, "It doesn't stop Death from knocking, sprout, it only delays him a while."

And then, when her mother lay dying in a hospital bed, she tried to cast the spell, just for a moment, just for a little more time—just a little more.

Just enough to—to what?

To say good-bye?

Only to cast it again, and again, when time ran out because there was never enough time for good-bye?

But still she tried, still she pulled on the magic—

Until her mother took her hands and squeezed them tightly and said, "It's okay to let things go."

But it wasn't. It never was.

And Tara, angry at her mother, left for the vending machines at the end of the hall. Left to cool off, and to come back, and try to find a good-bye—

But there were no good good-byes, and her mother died as Tara stood in the light of the desolate vending machines, trying to find words that she'd never say.

That was the last time she cast a spell.

The last time she called to magic, and it answered. The last time before the doors swung closed and locked themselves, cutting her off from that warm and light power. She had no right to believe that they would open now. She didn't even know how to ask. She was a dry and barren well, and there was nothing there to pull from, nothing to lace into her words, nothing to give the spell its spark.

But magic was a strange thing.

It wasn't a switch that could be turned off or on; it wasn't a poem she could forget or a face that slowly lost its definition. It was a living energy that came when it wanted, that chose who could wield it. It was a creature that knocked, and it was she who had to find a way to open the door.

Once, it had chosen her.

"Please," she whispered, her voice breaking. *"Please."*

But what if she failed again? What if she couldn't do anything? What if—like with her mother—she couldn't save him? Couldn't save anyone? Was her father right, and was she evil for simply trying?

Beneath her fingertips, Moss's heart stopped.

If this was evil? Trying to save someone?

Then so be it.

Something deep inside her flickered. Soft at first, then

louder and stronger. It thrummed beside her heart with every breath and sang in her veins like it was glad to be home.

And it was hers.

A rush of magic flooded into her fingertips, pooling there like rain droplets, and seeped down into Moss's chest. It shocked his heart, and underneath her fingers, it began to beat again. Slow, steadily waking, but there. His pain subsided, his body broken but still alive. Then he took a deeper breath.

And another.

His eyelids fluttered open and found her face.

"You," he rasped, staring at her with a mix of horror and surprise. His voice was stronger. *"You're— Aargh!"*

Something flared in him. That same dark magic she sensed before—and it bit at her like a rabid dog. As if to say, *Mine*. It came snarling back at her, a flash of teeth and fire and so much hatred it made her scream and recoil.

Moss writhed on the ground, his twisted arm twisting further—something burned into the back of his hand, where the dark magic was the hottest and most hateful. He began to scream. Loud. Shrieking. His eyes rolled into his skull—

Tara lurched toward him again, bringing her magic to her fingertips, but she wasn't powerful enough. Her spell faltered.

Her fingertips blistered from that terrible magic.

All she could do to keep him from screaming was—

Think, think, think.

Whatever this magic was, whatever hold it had, was tormenting him even now. She had to cut him off from it, shake off the influence, but she wasn't sure how. Until her eyes settled on the lavender Amala had tucked into Moss's shirt pocket.

She plucked it out, threw it away, and waved her hand over his face. "*Somnum.*"

And he slumped against the floor, unconscious, his face twisted into a half scream as he slept.

Shaking, she sat back on her knees. The burn on the back of his right hand was red and raw. Two opposing right angles meeting at their edges. She'd never seen the shape before, never mind burned into someone's *skin*. Like a brand.

Her brow furrowed.

A curse?

The west door to the library burst open. Footsteps rushed in. Heavy ones.

Panic pulsed through her. If someone caught her, they'd think she'd pushed the bookcase over—or worse, tried to kill Moss.

Tara killed Moss in the library with the bookcase.

She quickly pushed herself to her feet, but she was *much* too late. She barely managed to take a step before the person turned the corner of the aisle and found her.

Doc Martens, one unlaced, torn hose and wild dark hair.

Daphne Frost.

With a crossbow.

She drank in the scene with widening eyes as Tara's mouth fell open. *Run*, her heart screamed. *Run, run, run—*

"Wait," Daphne ordered, but Tara didn't listen as she turned on her heel and fled the library. "Wait—*Tara!*"

She knew what it looked like. She knew what Daphne saw. What she thought. And there was nothing she could do about it. Because all she saw on Daphne's face was the same look her father had given her after her mother died.

The look that said she was not good, or helpful, or human.

It was the look of someone facing a monster.

And Tara knew that no matter how far she ran, she'd never escape it. But she ran anyway. She didn't stop until she was out of the school and halfway down the pitch-black road to the main street. Dark fir trees towered around her, wind whispering through the tops, sounding like screams.

And in the distance—sirens.

Daphne must have called the ambulance. Good. It was more than Tara had done.

Halfway down the road, she saw the flash of blue and red lights and quickly hopped into the woods. The police passed, sirens blaring, as they tore into the school, an ambulance and firetruck following.

Moss would get help. He'd be fine, thanks to Daphne.

So she pulled her book bag higher on her back and set off through the woods toward Main Street. She was close enough to hear the cars when something large and white caught her attention. She glanced over her shoulder, still trying to catch her breath.

Between the large dark firs a horse stood solemnly, as white as snow.

But when she turned to face the animal, it shook its mane as if it was also spooked by her, bolted into the dense thicket—and was gone.

CHAPTER TWELVE

SWEET AS WHOLE

Her father's car was already in the driveway by the time she made it home. It must have been an early day for him. She hoped he wouldn't ask why she looked so flustered. She tried to straighten her blouse and smooth back her hair by the time she climbed up the steps and went inside.

He was waiting in his recliner. She wasn't sure what book he'd been reading—something either clerical or faux cerebral. He was a professor of religious studies. Her mother had been an adjunct professor of English—and they'd met at a college in Chicago. But he'd changed since her mother died.

He grew cold and distant, and at the same time, he tightened his grip on her—like he was afraid she'd die too early and too suddenly, like her mother.

Now he was teaching a theology course for a semester at the local college. That was the reason they were here in Vermont to begin with. He'd wanted to go somewhere far away, to divorce Tara from whatever memory she had of her mother and the magic they shared. To start fresh. And what better place, he reasoned, than a small and secluded town in Vermont?

She swallowed thickly. He'd been waiting for her.

"Welcome home," he began pleasantly, returning his gaze to his book. "How was school?"

"It was good. I had to stop by the—" She stopped midsentence. *Should* she tell him about the library? What if the local news reported Moss's accident?

"Stop where?"

"B-by the grocery store. But they d-didn't have what I was looking for," she said, quickly changing course, swallowing the knot in her throat. "Would chicken and pasta be okay for tonight?"

"That sounds delicious," he replied, and turned the page in his book. "Thank you, daughter."

Her muscles unwound a little, and she quickly hurried into the kitchen, put on a pot of pasta, and baked three chicken breasts. She was on autopilot, her anxiety still vibrating from the library. If her dad noticed that the chicken was a little overcooked, or that her hands shook a little more than normal, he didn't say anything. She set out their plates, equally portioned, and she and her father and brother, Donny, all sat down to eat.

Donny had taken their mother's passing a bit differently. He'd never inherited her magic, and Tara always suspected that he sort of resented it. That is, until her mother died and her father turned against magic. Donny seemed pretty unaffected by the whole thing, and Tara envied him for that.

"Tara," her father called from across the table, and she looked up from her dry baked chicken. "I've invited your cousin

Beth to look after you the weekend Donald and I are touring Dartmouth."

Dartmouth? She glanced at her brother, Donny, eating with one hand as he played his Game Boy with the other.

Tara hesitated. "I—I can look after myself, I think—"

"It will be good for you to have company," he interrupted quickly. "Besides, I'm sure you're nervous in a strange new town, and your cousin would like to come see you."

Her shoulders drooped a little. *Beth.* They never really saw eye to eye. If she were bolder, she'd say that Beth was the one who whispered into her dad's ear about demonic magic, but she could never be quite sure. "Yes, sir."

"It'll be good for you two," he added, dabbing his mouth with his napkin. "She's a very good influence, you know."

Of course she was. Pretty, perfect cousin Beth, who could do no wrong. She didn't have demon blood in her—being her father's sister's daughter—so she was the exemplary Maclay. Someone her father wanted her to follow. Being someone like Beth was much better than being someone like Evelyn Maclay.

After dinner, her father went back to the living room to finish his book, and Tara cleaned up the table. Her brother was supposed to help, but he just grabbed a bag of Bugle chips from the pantry and watched her wash dishes.

"So, only the store, huh?" he asked, popping a horn-shaped chip into his mouth.

"It was crowded," she replied hesitantly, eyeing him.

He shrugged. "As long as you aren't getting into that witchy shit again. You know Dad won't like that."

"I'm not."

"It'd really break his heart."

Her fingers curled around the sponge, remembering how good and whole the magic felt in her fingers again, like blood rushing back to a severed limb. "You know I won't," she said quietly.

Not again. It was a one-time thing, she promised herself.

"Mm-hmm. Just don't screw anything up here," he added, patting her on the shoulder, and left for his room. He'd flunked out of his second year at the community college, and his father had dreams of *Dartmouth* for him? Sure. She doubted he had the grades, but her father did have connections.

She had so much homework already. So much to catch up on. She doubted she'd get it all done tonight. And tomorrow, she'd have to find a tutor for precalc.

And Moss—how was Moss? Had the ambulance arrived in time?

Had Daphne told the police that she'd seen Tara fleeing the scene? Half the evening, she'd expected the police to come knocking on her door to ask her a few questions. If they did, she'd tell them *she* wasn't the one with a crossbow at school.

Why the hell would Daphne Frost have a *crossbow* at school?

Her father was in his chair again, reading the same book. "Study hard," he said as she passed him on the way to her bedroom.

"Y-yes, sir."

"And, Tara?"

She paused. Glanced over her shoulder. "Yes, sir?"

Licking his thumb, he flipped the page and then turned his brown eyes up to her. They softened a little, almost how he used to look at her before, and he said, "Happy early birthday."

She sucked in a surprised breath.

"You think I'd forget?" he went on with a laugh. "I put your present on your desk. In case I don't see you tomorrow morning."

"Thank you," she muttered, and quickly left for her room. She pressed her back against the closed door, finally alone, and stared around at all the boxes she still had left to unpack, and then to the bag sitting on her desk. She went over to it and took out a soft cardigan.

It was a loud pink—a color that her cousin Beth would wear. Tara had never really liked pink, though at least the sweater was warm.

She'd forgotten that it was her birthday tomorrow. Her mom would've never let her forget. Last year, she'd spent all night baking a cake to have it ready the second Tara woke up the next morning, candles already lit.

"The most special day for the most special witch," her mother would always say, wrapping her up in a warm hug.

But after the kind of day she'd just had, the memory felt like a very awful joke.

Still, she had somehow cast a spell again. She remembered the way her fingers tingled with the magic, the way her blood hummed. She grabbed the book from the box where she had thrown it in anger the other night, and picked at the singed edges.

"I'm sorry," she muttered to it. "I didn't mean to throw you."

She still remembered the feeling of the magic in her finger-tips, if only for a moment, before that horrid dark magic had taken hold of Moss again. Her mother could have easily fended it off. She'd been the most powerful witch Tara had ever known—though admittedly she didn't know many witches.

Tara had only gotten a fraction of her mom's power. A drop of it. Her mom could have saved Moss then and there. Her mom would have stayed when Daphne found them. Her mom would've set the record straight.

But Tara was not her mom.

Even as she opened the spellbook—even as she muttered the simplest spell, willing the magic into her veins—

All she could see was the look on Daphne's face, and how it mirrored the look her father gave her at the hospital.

Why couldn't you save her?

She slammed the book closed and tossed it into the box again. Tara was not her mother, no matter how much she wanted to be.

CHAPTER THIRTEEN
AFTER MATH

The news about Moss had quickly spread by the time school began on Tara's birthday. Everyone whispered to one another, wondering what had happened. As Tara followed the front walkway up to the school with the rest of the students, she caught bits of their conversations. Some thought he'd hurt himself, while others knew about the accident in the library. At least he wasn't dead—maybe her magic had helped him after all?

"Could someone have pushed it on him?"

"Did he get into a fight?"

"Who'd want to hurt *Moss*?"

"Who *wouldn't*?"

It almost made her wonder if she'd imagined the entire thing yesterday, but she held on to the feeling of that spell, the magic pooling in her fingertips. No, that hadn't been her imagination. None of it had. Not the awful, vibrating magic that swirled in the library, rocking the chandeliers. Not Moss's frightened screams. Not his ragged breaths as he lay dying.

It was all too real.

As she climbed the steps into the school, she heard her name called—"Tara!"—and glanced behind her.

Daphne kicked up her skateboard and made a beeline straight for her.

Panic built in her middle. She quickly turned back around and pretended that she hadn't heard her.

"Hey, Tara! Wait!"

Tara slipped into the school and disappeared into the crowd of students before Daphne could race up the steps. And Tara avoided Daphne like that for the better half of the morning, though if only she could avoid the rest of her classes the exact same way. Precalc was just as horrendous as it had been the previous days. She knew almost nothing and so she learned almost nothing, and Mrs. Dupont really loved picking on Tara because of it.

She lost count of how many times she answered wrong, only for Elaine or someone else to pipe in with the right answer.

When the bell rang to dismiss them to next period, Tara just wanted to sink into her desk and rot there.

Baz patted her shoulder gently as they walked to English. "It'll get better. Always does."

To which she replied, "I . . . doubt it." Then, quieter: "How's your friend?"

He gave her a strained smile. "Moss'll be fine. He's taken tougher hits on the field."

That made Tara feel a little better as she sat down in class.

Mrs. Albedo clapped and told everyone, "Get into teams of two!"

And the next thing Tara knew, she was one of the last two people who didn't have a partner. The other person was . . .

Tara glanced over to Daphne, who was waiting oh so patiently for her to slide her desk over, drumming her fingers on her closed notebook, her other hand propping up her head. "Guess it's us, cupcake," she said.

Tara pulled her desk over until it touched Daphne's. Then she sat quietly as Daphne stared at her. Tara waited for her to make the first move, but the silence was killing her. Everyone had huddled into their pairs, the chatter of students disguising everyone's conversations.

She finally whispered, "Why didn't you tell the police?"

Daphne quirked an eyebrow. "Because I want to get my facts straight first. Why were you in the library?"

"I was looking for a b-book. Then Moss came in and—and it l-looked like something was chasing him. He knocked the bookcase over, and it fell on him. I pulled him out. That was when you came in." Then she steeled herself to ask, "Why did you have a crossbow?"

"I—well—" She hesitated. "Doesn't, uh, everyone carry a crossbow around?"

"No."

Daphne winced. "I just came from archery practice?"

"I don't think they use crossbows." Tara paused. "And I think archery is a spring sport."

Daphne caved. "I left before the police arrived, too. What book were you looking for?"

"*Macbeth*," she admitted, "but it wasn't there."

"You can borrow mine, if you'd like." Daphne took hers out of her book bag and scooted it across the desk. "It was Brian's, so I hope you don't mind breasts doodled in the margins."

Tara couldn't help but gasp a laugh before quickly covering her mouth to keep herself quiet. "You wouldn't mind?"

"No," Daphne replied, and leaned closer. "Besides, it'll give me an excuse to keep a closer eye on you, yeah?"

Tara felt her skin prickle.

"Just in case, you know, you aren't telling the truth."

Tara picked at her nails, staring down at her desk. "Well, neither are you," she mustered up the courage to reply. "So I probably shouldn't trust you either."

"I guess not."

And that was that.

Mrs. Albedo handed out their project assignment and went over what they had to do. The project was easy, at least. Do a presentation on one of the three themes in *Macbeth*: kingship, ambition, or fate versus free will.

It was a no-brainer for either of them.

"Free will," said Tara.

"Fate," said Daphne at the same time.

They gave each other the same look.

Mrs. Albedo laughed as she walked by. "Well! Your discussion should be interesting, then." She left for the next group.

Daphne glared at the teacher and then skimmed the handout. A fifteen-minute presentation. With a visual aid. And a two-page essay.

"I can write the essay, if you'll do the presentation," Tara said, because she'd rather write a hundred-page dissertation than stand in front of a classroom. "We can both work on the visual aid. Maybe a poster—or a worksheet?"

For a long moment, Daphne tapped her pencil on the desk. Then she said, "Maybe we should start by agreeing on our stance."

"And I feel you aren't going to budge."

"But neither are you." Daphne folded the handout in half, and then again, her long fingers pressing against the edges to flatten them in a seamless motion. Her nails glittered, but a few were chipped now. "I think the families we're born into, the cultures, the circumstances, dictate who we are to the rest of the world. It's not that I don't believe we can't be anyone or whatever, it's just . . ." Her gaze looked a thousand miles away. She shook her head. "Doesn't matter. Why're you Team Free Will?"

Truth be told, Tara didn't know. It wasn't like her life was hers to live. Maybe once, when she watched her parents dance in the garden, she believed that life was limitless with possibilities. But now that was far from the truth. Her fate had been decided for her before she was even born—because of the magic she carried. The demon blood, her father said. And now all he wanted to do was keep her safe and coddled and protected, far away from the evil of the world.

He held on so tightly it felt almost impossible to breathe.

"I like the idea," she finally said.

"Fate gives me purpose," Daphne replied.

"Free will gives me hope." She glanced over to Daphne, who was looking at her with pursed lips, and for the briefest moment, she thought maybe Daphne saw through her words, down into the dark crevices she'd rather not think about.

Daphne rested her chin on her hand and leaned in toward

her, studying her from underneath those thick, dark lashes, and she couldn't help but feel a chill curl up her spine. Not an unpleasant one—the kind that made her heart race a little bit faster. Tara imagined what Daphne saw. A pale white girl with long hair that wasn't quite blond and wasn't quite brown. A color Tara's mother called *honey* because it shifted depending on the season. Daphne probably saw that her nails were bitten to the quick, that her uniform was the same one she wore yesterday, that she had a pimple on the side of her nose. Someone not at all interesting, so why did Daphne look at her like she was?

"There's something about you, Maclay," Daphne Frost said.

"A good thing?"

"I'm not sure yet."

Tara's heart rose in her throat, and though she tried to swallow it, she couldn't. She wasn't sure if she wanted to turn invisible or ask to be read like a book—pages open, honest and sincere. The latter sounded like it could hurt a lot more in the end.

Suddenly, a sharp knock came from the classroom door.

Daphne and Tara tore their gazes away from each other.

The principal poked his head in and called Mrs. Albedo out of the classroom. A feeling of foreboding swept away Tara's burgeoning good mood. Everyone else seemed to feel the same way, because they were quiet—too quiet for a classroom just left unattended, as if they were straining their ears to hear the conversation on the other side of the door.

After a few moments, Mrs. Albedo returned to her classroom with the principal. She was white as a sheet, fidgeting with her blouse sleeves. "Class . . . it will be announced later today, but we—the principal and I—thought it would be better if you heard it from us." She looked at the principal, who gave a single solemn nod, and then said, "Moss Jedon . . . has passed away."

Tara felt her breath catch in her throat.

He'd *died*? Her blood ran icy at the memory of that dark magic on his hand. She thought she'd cast a spell strong enough to save him—to give him time. But her magic had been too weak. Her thoughts spun so fast, she was oblivious to the shriek that escaped Elaine's lips. The way the rest of the class fell into a shocked, horrible silence. The look on Baz's face—a look of pure terror. The only person who didn't react was Daphne. She gripped her pencil tighter and turned her gaze out the window again.

The rest of class . . . wasn't a class.

It was quiet, and it was sobbing, and it was a prison.

The second the bell rang, everyone flooded out of English like it was a sinking ship. By then news of Moss's death had spread like wildfire throughout the school. Tara tried to ignore the gossip. But the wildfire turned into whispers, and every hall she walked down, she heard rumors growing louder and louder.

One was unfortunate.

Two was a coincidence.

Three dead boys?

That was intentional.

"They're being *murdered*," someone said as Tara closed her locker door and headed to lunch.

Someone else said, "This can't be an accident."

"Of course it was—the bookcase fell on him. Head trauma?"

"Is it the Red Witch?"

"And Brian? He slipped between the bleachers."

"Chad could've been shoved into the clothes hook. . . ."

"Who'd want to kill them?"

No one saw you in the library, she thought, training her eyes on her desk. *Except Daphne.*

She just needed to lay low. Not make any more waves.

She didn't know these boys. She didn't have history with them. She didn't need to be snooping around in things that didn't concern her. Yesterday she was just in the wrong place at the wrong time, and she already had someone suspicious of her.

Tara kept her head down for the rest of the day, so she didn't notice the accusing look Elaine began to give her, tear-filled and hateful, or the way she whispered to her friends at the lunch table, or the rumors that began to spiral after school and into the weekend.

Tara didn't notice any of it.

At least, not until it was too late.

CHAPTER FOURTEEN
I HEARD A RUMOR

Monday at school felt quiet.

Things always did before a storm.

Tara didn't know about the storm, though. She'd spent the entire weekend trying to understand what the heck a polynomial was and why it was so important to her life that she know about it. Wouldn't it be more helpful if instead of teaching a type of math that she'd never use again, the class would teach how to file taxes? That felt like a much better use of everyone's time.

Taxes seemed easy compared to the numbers in Tara's precalc book.

"Maclay!" she heard someone call, and looked up. Daphne was waiting for her at the entrance to the school with her skateboard in her hands. Tara avoided her eye as Daphne asked, "Nice morning, isn't it? Looking forward to the assembly today?"

Tara hadn't known there was an assembly, so she muttered, "I d-don't know," as she shouldered past her into the school.

Head down. Stay invisible. That was her plan. And thankfully, Daphne got the hint and left her alone. The halls were quieter than usual, but Tara chalked that up to Moss's death on Friday. It was still surprising. It had been all weekend, and she woke up surprised again this morning.

The spell should've kept him alive. It should've healed him. She didn't understand. . . . Had she done something wrong?

As she sat down at her desk in precalc, Hailey came over and leaned against the desk beside her. "Good morning," she said pleasantly to Tara. "Is everything okay?"

Tara hesitated. "What? Oh—yes. I'm sorry, by the way. About your friend . . ."

Hailey's good mood faltered. "And I'm sorry about the rumors."

The *rumors*?

But before Tara could ask her what she meant, the bell for first period rang and everyone settled into their assigned seats. Even though she'd studied all weekend, she was still so lost in precalc the teacher might as well have just failed her then and there. She was so stressed out over that that she forgot about the rumors Hailey mentioned almost instantly.

She remembered, however, the moment she walked into English and was met by the scowling face of Elaine and all of her popular friends. With the exception of Baz, who wouldn't look at her at all. And Hailey, absently braiding her own hair.

When Daphne finally sat down beside her, Tara asked quietly, "C-can I ask you a question?"

Daphne gave her a skeptical look. "What's that worried look for?"

She tried to school her face, but she only made herself look more petrified than she already was. "What—what are the r-rumors about me?"

"I didn't spread them, if that's what you're asking—"

"No! I know, I just—"

Mrs. Albedo interrupted loudly, "Is there something you'd like to share with the class, Miss Frost? Miss Maclay?"

Tara winced and ducked her head. Daphne replied, "No, ma'am, I was just telling her how horrible it is that she still doesn't have a textbook."

The teacher sighed. "And that is something I have gone to Principal Greaves about. Until then, you and Miss Maclay will share," she said matter-of-factly, and returned to writing out today's thematic questions onto the board.

The class muttered, glancing back to the two new girls conspiratorially, before Mrs. Albedo began to call on random students to answer today's reading questions.

Daphne sank down in her chair and flipped open her notebook. She scribbled on a blank page, *Everyone is afraid. So, they had to find someone to blame.*

Tara unzipped her pencil case to get a pen, clicked out the tip, and wrote, *So they blame me?* on the line below.

Elaine's been spreading rumors—that you were in the library before Moss died.

"I was looking for *Macbeth*," she muttered, her stomach dropping into her toes. She *had* bumped into Elaine that afternoon. Right in front of the library. And suddenly, she could see all of the cutting looks the other students gave her out of the corner of their eyes. Clenching their fists. Angling away from her like she was—like she was some sort of—

Ignore them, Daphne wrote.

Tara was about to say how that sounded easier said than done, when Mrs. Albedo clapped as she walked to the front of the class. "Now! Take out your books and turn to page three hundred and eighty-seven. We're going to talk about the last act! And murder most foul!" Then her eyes widened, realizing her words had been in poor taste. "Oh, I meant—not *real* murder. The Bard is fiction, class. We all know this. And that line was from *Hamlet*, another of Shakespeare's . . ."

Tara finally reached into her book bag and took out her notebook, feeling every eye on her whenever she moved as if she had already been found guilty. She hoped that the rest of the day would go by a lot faster.

CHAPTER FIFTEEN

ASSEMBLY REQUIRED

I t did not.

Tara survived until lunch, which was longer than she expected. But lunch itself? *So* much worse than she could've imagined. The second she stepped into the cafeteria, she felt dozens of eyes on her, watching her, people whispering behind their hands as she went to sit at a vacant table.

"Did you hear about poor Amala? She's not coming back. They are moving out of Hellborne—can't say I blame them. . . ."

"Do you think the new girl could've done it?"

"She moved here *after* Brian and Chad died. . . ."

"But Elaine saw what she saw—she *was* in the library before the police found Moss. . . ."

Tara wanted the earth to swallow her whole. She thought she could handle those kinds of sharp, accusing looks from her dad, but now they were amplified. Everyone gave her the same look he had in the hospital, after she couldn't save her mother. . . .

If Elaine accused her of killing Moss, it would be Elaine's word against hers, wouldn't it? That wasn't great.

And if Daphne backed her up . . .

Suddenly, she felt like Goody Proctor. And the history of Hellborne didn't make her feel any better.

If she'd just never gone to the library to begin with, then she wouldn't have been dragged into any of this. She saved Moss's life, and how did that end up? With Moss dead. *Still.* Saving his life had been pointless. It *had*, in fact, only given him a little bit of time.

She hadn't been strong enough.

Baz glanced over at her five times during lunch—she counted because she was nervous and spiraling in her anxiety. Were they rumor-mill glances? Or checking-in-on-her glances?

She decided on the latter because it made her anxiety spiral a little less, to think she still had favor with the one person who'd liked her right off the bat, and she forced down a piece of mystery-meat nugget.

Daphne didn't show up to lunch at all, or the next two classes. Not that Tara was looking for her.

"You're looking for Daphne," Baz said as the bell rang for last period. He caught up to her in two quick strides, hoisting his book bag over his shoulder.

Tara, flustered, quickened her pace. "I am n-*not.*"

Baz rolled his eyes. "Oh, come *on*, don't make me spell it out. I've a good nose for this kind of stuff," he added, tapping the side of his nose with a wink.

"Well, then your nose is wrong." She turned down the hall toward her next class—

And Baz caught her book bag by the handle, stopping her in her tracks. She twisted away. He held up his hands innocently and nudged his head in the opposite direction. "Slow down, New Girl, we've got an assembly this afternoon. Remember?"

". . . I forgot," she admitted. Daphne *had* mentioned an assembly this morning.

"I can walk with you," he said. "It's in the auditorium. I don't think you've been there yet."

She hadn't, and she didn't really know how to get there, either. She knew the auditorium was somewhere in the vague area to the north side of campus. Beyond that, it was one massive shrug.

"You don't—you won't get in trouble with your friends?" she mumbled. "I heard about Amala. . . ."

"Yeah. She's not even staying for Moss's funeral. It's closed casket, anyway. You know, because he . . ." He trailed off into silence and then cleared his throat. "Elaine said she saw you in the library before he . . ."

She squared her shoulders. "I didn't, if that's what you're asking."

He gave her a sympathetic look. "I wouldn't be walking with you if I thought you did. I was just going to ask if you saw anything. Something that could help us figure out what's happening?"

It's dark magic, she wanted to say, but he'd look at her like she was out of her mind. Or a liar. And neither of those were looks that she wanted at the moment.

They passed the library, which had been cordoned off since the incident. A foreboding feeling twisted her stomach, and she swallowed the bile rising in her throat. If only she'd been stronger. If only her magic had cooperated. But it hadn't.

And she had failed.

"No," she finally muttered, her throat tight. "I wasn't there when it happened."

"Oh." Baz sounded disappointed. "Right—sorry. Of course you weren't, you know? Let's stop talking about murders and witches," he added, holding the door open for her as they entered the auditorium. "What do you think about the Spice Girls?"

". . . Who?"

"The Spice Girls!" he said incredulously, and hummed a few bars, but none of it rang a bell for Tara. "Huh. Well, I like them better than the *NSYNC boys."

"I don't think that's a band."

"'Course it is—*It's tearing up my heart, as long as you love me?* Masterful lyrics."

Tara laughed despite herself. She'd listened to a few songs on the radio on the road trip from Utah to Vermont, and she knew for a fact that wasn't how *either* of those songs went.

The student body funneled through the rows of chairs in the auditorium. There were a lot more people than Tara expected. She'd never really gotten a proper read on the school—since most of her classes were on the third floor—but it was surprisingly big. A little overwhelming.

"Do you know what this assembly's about?" she asked Baz as they sat down near the back of the audience. She glanced around, but Daphne was strangely nowhere to be seen.

"Yeah. Same thing it is every year—oh, there's Leelee." His face softened at the name, and she followed his line of sight to . . . Hailey Conrad standing up on the stage. "You know she probably practiced this speech a hundred times in the mirror even though she's had it memorized for weeks now. She's always a lot more anxious than she looks. She works so hard, and no one ever sees it."

There was admiration in his voice, so much of it that Tara suspected there was more to Baz and Hailey than school friends. He talked about her with the kind of reverence that she'd only read about in poetry. Not as eloquently, but the feeling was there.

Baz caught her staring and turned to her with a grin. "What?"

"I . . . Nothing," she quickly replied, because he must not have been aware of it, the way he looked at Hailey, and it wasn't her place to say anything.

Principal Greaves walked across the stage to the podium and ushered everyone to their seats. Tara shifted uncomfortably in her chair. She had tried to ignore it when she first met the man, but he had a strange aura about him. It wasn't malignant or magical, but it was . . . something. *Guarded*, she decided. "Quiet down, quiet down now!" And when the student body finally did fall into silence, he began, "It's been a horrific first few weeks here at Hellborne Academy. I never thought my starting year here would be rife with such . . . *tragedies*, but we will get through this together! If you need to talk to a counselor about anything that's happened, Ms. West's and Mrs. Apperson's doors are always open to you. And furthermore, if you have any information about Mr. Jedon's death, please speak with the police. Now," he added, clasping his hands together, "with that out of the way, please give a warm welcome to Miss Hailey Conrad, senior class president!"

Hailey stepped up to the podium amid the applause and adjusted the mic.

"Huh," Baz muttered, frowning, "she usually has her index cards with her. . . ."

"Fellow students," Hailey began boldly, "October is always a strange month in Hellborne, but this year, Hellborne Academy has been cursed with tragedy after tragedy as we mourn the loss of three of our most talented students. . . ."

"Moss, *talented*?" Tara heard someone behind her whisper.

"Yeah, most talented *cheater*."

"Poor Amala . . ."

"Did you hear? I heard Brian tried to pressure—"

Suddenly, Baz whipped a glare over his shoulder. The girls quieted instantly.

Hailey went on. "Which is why I believe that instead of postponing our yearly tradition of the Burning, we must fight for our right to celebrate it as we have every year before. We mourn our fellow students, but they would never want us to change our traditions because of them, and Principal Greaves agrees. Moss *loved* the town decorations. Chad always volunteered as one of the townsfolk! And Brian . . . well, no one misses Brian more than I do, and he would never have wanted me to sit in the sadness of losing him. We shouldn't—we won't. Which is why I'm announcing the ballots for this year's Red Witch!"

That caught Tara's attention. "Doesn't Elaine want to be the Red Witch?"

Baz leaned into her and murmured, "Yeah, but we all gotta vote on it. The winner's announced at the homecoming football game this Friday. The senior who gets voted as the Red Witch gets a five-thousand-dollar scholarship to college, so that's the big thing."

"Well, at least they get paid to get burned, I guess."

"No actual fire. Nowhere near them."

Still, it seemed like a lot to Tara. Make-believe sacrificing a young woman on a pyre, even in the name of tradition.

Then again, Hellborne itself *was* a lot.

"And now," Hailey added, holding up a box, "it's Red Witch time! We'll be taking votes this week at lunch and all first quarter at homecoming Friday night, so you better choose your favorite! It's going to be totally magical. I, *personally*, am voting for Elaine O'To—"

"Thank you, Miss Conrad," Principal Greaves interrupted, standing from his chair behind her. He smiled as he gently shooed her off the podium. "We can't influence the election, now, can we?" he said with a laugh, adjusting his favorite pin-striped suit, his graying hair pushed back. He went over a few other key points to the coming weeks—the Burning and a field trip to the Hellborne Museum next week.

Which, again, Tara felt a bit strange about.

"It's a field trip," Baz said with a shrug as they filed out of the auditorium. The assembly took up the last bit of class, so the principal had dismissed them for the day. "We go every year. It's boring as hell but a free grade. Lots of old shit in glass boxes."

"Is it optional?"

"Nothing Founders-related is optional."

"And the pyre?"

"Gotta get voted to burn," he replied, tsking. "Weren't you listening?"

She *was*, but she rather hoped she'd heard wrong. The Burning. The Red Witch. Never mind the three dead boys. And the dark magic . . . A town with a history of witchcraft suddenly assaulted by it again?

That couldn't be a coincidence.

As Baz walked beside her, he reached into his jacket pocket to take out a lighter. He flicked it open and closed, open and closed. He did that a lot when he was seated at the lunch table. Was he nervous? Why?

Before she could ask, someone called his name from down the hall.

Hailey.

"Bastion!" She came over with her entourage. "Aren't you coming with us? We're throwing a going-away party for Amala today! Oh, Tara, hello again."

"Hi," she murmured. Hailey smiled at her, and she tried to return it, but Elaine gave her a glare so fierce, she winced and averted her gaze.

A tall white guy slung his arm around Cory and leaned in toward Baz. He did, in fact, remind Tara of Shaggy from *Scooby-Doo*. "Dude, you coming or what?" Harris finally in the flesh, Tara guessed. "It's gonna be *so fly*."

"Sorry," Baz said with a grin, "gotta head home today. Can you give Amala my good-byes?"

"Sure, sure. Somethin' up with your parentals?"

"No," he admitted, glancing at Tara as if he was afraid to say too much. "Chores. Forgot to do them yesterday—I was helping the equestrian club try to catch that horse that's on the loose."

Cory snorted. "You mean the one *Hailey* let out?"

"I didn't mean to!" Hailey cried indignantly.

"It's just surprising," Baz said. "You're usually so good with horses."

"Well, the *horse* got spooked, Bastion. And people change. Fine, as long as you're sure you don't wanna come, then we'll miss you. Don't forget to vote for Elaine this week!"

"I've been working for this moment for years. *Nothing* will stop me," Elaine said, and turned prickly when she glanced at Tara. "And no one will kill me before I get it."

Baz ignored the jab, putting himself between Elaine and Tara. "I'd never vote for anyone else," he replied warmly. "I'll catch up with you guys tomorrow morning?"

Harris rolled his eyes. "Buzzkill! But fine, fine, bro. See you in the a.m.," he said, and the group walked away. Hailey gave one last look at Tara before she followed them. They were swallowed by the hall of students in moments.

Baz let out a soft sigh. The aura around him flickered bluish-gray.

She inclined her head. "You lied to them."

"A small one," he admitted.

"Why?"

"Big lies get caught," he replied. She stared at him, refusing to budge, until he relented. "I don't do well with a lot of big emotion for a long period of time. It's all hard to digest."

"Anxiety?"

His lips twitched into an almost smile. "Something like that." He nudged his head toward the school's exit, and together they walked in silence down the winding road to Main Street. The evergreens were tightly packed around the town, bending softly in the coming winter breeze. Most Hellborne Academy students walked home, or they drove. It was a small enough town that they could, though there was a biting chill to the air that hadn't been there a few days before.

He elbowed her in the side to get her attention and pointed ahead to the girl shuffling her way down the street ahead of them. "Isn't that your girlfriend?"

"M-my *what*?"

"Goth girl, I totally said goth girl," he lied, and cupped his hands around his mouth and shouted, "Hey! Icy Hot!"

Tara wanted to hide.

Daphne didn't even twitch. She just kept walking.

"Don't ignore me! Yo! Queen of Shadows!"

At that, Daphne *did* stop in her tracks—and turned on her heel. Tara felt the deathly chill of her glare, and even though it wasn't even on *her*, it still made her want to crawl under a rock and die. "What do you *want*, jock."

Not a question.

Tara definitely wanted to hide, but Baz had a hand on her shoulder so she couldn't go anywhere. She took it back; she wanted to walk home alone now. It was better than with people. At least alone she was sure she wasn't going to get murdered. Mostly.

"I wanted to ask how you got out of assembly, I've been try-ing for *years*," he said with a big old smile that fooled *no one*. What was his motive? "Let's walk together, yeah?"

"I'd rather die," Daphne said nobly.

"Death would be preferable," Tara agreed.

Baz's hand on her shoulder tightened. "Oh, come on, we're all walking the same way, and I'm sure you're both excited for homecoming on Friday?"

Daphne rolled her eyes and pulled her book bag higher, resuming her steady march down Main Street. "Not really," she replied, her voice level and void of emotion. "It's ridiculous. My old school never had any of this."

"Mine either," Tara agreed. "They would've been . . . getting lost in corn mazes and riding in haybales."

"You had corn mazes?" Daphne asked.

"A few."

"We had snow. Michigan," she added, and then turned to Tara. "Well, since you're here, we should talk about our English project."

Tara felt herself go rigid. *Now?* After school? She wondered if Daphne had that crossbow hidden somewhere in her backpack. "Um, well—"

"You haven't picked a topic yet?" Baz *tsk*ed. "You need to get on that. I can leave you two to it if you'd like?"

Tara panicked. "Uh—no, it's—"

"Okay," Daphne said.

"Excellent." Baz winked at Tara and turned to leave when she reached out and grabbed him by the sleeve of his letterman jacket.

She hissed quietly when Daphne was out of earshot, "Wh-what are you *doing*?"

"I have no idea what you're so mad about," he whisper-replied innocently.

"You're incorrigible."

"Aw, shucks, don't use such big words. I don't know 'em. I'm that way," he added, prying her white-knuckled grip from his sleeve. He gestured toward the opposite direction when they finally got to the Crossroads. Back the way they came. So his way home *wasn't* in the same direction she went. He lied again—why? To get her and Daphne together?

"You lied again," she accused.

"Small one. Insignificant, really." He patted her on the shoulder. "See you at school!"

Then he turned with a wave good-bye, leaving her helpless and stranded, and disappeared up South Street. Tara wondered whether or not she should make a run for it. She definitely didn't want to stay here and be questioned, *again*, by Daphne.

Even though she didn't kill Moss, Elaine was apparently evidence enough to put her at the scene of the crime. All the police needed was for Daphne to go to them and report what she saw—so why hadn't she already? And when Tara's father found out about all of this . . .

She didn't want to think about the consequences. Even if she didn't get convicted of a crime she didn't do, her father wouldn't just pick up and move them again—he'd send her somewhere.

And it'd be worse than Vermont.

When her mother first died, her cousin Beth had given him a brochure for an all-girls school in Ohio. A finishing school. The kind that taught young women manners on how to conduct themselves in proper society. Her father had lingered on that brochure too long, but in the end, he said he loved Tara too much to let her go somewhere far away.

"I will send you there if I have to," her father had said as he hugged her in the packed-up kitchen of their old home. "But I love you. I will do whatever I have to. Let's try to start new first."

So they had moved to Vermont. Which was bad, but not as bad as the school in that brochure. All the young women in it had these lifeless smiles and beady eyes, and just thinking about it sent a shiver up her spine.

No, she had to keep her head down. Stay quiet.

And—

Her feet were moving to get away before she realized it herself, until Daphne slid in front of her to stop her. Tara muttered, "Y-yes?"

Daphne said, "It doesn't make sense that people think you have anything to do with these deaths."

"Because I don't."

Except that was a lie. She'd failed to save Moss, and now he was dead, so wasn't that a little bit her fault? She should've kept her nose in her own business. Because she wanted nothing to do with this twisted, terrible thing that was lurking in Hellborne, Vermont. Because she wanted nothing to do with magic ever again. But she couldn't say any of those things. It wasn't like Daphne would believe her, anyway.

"Then *what*," Daphne went on, "are you trying to hide?"

Tara gave a start. "Hiding? I'm—I'm not—I'm not hiding—" Anger flared in her middle. She was so sick and tired of being told what she *should* do. "Do you really think I did it?"

"I'm saying—"

"Well, I *didn't*! I couldn't have! I d-didn't kill Moss, and I didn't kill Chad or Brian. I wasn't even here. I don't *want* to be here."

It was the first time she'd ever said the secret aloud. That she didn't want to be here. Was here Vermont? Or here . . . *here*? Everything had become so dull and gray since her mother died. The world had flipped upside down and something inside her had cracked and broken on the ground and nothing was ever going to be the same.

Her magic would never be the same. Her life. Her *family*.

She didn't want to be here, and she wasn't quite sure herself what she meant. It wasn't that she wanted to die. It was just . . .

She wanted her mom. She wanted long talks in their garden.

And those were both things she'd never have again.

Daphne inclined her head. "I was *going* to say I don't think you did it. As you said, you weren't here for Chad or Brian's murders. It doesn't make sense."

"Then what do you want from me?" she asked in a tiny voice, because she wasn't sure what she could give.

"I also didn't want to come here. I've been the new kid so many times. It's . . . exhausting? And right when I think I might've found a groove, my parents up and drag me to some other godforsaken part of the country. They usually don't even ask me."

Tara averted her eyes, picking at her cuticles. "My dad didn't ask me, either. He just told me it was for my own good."

"And isn't that *bullshit*? I love my parents, but I'd like a say in my own life, you know?"

She nodded. "More than you think."

There was a spark in Daphne's eyes. "Then let's take charge of it, yeah? Prove to Elaine and everyone else that you aren't the murderer and that I . . . that my parents can trust me. Let's find the killer."

Tara couldn't have heard correctly. "*What?*"

"Help me find out who's killing people at Hellborne." Then Daphne offered her hand. The dusk light glinted in the silver rings on her fingers. "So? What do you say? You're the only person who saw what happened to Moss, and I don't want another person to die because I'm too slow."

Too slow . . . ? Tara looked at Daphne's offered hand,

and she clasped it tightly. Daphne's hand was rough and callused, and her fingers held tightly, sturdy. She let go, and Tara quickly pulled her hand back. "Does this have to do with your crossbow?"

Daphne smirked. "It does. But what I'm about to tell you is going to be really weird."

"Weird how?"

In reply, Daphne Frost looked her straight in the eyes and said, "Because I'm here to kill a witch."

CHAPTER SIXTEEN
MURDER BOARDS

"Like a . . . *witch hunter*?"

Daphne threw her head back with a laugh.

Tara visibly wilted. "Oh, well, that's a relief—"

"It'd be boring if we *only* hunted witches. We hunt other monsters, too. We only *specialize* in witches."

Oh. That . . . was probably a little worse. Tara wasn't really sure what she had expected, but witch hunter had not been on her bingo card.

Considering the crossbow, maybe it should have been.

Daphne went on, not noticing Tara had begun to hyperventilate. "I know it sounds wild—witches! They don't exist! Yada, yada, but hear me out: They do. And Brian, Chad, and Moss all fell victim to one. I just . . . don't know *who*. And time's running out. And you're the only lead I have."

Except Tara was a witch, too, and teaming up with a witch hunter felt like a kind of Shakespearean tragedy.

If she slipped and accidentally used her magic, would Daphne even blink an eye before plunging a stake in her? *Did* witch hunters use stakes? Arrows? Guns? Tara knew she bled like everyone else.

But if these rumors kept spiraling . . .

Her father would hear about the rumors, and then she'd be off to that finishing school. Or maybe something worse. He'd never let her do anything without his supervision again. So she was faced with a choice: hope that her father didn't hear the gossip in town or help a witch hunter catch a murderous witch.

What would my mom do? she asked herself, but she didn't really need to think long to know that answer.

She said, "Before Moss ran himself into the bookcase, he seemed to be talking to someone. Someone he knew. But there was no one else there. He said, 'I didn't tell anyone. I didn't do anything. You got what you deserved.'"

"Verbatim?"

"I'm pretty sure. I have a good memory."

Daphne pursed her lips. She debated for a long moment. "Okay. Let's get to work, then. C'mon, we'll go back to my house."

Tara gave a start. "N-now?"

"Time's ticking, so yeah. Unless you have somewhere else to be?"

She hesitated, glancing down in the direction of her house. Her father wouldn't be off work until 5:00 p.m., and it was just 3:30 p.m. She had time if she returned before he did, and they still had leftover lasagna from yesterday. "What . . . what do you have in mind?"

The witch hunter smirked. "I've got a murder board."

"A . . . wh-what?"

Daphne rolled her eyes. "I'm working with a novice."

Daphne lived in an unassuming brick house on the other side of town. And while that might've sounded like a far walk, it really wasn't, because Hellborne was so small. It was—*maybe*—a ten-minute stroll, though Tara didn't remember a single moment between that dumpster and the Frosts' driveway. Her nerves vibrated.

There was a single car parked in the driveway, a beat-up blue van that looked like it had come straight out of the '70s. Rust included. There was also a motorcycle in the driveway, but without its front wheel, it looked certifiably undriveable.

She followed Daphne up the front steps, which were overflowing with asters and goldenrod, as she fished for her keys in her black backpack. Just before she inserted the key, she paused and turned on her heel to face Tara. "If we run into the twins or my parents," she said, "you're gonna say you're over because of *Macbeth*. Our essay."

"That makes sense. . . ."

"Dad's not really keen on non-hunters poking around the business."

She tried to not look too alarmed. "Business? So, your entire family . . ."

"All of 'em. But they can't help me with this case; it's the rule. This is my rite of passage, yada, yada," Daphne said, unlocking the door. "Though it's a bit bigger than I thought it'd be, so lesson forty-seven: Pride will often get in the way of good work. So, ergo, you're helping me."

"Oh." But that only gave her more questions than answers. What kind of rite of passage was this? There were *rules*? It was all so strange. A bit like witches, come to think of it. She heard rumors of different communities of different kinds of witches, but hunters? She hadn't thought much about them.

Daphne called out into the house that she was home with a friend, and Tara followed her inside quietly. First sign of trouble, and she was leaving. She'd feign sick, or that her father needed her home—something.

Mom would help, she thought, but then a doubtful voice added,

But you aren't your mom. She's dead.

Two boys around Tara's brother's age looked up from the kitchen table, both with the same dark hair as Daphne and dark eyes. In front of them were bits and pieces of . . . crossbows? Bolts and strings and other odds and ends to the weapon that Tara couldn't even begin to understand.

"Uh, what's a friend doing here?" the left twin asked, alarmed, grabbing a bag to swipe all the crossbow mechanisms into.

"Her name's Tara, and it's fine—you can keep your things out," Daphne quickly replied. "She's cool. I told her y'all like to go *hunting*."

Well, *now* Tara knew.

The left twin visibly wilted and sat down again. "Thank *god*, we just got old Winnie apart." And then he patted the butt of the crossbow like it was a dear pet, and whispered, "Good

Winnie, all dirty and oily, but we're getting you in tip-top shape."

"Gabe, stop being weird," Daphne sighed, and said, "Gabriel, and the one with his face on the table is Michael."

"Mike," the right twin said, facedown on the table. He picked his head up. "You never bring friends home. Who's she?"

"This is Maclay—erm, I mean Tara," she said, motioning back to her. Tara's ears burned at the tips because she liked how Daphne said her first name. Soft at the beginning, a growl at the end. "We're doing a project together. *Macbeth*."

Gabe made a face. "I hated that one in school."

"It's not my favorite. Oh—did Mr. Giles call?"

Michael shook his head. "Not yet."

"Damn," Daphne complained, making her way down one of the hallways. Tara quickly followed. "We're going to spread out in Dads' study!"

Gabe shouted after them, "Hey, just remember she can't help with *your solo homework*!"

Solo homework—the hunting stuff?

Daphne didn't deign to give him a response as she opened the garage door and welcomed Tara inside. She expected a car and maybe a workstation, but the garage had been converted into another room. Bookshelves lined the walls and were filled with manuscripts and concoctions—poisons—and plants in jars, organs in murky liquids, and deadly weapons. The books, however, all had a strange aura. Tara could sense it the moment she laid eyes on them.

They were the kinds of books her mother had. The ones whose ashes still simmered with magic.

Tara ran her fingers along the books on the shelves. Beside them was a crafting table with more crossbows and bolts and . . . stakes?

"For vampires," Daphne explained.

Tara gave her a confused look. "The . . . blood-sucking kind?"

"Mostly. You know how there are witches? Well, there are also vampires and demons and angels and all sort of other creatures, most of them better off dusted."

That was . . . a lot to take in at once. She knew she had demon blood, but she hadn't thought about the wider implications of that. That demons were in the world, walking among everyone else. And, apparently, so were vampires and angels and all manner of things that went bump in the night. Her common sense told her they were fictional—stories that parents told children to keep them in bed at night—but she couldn't really believe that with all of these books on the shelves. Books about types of demons, about vampires, about angelic thousand-eyed monsters.

If there were witches like her, then why not demons and vampires and werewolves and stranger things?

Daphne went on, "My dads say there's a slayer in Sunnydale, California, doing all the fun stuff."

"Slayer?"

"Someone chosen by fate or whatever to kick ass and take names," Daphne said, flipping over a whiteboard. "If only we could all be so lucky. My parents and I travel wherever we're told to go. Someone puts out a bounty for a witch or vampire or demon or whatever who turns dark, and we go and take care of it. Which, you know, means I'm always the new girl." On the other side was an intricate web of information and victims and

Hellborne history. She rapped her knuckles on it. "Say hello to Miss Murder Board."

Tara stared, agog. "She is . . . intricate. . . ."

"That she is. Here's what I got so far about all of the victims. Some of the info I got from . . . dubious sources."

"I was about to ask about the autopsy reports."

"Don't think too hard." Daphne came to stand beside her and folded her arms over her chest in a thoughtful pose. "I think I've stared at all this info so long, I can't see what's right in front of me."

Tara frowned. It *was* a lot of information, intersecting strings, newspaper printouts, xeroxed autopsy reports, and sloppily jotted notes. She stepped closer to read Daphne's scratchy handwriting.

BRIAN SHORTER
- 1st Death, Sept 19
- Last seen after lacrosse practice
- Found in the bleachers upside down having "accidentally" hanged himself between the slats
- Burn mark on hand
- Cause of death: embolism of the brain

CHAD JACKSON
- 2nd death, October 2
- Same friend group as Brian
- Last seen after tutoring in the library with Elaine
- Found in the boys' locker room, having tripped backward into a locker; coat hook went through skull

— Burn mark on hand

— Cause of death: head trauma

MOSS JEDON

— 3rd death, October 17

— Saved him in the library with new girl (Maclay), was taken to the hospital

— Died later at the hospital (from his injuries sustained in attack on the 16th? Unsure)

— Burn mark on hand

— Cause of death: self-defenestration

Around the information were questions like *Are they all linked to one event?* and *All look like accidents???*

But the question that wasn't written in any of the white margins was one that Tara wrote as she picked up the dry-erase marker and uncapped it: *Why death?*

"What do you mean?" Daphne asked.

Tara snapped the cap back on, rolling her knowledge around on her tongue as she recalled a passage from one of her mother's books—it wasn't a spellbook, but a philosophy book written in the 1560s. "If it is a witch, as you say, why death? Aren't there other spells? To make people suffer instead? Why murder them? Maybe if we find out why, we can figure out who. It might be part of the witch's . . ."

"Revenge?" Daphne filled in.

"If it was revenge, wouldn't the witch want them to suffer? Why kill them so quickly?"

"You have a point," she replied, scratching the side of her

neck. "And almost everyone at the school has grudges against these guys. They were shits."

"Do you know who might be next?"

"Could be anyone, but if I had to bet, it'd be someone in the popular group—Cory or Harris or your buddy Baz."

Tara inclined her head toward the names again. "Why not Elaine or Amala or Hailey?"

"The victims have all been guys so far. Don't you think if the witch hated everyone in that group, they would've gone after Elaine first?"

Tara tried not to smile. "Probably."

Daphne set her hands on her hips. "Exactly. Also," she added, "the girls all have alibis. When Brian died, Elaine was at the mall, and when Chad died, she had dance lessons. Amala's on the dressage team, so she doesn't have time to be a witch."

"And horses are pretty good judges of character," Tara agreed. "And Hailey?"

Daphne scoffed. "Our perfect senior-class-president princess? She's clear. Has so many extracurriculars she has alibis for *ages*. I don't know how she sleeps, honestly. The day Brian died, she was at the mall with Elaine, and she worked at the bookstore in town on the night Chad was killed, so we've got multiple eyewitnesses there. With Moss, I haven't checked, but . . ."

"I saw Elaine outside the library that day," Tara said.

"And that's where that rumor started," Daphne realized, nodding. "Since we don't know who it might be, maybe we should start with how they died. Which is . . . different for every one of them. That doesn't help. The only thing linking them is that they were all friends."

"What about the mark on Moss's hand?" Tara asked.

"You saw it, too?"

She nodded.

"It was on Chad's and Brian's hands as well. Here, look." Daphne shuffled through the pages on the murder board until she brought one to the forefront. It was a sketch of what the burn looked like: two opposite right angles crossed together. "I dunno what the sign is or what it means—I've been scouring everywhere. Asked a friend of my dads' to try to help us identify it, but he hasn't replied yet."

"This Mr. Giles person?"

She nodded. "He's a Watcher—they're basically people who are *super* knowledgeable in everything and live forever, so if anyone knows about whatever it is, it'd be him, but . . . I think he's kind of preoccupied right now."

"Hmm." Tara traced her fingers over the sketch.

"It could just be the witch's calling card—you know, like how serial killers leave notes or brands on their victims?"

Something bothered Tara about that. "How are you so sure it's a witch?"

"Oh, it *could* be a demon or something else in any other cir-cumstance, but in this case, we were contacted directly by the higher-ups. They thought this would be a good rite of passage for me. They gave me minimal details—that the Devon Coven said that there was a witch in Hellborne, Vermont, who needs to be dealt with. And that's it."

Tara guessed this Devon Coven didn't even consider there could be two witches in Hellborne. Not that she'd kill anyone.

Daphne turned and went to sit in one of the two chairs and sank deep into the cushions. "Everyone who has died so far was part of your friend Baz's popular group, so it's safe to say the murderer is *someone* in that group. Or maybe close to it."

"Baz isn't a friend," she quickly retorted. "He's just—helping me. Sort of."

"Seems pretty friendly to you."

Tara eyed her, frowning. "You could have been friends with him, too."

Daphne scrunched her nose and looked away. "After this job, we're packing up and going to the next one. So, there's no need to get close to anyone."

"Ah."

Including her. Good. Perhaps that would keep Daphne far enough away from her so she wouldn't ever catch on to her secret.

Tara reached for the marker and uncapped it. She drew a box in the corner of the whiteboard where there wasn't any information. "Well, I think we should figure out a list of suspects and cross them off one by one. At least, that's what Agatha Christie heroines would do."

Daphne sighed. "I'm no good at detective work."

"Your murder board is great."

"You don't have to be so nice."

"It also happens to be the truth." Tara wrote down the names of the three remaining boys in the popular group, though writing Bastion's name pained her. "Cory, Harris, and Baz . . . they'd have the most motive, theoretically. Anyone else? Anyone who might have a grudge?"

Daphne grabbed a skull from the end table and began to toss it up and catch it. "Like, literally *everyone*. Wait, what about that girl who fought with Moss in bio? Marieke? Madison?"

"Marissa?"

"That's her! She seemed kinda suspicious. I think she used to be part of their group."

Tara added Marissa's name to the board, thinking the same thing. "Also, Principal Greaves."

"What, *really*?"

She nodded. "I get . . . a bad vibe from him." By *bad vibe* she meant a strange aura, but she couldn't tell Daphne that. "Besides, he's new to the school, too, right? And the murders began only after he became principal. That's suspicious."

Daphne nodded. "Greaves, then."

Tara capped the marker and stepped back to look at the board. It wasn't a long list.

She didn't realize Daphne had come up beside her until she said, "Well, at least it's a start." She eyed Tara. "We don't make a terrible team."

"Yes, well"—she handed the marker to Daphne again—"I'm trying to be useful. I've never done this before."

"Me neither, if you can't tell." Daphne sighed, scratching the side of her face with the marker. "Man, I really wish I could ask my parents. . . ."

That made Tara curious. "Why can't they help?"

"It's the rite of passage thing—every hunter has to prove themselves by solving the mission in question. This mission just happened to be tracking and putting a stop to a witch. Hopefully before she murders too many people," she added under her breath. "Why did it have to be a *witch*?"

"Do you hate all witches?"

"*Hate*?" Daphne scrunched her nose. "That's kinda strong, cupcake."

Was it? Tara's father did—very easily. She could see it in his eyes every time he looked at her. Maybe it was easy enough to admit to Daphne that she was also a witch, but what if Daphne started looking at her the same way her father did?

She . . . she wasn't sure she could stomach that.

"I—I just thought . . ." Tara began, but the witch hunter gave a shrug.

"I'm sure I don't hate all of them. I've only ever dealt with bad ones, though, so I haven't met anyone else, to be honest," she said, eyeing Tara thoughtfully. "Have you?"

Tara felt her spine straighten. If she said no, she hadn't met any witches, then she might get caught in that lie later. But if she said yes, then would Daphne think less of her? Or—worse—think that she was the murderer? There wasn't a right answer here. "I—I mean, I don't— I've never *seen a*— Maybe," she said, training her eyes on the ground. "They seem danger-ous. All of them."

"My dads say the only thing more dangerous than a monster is a well-read monster-hunter. Thus the books. I've seen you eyeing them, Maclay. Don't look so shy."

Tara fought a smile. "There's just so *many*."

The shelves were lined with titles she'd never heard of. She wondered where Daphne's family got them. Tara's mother had said all her books had been passed down to her from her mother, who had died when Tara was seven. She didn't remember much about her, just hazy memories of cable-knit sweaters and honey perfumes. Would she start to forget about her mom the same way? Lose the memory of how the sunlight touched the gray strands in her blond hair and turned them silver? Of her soft smile when-ever Tara asked a question about secret, hushed things? Of the sweet glimmer of magic when her mother talked to her flowers?

Her mother had always taught her that there was light magic—good magic—just as there was dark magic. The kind that lured you in, promising power. Whatever you wanted. Whatever you yearned for.

"Magic should never be used for what you want," her mother had once said gently as a rose bloomed in Tara's cupped hands, "only what you need."

"How do I know what I want isn't what I need?"

"Your heart will tell you."

Would it, though?

Daphne waved her hand toward the shelves. "Well, if you're going to help me find the witch, you might as well learn about them. These are my dads' books. They make moving a pain in the ass."

"They're nice. I mean, th-the books."

Daphne grinned. "You can borrow them if you want. Any of them. Just lemme know which ones you want, and I'll write them down so they'll know."

Tara felt her heart twist with excitement. "*Any* of them?"

"As many as you can carry."

Was this a test? Was this how Daphne would trap her, prove that she was a witch? She ran her fingers across the spines of novels. *Ancient Rituals of the Lei-Ach. Taglarin Mystic Rites. Auras and Their Secrets.*

It was a risk she ached to take.

What kind of witch would she be, she wondered, if she had access to all these kinds of books?

Contented, she thought.

"I'd love to," she replied.

"Good, and besides, it's nice, you know? To talk to someone who doesn't think I'm crazy."

She gave Daphne a surprised look. "Why would I think that?"

"The whole witch-hunter business. Magic. Demons. You know, normal people would think I'm out of my mind."

Tara shook her head. "Everyone derided Mary Wollstonecraft for over a hundred years for writing that women were capable of the same intellectual achievements as men. She was right, of course. People were just . . . they're just scared of things they don't understand." She absently rubbed her thumb along the spine of a book she'd never known existed—so many of them. Books on magic and lore and legends. Books on rituals. Books on demons, and angels, and strange shadows that whispered in the night. "I'm comforted by the things I don't understand."

"Why?"

Tara turned her gaze away from the books to Daphne and gave her the smallest, most secret smile. "Because I barely know myself— Oh, is that strange?"

"A little, but I don't mind. You're cute," Daphne replied with the softest hint of a smile, like she understood. The smile looked good on her, like a tailored jacket and well-fitted boots. It fit. And for the first time in . . . *forever*, Tara felt a little less on edge. A little duller, a little softer. She didn't need to be prickly here, which was strange, because by all accounts she was sitting in the mouth of a wolf that would gobble her whole.

Then, suddenly, Daphne realized exactly what she had said and added in a fluster, "I—I mean—*it's* cute, not you. I mean, you're *also* cute, but your face, the way you look at books, it's just— I didn't mean—well, I *did*, but—oh my god," she groaned, rubbing her hands over her face, "I'm just digging my grave, aren't I?"

"It's very deep so far," Tara agreed, trying not to laugh.

"Maybe I can dig myself a one-way trip to hell, thank you. What I meant was— Are you *laughing* at me? No laughing! Please! I'm mortif—"

"Daphne!" a male voice called from the other side of the door, mercifully saving Daphne from her tailspin. There was a knock on the door before he popped his head inside. Mid-forties, tight black curls, brown skin like Daphne, and large thick black-framed glasses. "Oh! You've got a friend. In . . . our study."

"This is Tara," Daphne quickly replied, flipping over the whiteboard to the blank side again. "She's a friend."

"A friend in my study?"

"It's quiet," she said, and Tara nodded.

"These are strange books," Tara added, to sell their innocence. It must've worked, thanks to her large doe eyes and her curious brow, because he laughed.

"It's a bunch of gibberish. Hope you girls are hungry. We've got Taco Bell for dinner. Fred went by and grabbed it on his way home from work, so you two better get some before the twins eat everything."

Mexican sounded delicious, and Tara was a little hungry— until a thought occurred to her with a bolt of dread. "O-oh, what time is it?"

He checked his Rolex. "Five thirty."

"I—I have to get home," she said in a panic, grabbing her book bag. "I'm going to be late."

"You can call," Daphne suggested, giving her a worried look. "Can't you? Is everything okay?"

"Yes, but . . ." She hesitated but thought perhaps calling *was* the best thing to do, anyway. They were planning to eat leftovers, and if it was for school, surely her dad wouldn't mind? Especially if he knew where she was. "I can call him, yes," she agreed, so Daphne led her to the phone in the kitchen, by the laundry room.

There was another man setting the table, with ginger hair, save for a streak of white at the front, and a smattering of freckles across his cheeks. Fred.

As she dialed her home phone and waited for it to ring, she watched Daphne's dad kiss the ginger-haired man on the mouth, and she quickly looked away.

Her parents had never kissed in front of her.

They never said they loved each other, either.

The phone rang long enough for her to decide that either no one was home, or her brother was listening to the Foo Fighters so loud he couldn't hear the phone. And either way, that meant her father wasn't home. Should she leave anyway, and risk her father's wrath?

Or . . .

"Yeah," her brother answered on the ninth ring.

"Hi, Donny, it's Tara."

"Yeah."

"I'll be a little late coming home, but there's leftovers in the refrigerator. I'm . . . studying. There's a lot to catch up on."

"Right, okay."

"Will you let Dad know?"

"Yeah, yeah." And he hung up before she could thank him.

Her brother didn't sound like he was in the best mood. Maybe she should go home, just in case. . . .

Daphne's father—the one with the dark hair—put his hands on his hips and looked at Tara expectantly. "So? What's the verdict, kiddo?"

Kiddo, like she was already a part of their family. Her father had never called her anything other than *Tara* or *daughter*. He'd never met any of her friends.

Not that she had many. Not that she'd ever brought any home.

And just that possibility, that daydream of a friend and a normal family and a seat at a dark oak table set with brightly colored plates and the smell of fresh Mexican food—it made her bold.

She placed the phone back on the hook and said, "M-may I stay for dinner?"

CHAPTER SEVENTEEN
FAMILY MATTERS

The Frosts were the kind of family Tara only read about in books. They laughed together as they talked about their day, shared inside jokes, and ribbed each other with broad grins on their faces. Sean had a professorship at the university an hour away—much like her own father, but somehow a world apart, while Fred worked at the local hardware store. The twins were taking a gap year—like Tara's brother—and they were focusing on making a feature-length film that looked like found footage. About a witch terrorizing a group of campers.

"We'll call it *Stalking the Witch*," Mike said, nodding, but his twin brother made a face.

"I hate that name. It needs to feel more organic—like it's *real*."

Daphne rolled her eyes and leaned over to Tara, whispering out of the corner of her mouth, "They've been stuck on this fight for *months*."

"About the name?"

"They're *obsessed* with making it perfect."

"Because it has to be!" Gabe cried, overhearing them, waving a spoon full of sour cream in the air. "The title's gotta draw you in. People didn't go see *Scream* because of the weird ghostmask dude, did they? No!"

"I did," Daphne pointed out. "*Scream* was a weird title."

"It was *memorable*," Mike argued. "You just don't have taste."

"How about something more academic-sounding?" Tara offered. "*The Witch Files*?"

Gabe gasped. "Ooh! *The Witch Files*!"

"How about project?" Daphne added. "*The Witch Project*?"

"But what kind of witch?" Tara mused.

"Like the one here," Gabe replied. "You know, the legend of the Red Witch? Have you made any headway on that, Daph?"

"We don't talk about *homework* at the table," Sean reminded them, his voice pleasant but stern, and grabbed a taco from the middle platter, loading it up with salsa and hot sauce. He had a napkin tucked into his collar so he wouldn't get it on his catprint button-down.

Fred shook his head and told his husband, "Kids and their creativity."

Tara hid a smile and bit into her taco. People actually lived with each other like this? They joked and shared stories over dinner? She thought that her memories of normal dinners had been a dream. Her mom burning the chicken and bashfully taking out a salad. Her father laughing and kissing her hand, and telling her it was delicious nonetheless. They felt like scenes from a different life.

When Gabe and Sean started arguing about whose turn it was to take out the trash, Tara tensed for a moment, expecting a fight, before Gabe gave in with an indignant sniff and said, "Fine, I'll do it this time—but you owe me."

"Thank you," Sean replied, and he and Fred cleaned up everyone's plates and wiped down the table. "So, Daph, *do* you have any leads?"

Fred observed wryly, "I thought you said no work at the table?"

"I did, didn't I," his husband agreed cheekily, "but we're done with dinner now, aren't we?"

"You and your semantics," Fred sighed, and they carried the dirty dishes to the sink. Tara wanted to burn this dinner into her memory. She wanted to have a hundred more like it. Dinner with a table full of friends—a Scooby gang.

Stupid, she scolded herself as she followed Daphne back to the study. She checked the clock above the fireplace as she went. It was almost seven. She should be getting home.

Daphne grabbed a few books from the shelf in the study and offered them to her. "Here. I saw you were kind of eyeballing these earlier."

"Um, oh—I can't possibly—"

"*Take* them, Maclay," Daphne groaned, pushing them into her arms. "And remember to return them."

"You just want me to come back," she replied, teasing, before she could stop herself. What had come over her? She wasn't used to being forward like this.

"I have to keep an eye on you, remember?" Daphne quirked an eyebrow.

Tara put the books into her backpack, almost afraid Daphne would change her mind. "I'll read them quickly so I can come back."

"You can come back without them, too."

Her heart fluttered at the thought. "Thank you. Your family's really nice," she added, zipping up her book bag. "They're . . . normal."

Daphne snorted. "No one's ever called my family that before. My dads? They're some of the best hunters in the business. My brothers aced their rites of passage within a day of getting their mission. I feel . . . like I'm the odd one out, really."

"I th-think you're exceptional."

Daphne bit back a grin. "You barely know me, cupcake." Then she went to the other side of the library and added, changing the subject a bit too quickly, "Maybe we should be looking at Nordic runes. . . ."

"Aren't you afraid?" Tara blurted. "Of killing?"

Daphne gave a one-shouldered shrug, but she was facing away from Tara so she couldn't read her face. "Sometimes witches turn dark, and they hurt people. Those are the ones we hunt down."

"And the ones who don't?"

"I haven't met any yet."

But if you did? she wanted to ask. *Would you also hate me, like my dad?* But Daphne was too close to crossbows, to knives, to stakes meant for undead hearts. "Oh."

"You won't have to do the hard part," Daphne promised then, as if that was what Tara was worried about. "We should start crossing people off the suspect list tomorrow," she added more quietly, glancing around to make sure her family wasn't listening. "Who do you think would be the easiest?"

"I'm not sure. . . ."

"We'll figure it out. Do you need a ride home?"

Tara shook her head. The brisk night air would clear her mind. Let her think. "I don't think so. Thank you, though. I should probably go." So she just waved good-bye to Daphne and her family, thinking that perhaps if she had been anyone else, she could've fit in here, too.

But she wasn't. And she couldn't.

She was Tara Maclay, and she'd learned a long time ago that she didn't fit in anywhere.

CHAPTER EIGHTEEN
DEATH AFTER DARK

Her father was waiting in his reading chair when Tara got home. The living room lights were off save for the one lamp behind his head, so the shadows painted him in a stark silhouette. He licked his finger and flipped the page.

"Your brother told me you had dinner with a friend tonight," he said, his voice so soft and even, she felt like she was walking on land mines.

"Y-yes," she replied. "I w-went over to get help on a project, and I stayed a bit late. . . . I'm sorry. I c-called Donny to let you know."

"Don't you think it was a bit last-minute?"

Her hand tightened around her book bag strap. "I'm sorry," she repeated.

"Do I even know who you ate dinner with?"

"They—they're nice people. The Frosts. They live—"

"Did you even *think* to introduce me to them before you went and did something dangerous?"

Dangerous? She decided not to take the bait. "I'm sorry."

"I know you are, but you know what I say about sorry—you only mean it if you never do it again. I was worried, Tara."

"It won't happen again," she promised.

He nodded and licked his thumb to turn the page again. "That's all I ask. I assume you aren't hungry, since you already had dinner. Why don't you go to your room to study?"

It was more of a command than a question, but she nodded *Yes, sir* and quickly scuttled off to her room and closed the door. Her heart hammered in her chest. Her father was *furious*, and she did feel bad that she'd made him worry. She should've known better, but dinner with the Frosts had been . . .

It had been really nice, and that was saying something, since they were all witch hunters.

Somewhere in the middle of studying how to compose functions and inverse functions, Tara fell asleep. And began to dream.

About her mother.

She didn't dream often, but when she did, it was always about her mother. Her mother stood in the backyard surrounded by sunflowers and ivy and violet wolfsbane, the sun streaking through the emerald leaves of the broad oak behind her. It was a good memory, the best one Tara had. So it was her best dream, too. Even though she couldn't feel the sunlight or remember what day of spring it was, she knew it had happened, once upon a time.

Sometimes she'd have conversations with her mom in the garden and tell her how much she missed her.

Sometimes her mom would just laugh and kiss her forehead, as if to say, *You're here again? It's okay; you can stay for a little while.*

Tara remembered things very well, too well. She could quote the magic books her mom kept locked in the suitcase in her closet. She could pull facts from their pages, recall spells and sutures that could tie the world back together.

There were spells of love, spells of happiness, spells to bloom a sunflower.

But there were no spells against death.

Unnatural spells, yes, but not natural ones. Not human ones.

And what good was magic if it couldn't save the person she loved the most? Maybe that was why she closed her magic away. Or maybe the magic of the world had closed itself off from her, ignored like a dying limb on a tree.

So, Tara, even in this sun-soaked dream, felt cold and alone. Her mother gone, and now also her magic.

Her mother smiled this time, though, and said, "It won't be forever. Remember that willow we always sat under? You'll find one again, and you'll be happy."

Of course her mother would say that.

"I miss you," Tara whispered, a quiet secret, an admonishment. "I miss you so much."

Her mother's smile saddened, and she reached out to cup Tara's cheek in her hand. "I know, sprout, and I'm sorry, but you need to wake up. There's something strange happening, and I'm afraid you won't see it if you stay here."

Tara's eyes widened. "Strange how? Wait, *Mom*—"

The sunlight disappeared, and the shadow crept in. She glanced up into the creaking boughs of the oak tree, and when she looked back to her mother, she was gone. And in her place stood Daphne Frost, eyes sunken and lips blue. Dead.

Tara screamed—

And awoke with a sudden gasp. She was alone in her room. No one was there. Was that a warning? From her mom? Daphne wasn't dead yet—she *wouldn't* die.

Not if Tara had anything to say about it.

CHAPTER NINETEEN

MARISSA

Tara had to find Daphne.

She hadn't seen her on the walk to school, so Tara was already thinking the worst had happened, that while she'd dreamed Daphne had . . .

Stop it, she's fine, she's fine, she told herself. Common sense told her not to feel anything for the witch hunter, and she usually liked common sense, but now all she wanted to do was shove it into a box and duct-tape it closed so it couldn't tell her what a terrible idea it was to like Daphne Frost. As a friend—or anything more.

"I need to find her," she muttered as she walked into the school. "I just need to find—"

"Who?"

Her heart swelling, she whirled around, and there was Daphne, kicking up her longboard and taking off her helmet. Worry crossed Daphne's face. "Is something up, Maclay?"

"O-oh, no. I was just—" Tara racked her brain for some excuse, since she couldn't exactly tell Daphne she was worried Daphne had *died* because of a nightmare, but she was drawing a blank. "I . . . um . . ." Then the multicolored hair of Marissa caught her eye as she climbed the steps of the school. "I think we should go after Marissa first."

Daphne cocked her head. "Oh?"

"Y-yeah."

"I think maybe you're right. . . . She'd be pretty easy to cross off the list. Just interrogate her, you know. I've also got a stone that'll glow if a witch bleeds on it. We can cut her finger and—"

"Maybe we can talk to her first? See where she was the nights the guys were attacked? And then . . . go from there?"

"And if she's the witch and just decides to blow us up?"

"Which is why we should probably handle this delicately."

Daphne sighed. "I'm not very good at that part."

"Well," she replied, "isn't that why we're a team?"

Daphne smiled at her. "Yeah."

There was a strange warmth in her belly, one that made her feel light and buoyant whenever Daphne looked at her with those dark, dazzling eyes. Her common sense told her *Beware, beware,* but for once, Tara didn't want to heed the warnings.

Maybe the fall was going to hurt, but at the moment, at least she liked the view.

Over the next few days, between homework and the investigation, Daphne and Tara decided that the best time to talk to Marissa was during PE. So that Friday, which was also, tragically, the day of homecoming, they put their plan into motion. Everyone was festooned in Hellborne Academy's colors—bloodred and gold, devils painted on their cheeks, knee-high socks, anything the school's uniform code would allow. Even if Tara didn't *already* know it was homecoming, Baz certainly reminded her when he tied a ribbon in her hair before class and said, "You look cute in red," with a wink.

For the last few days, Coach Lee had tossed them a dodgeball, and it had been living hell. Daphne wasn't the only one who usually got out of gym every day—Marissa also miraculously disappeared halfway through class, and she never came back until just before the bell rang.

"Maybe that's when she scopes out her next victim," Daphne said, chewing her thumb. They huddled together in English, pretending to work on *Macbeth*. "Prepares her spells?"

"I don't know. . . ."

"Well, I'll get to the bottom of it."

Tara had no doubt. "Be gentle."

Daphne pressed a hand to her heart, aghast. "Aren't I always, Maclay?"

She wanted to point out that Daphne had suggested cutting the poor girl's finger earlier to bleed on a witchstone, but she decided against it.

So now they were in PE, and Tara again smelled like old mothballs and regret. She really needed to take the clothes home, but she kept forgetting. The coach had split them up into boys and girls so they didn't have to play dodgeball against each other—"Girls, I'm giving you a fighting chance when you play among yourselves," he'd said—and like clockwork, for the third day in a row, Marissa excused herself to take care of "female issues."

The coach didn't even blink an eye. He didn't want to hear about it at all. "Yes—go, go, do whatever you do."

Daphne threw the ball to another student and said, "Hey, Coach, can I—"

"No, Miss Frost," he replied.

"But—"

"No."

Tara gave her a skeptical look. "What now?"

Daphne sighed, but then she brightened at an idea. "I'll distract the bastard. You go see what she's up to?"

"B-but I—"

"I super believe in you, Maclay!" she called as she went racing after a dodgeball heading their way, scooped it up, and then whiffed her throw so hard the ball sailed into the back of the coach's head. It bounced off and rolled to a stop by the bleachers. "Oops! Sorry, Coach!"

"FROST!"

With Coach Lee distracted, Tara—quiet as ever—slipped out of the gym.

"YOU THROW IT LIKE *THIS*. UNDERHAND FOR WOMEN. DO YOU GET IT?"

"It was an honest mistake, Coach. I think I broke a nail. . . ."

"YOU ALSO HIT ME!"

"Well, I didn't feel *that*. . . ."

Tara bit the inside of her cheek as she quietly closed the gym door and the blissful quiet of the hall surrounded her. She wouldn't have very long before the coach realized she was

missing, so she needed to figure out where Marissa had gone—
and fast.

As she went to push open the girls' locker room door, she
noticed a shadow out of the corner of her eye. Marissa? The
shadow slipped down the hall and around the corner.

Steeling her courage, she followed.

In truth, Marissa was the obvious choice for the rogue witch.
She had a bone to pick with the popular crowd, especially if she
used to be one of them. Tara didn't know much about what it
took to be popular—or to have friends at all, really. She'd never
had many. It came with the territory of being who she was.
Though here, at Hellborne, she found herself somehow inter-
acting with more people than she had all last year.

Baz couldn't be considered a friend, and Daphne was . . .

Was Daphne a friend? Tara wasn't very good at those.

But of all the friend groups to be in, wouldn't the popular
one be the one you'd want to *stay* in if you got the chance?

No one picked on you. No one called you weird or frumpy.
You were the bully.

Tara didn't suppose she really liked that, either.

The hall led to a dead end, Coach Lee's office on the left and
an emergency exit door on the right. She doubted Marissa had
gone into the office, and the exit door was wedged slightly ajar
with a wooden peg, so she cobbled her thoughts together—ask
about whereabouts, be friendly, *don't* make Marissa suspicious . . .

Easy.

She pushed the door open.

Marissa, leaning against the brick building, quickly
stomped out her cigarette and whirled around to Tara. "I swear

I wasn't—" Her shoulders quickly unwound. "Oh, shit. It's just you. I thought you were Coach Lee." Then she looked down at her stomped cigarette and frowned. "Damn, I wasted it. Did the coach tell you to come looking for me?"

"N-no . . ." Tara stepped out of the emergency exit to the concrete port. Cigarette butts littered the ground, all the same yellow ends. Things clicked—Marissa came out here to smoke during PE. Nothing more nefarious than that.

And a bit farther was a shovel in the ground, surrounded by wilting tomato plants and herbs. That reminded her—hadn't Amala said she was president of the garden club? What happened to the club now that she was gone?

"Good, means I got a few more minutes," Marissa replied, heading over to the shovel and taking the gloves that were hanging from the handle. Then she eyed Tara. "Why're you standing there?"

"I just wanted some f-fresh air," she lied, though not really. The gym *was* stuffy, and even the industrial fans couldn't keep it from smelling like BO and rubber all the time. *Be friendly*, she told herself, but she was quickly realizing that she *wasn't* cut out for this kind of sting operation. "Um—is that the school garden?"

"Yeah." Marissa crouched down and started weeding. "Since Amala's gone, it's gonna go to shit fast."

"And so you—you're keeping it up?"

"Someone's gotta." She tossed a weed behind her and reached for another. Tara felt a little useless just watching, so she came over and knelt down beside her to help.

"The basil will probably die after the first frost, so you should probably pick most of it now," she recommended.

Marissa frowned. "Oh. Okay. Amala really didn't give me much in the way of directions."

"My mother used to tend a garden." She scanned the rest of the garden. "The oregano should be fine for winter—and the mint, too."

"Thanks. When Amala moved here, she read up on them. But now she's gone again, so I guess it's up to me." Then Marissa placed the basil in a plastic bag she pulled out of her pocket, and gave Tara a thoughtful look. "You're Tara, right? The new girl Baz's been all over."

That made her skin prickle. "H-he's not . . ."

Marissa barked a laugh. "Oh, I know he's not! He's still hung up over . . ." But her voice dropped off, and she went back to pinching the dead leaves off the basil. "You might want to be careful around your new friends."

There it was. Tara's in to talk about them. To see if Marissa had any ill will toward them. It seemed way too easy. Her aura would flicker red if she wanted to hurt them, like it had in history class, so Tara studied her. There was a thin grayish aura around her; it waved and pulsed quietly, neutral. "I—I wouldn't s-s-say they're my friends. . . ." she began.

"Good. Because they'll be your friends just as long as you fit into their neat little mold, but the second you admit that you want to kiss a girl, they want nothing to do with you."

Her eyes widened. Instead of red—intent, murderous, bloody—Marissa's aura bloomed with purple sadness.

"And when that girl's Elaine and you're drunk at one of her house parties and would never *dream* of admitting it sober and you try to apologize and they just look at you like you're . . . why am I telling you this?" she murmured, giving Tara an incredulous look. "Maybe it's because I don't know you, but stay away from Elaine and Baz and the whole lot. They'll just hate you for being different."

"But . . . not Amala?"

A smile flickered across Marissa's lips, sad and soft. "No. But she left, too, and so I'm stuck here every day after school tending to her garden."

And if Marissa was here, she couldn't have been in the library when the witch attacked Moss. And Tara was sure Amala would testify to that, too.

Furthermore, her aura didn't fit the magic that had attacked Moss.

"And you know what?" Marissa went on. "I can't say I blame whoever's taking those assholes out. Good riddance, actually—"

Suddenly, the emergency exit door burst open.

Coach Lee poked his head out. His face grew three shades redder than a tomato when he found Tara out there with Marissa. "*Both* of you? Inside! *Now!* Miss Ellis, what are you *doing*?"

In reply, Marissa stood and took off her gloves. "Not doing PE, Coach."

Tara could hear Coach Lee yelling at Marissa as the two walked into the school. She hung back a moment longer, digging her fingers into the soil. It was clear that Marissa really didn't know much about gardening, but she was trying, and it was so evident that Amala had given care and kindness to the plants before she left. If Tara had been stronger, if she'd been able to save Moss, maybe Amala would have stayed. Maybe then Marissa wouldn't be caring for these plants alone.

Her fingers burrowed into the soil, and she closed her eyes.

"Please," she muttered to the air and sky and earth. To the power that flowed around them, in the soil, in the clouds. She just wanted to help a little.

To give Marissa help.

She concentrated like her mother taught her in the garden in their backyard, beneath the bowing willow tree, remembering the rush of magic as it brimmed in her body and spread through the soil like roots of a tree. Sun-drenched afternoons and lemonade and the smell of lavender and honey in the air. Her mother's laughter. The taste of magic.

The soil warmed like a summer day. And she could feel the earthworms dance and the pill bugs crawl and the leaves of the mint and oregano and basil and lavender and rosemary and thyme, unfurling and rushing toward the sky—

"Miss Maclay!" Coach Lee cried as he opened the emergency exit once more.

She snapped her eyes open and pulled her fingers out of the soil. The garden had overgrown itself, herbs snarling on each other in a plush thicket. Had *she* done that? She stared at her fingers, and then at the garden again—

She could *feel* it. Her magic. It ebbed and flowed in her, soft and swaying like an ocean.

And it stayed.

"Miss *Maclay*!" Coach Lee called.

"Coming!" Tara pushed herself to her feet, brushing the dirt off her knees, and hurried in after them, and back to the dodgeball game.

The rest of PE went by in a blur as Tara lingered in the back of the court, waiting for a dodgeball to come flying her way. Daphne was hungry to get to her after Coach Lee dismissed them to go get changed. She found Tara in the locker rooms as she tugged on her black T-shirt smelling of citrus and mint.

"So? Anything?" Daphne asked.

Tara shook her head. "Nothing. Marissa was working in the garden—probably with Amala—when Moss was attacked."

"Damn! Well, at least that's another crossed off. Oh! I have a thought," she said as Tara reapplied deodorant and—a little clumsily—quickly exchanged her moth-smelling T-shirt for her blouse. She hated changing in locker rooms. Daphne leaned in close so she could whisper, "All our targets are gonna be at the homecoming game tonight, right? Baz and Harris play on the team, Cory's probably going to be there with Hailey and Elaine to watch Elaine get crowned the Red Witch or whatever. I think we should go."

"O-oh." Tara frowned as she sat down and put on her brown loafers again. The garden's dirt felt gritty under her fingers. Her blood still hummed with magic. "I . . . I'm not sure I'll be able to . . ."

"Your dad?"

"He's . . . strict."

"I get it, I get it," Daphne sighed. "I'll report back?"

Tara nodded, though she wished she could go. She wanted to. If for no other reason than to keep her nightmare from becoming reality. It couldn't come true. She picked the dirt out from under her fingers as she followed Daphne to next period. If her magic had returned, then maybe she could do something, after all.

Save one person.

Daphne.

CHAPTER TWENTY
BRANDING

"Class, this week instead of focusing on the Reynolds Pamphlets, I thought we'd spend some time talking about our own Hellborne's history," Mr. Samuels said, sitting on the edge of his desk. Tara had only ever seen teachers do that in teen movies—though Mr. Samuels did think he was too cool, and not in an actual cool way. "Who wants to tell me who the founder of Hellborne is?"

Elaine's hand shot up instantly.

Mr. Samuels sighed. "All right, Miss O'Toole, have at it."

"Hellborne was founded by my great-great-great-great-great-great-great-*great*-grandfather Atticus Herold O'Toole the Third," Elaine said smartly. "He is *also* the father of the man who decided to burn the Red Witch."

"One of many men, I assure you," Mr. Samuels replied. "Does anyone know the date it was founded?"

Elaine's hand shot up again.

So, incidentally, did Hailey's.

Tara didn't know any of these answers. So she resigned herself to taking out her notebook and at least jotting some down. Maybe the history of Hellborne would come in handy when finding the murderer.

"Yes, Miss Conrad?"

Elaine pouted, dropping her hand, as Hailey said, "It was founded in 1716, though it didn't become a *settlement* until after the French and Indian War and the 1763 Treaty of Paris that gave the region to the British."

"That is correct! Now, does anyone know . . . ?"

Tara's notebook felt weird in her hands. Lumpy. She frowned. Maybe she'd shoved it into her locker wrong and bent it?

She opened to a new page—

And suddenly little black dots spilled out from between the pages.

No—not *dots*.

Spiders.

They sprang up from the page, from letters she'd written, the notes, the bullet points, ink morphing into plump black dots with eight legs.

One crawled onto her hand and sank its fangs into her. A terrible blistering pain throbbed up her arm. She shrieked and jumped to her feet, recoiling from the book. Spiders swarmed out, scurrying everywhere in ripples.

"What the devil?" Mr. Samuels cried. He jumped to his feet and marched down the aisle as students began to leap up, abandoning their desks as the spiders spread. Tara had pushed herself up onto the desk behind her, almost on top of Baz, scrambling to get away.

"Miss *Maclay*, what are you— Are those— Is that—"

A few spiders began to crawl up his shoes. He shrieked.

Then his eyes rolled into the back of his head, and he fainted.

Daphne cried, *"Jesus!* Toss it! Toss the stupid notebook!" Baz grabbed the notebook, opened the window with a shove so forceful it popped the safety lock clean off, and lobbed it out of the window. The notebook went arcing through the air and landed in the school's fountain.

"I'll go get the nurse!" Hailey shouted, ducking out of class.

Tara felt her skin prickling. Her breath came in short bursts. Magic—someone had used *magic* on her.

Daphne caught her by the hands. "Breathe. You okay? They didn't bite you, did they?"

But she couldn't take her eyes off her notebook floating in the fountain outside, spiders spilling out still, bleeding black into the water.

Daphne cupped her cheek and gently guided her face away. "Hey, eyes on me, Maclay," she whispered, and Tara finally did look at her. They held each other's gaze for one breath, two, three—

Daphne's eyes were dark like an abyss, deep and warm and soothing. Tara's heart calmed down enough for her to nod.

Daphne smiled. "See? You're okay."

Other students who weren't afraid of spiders were smashing them with their feet, even though Baz asked them nicely not to. "Bro, please, just pick them up and stick 'em out the window. You're getting the floor dirty. Mrs. Connie's gonna have to mop up the whole damn classroom if you do that."

When Daphne went to help them sweep up the bugs, Tara finally looked at her bitten hand again. She expected to see a red bite, but what she found was a lot more terrifying.

It was a mark, red and blistered like someone had branded her with a cattle prod.

"E-excuse me," she muttered, pulling her jacket sleeve over her hand, and quickly left the classroom. She hugged her hand tightly to her chest.

It wasn't the mark. It *wasn't*.

It couldn't be.

She repeated that mantra all the way to the bathroom at the end of the hall, and there she closed herself inside one of the stalls. She sucked in a deep breath. Gathered her courage. And finally pulled her sleeve up from her hand.

It was painfully burnt and with a swell of relief she saw that it *wasn't* the same mark as the ones on the boys' hands.

It wasn't a mark at all.

Once she actually gave it a good look, the burns migrated across her hand, rearranging themselves into words. Her relief was short-lived as she read the warning on her hand.

LEAVE IT ALONE.

The letters pulsed, gently, though she wasn't sure if that was from the pain or the magic. She gently touched her fingertips to the words, closing her eyes to try to sense the aura—but there was nothing.

So, magical, but not cursed. Just a burn.

A warning.

So the witch knew she was looking into the murders—then did that mean they knew Daphne was, too? Why didn't she get a warning? Unless Daphne was a part of the plan. And why would the witch *warn* her? A courtesy to another witch?

Or was it something else?

She didn't know, but if the witch thought they'd scare her away with a warning, they didn't know Tara at all. She didn't like getting bossed around or told what to do.

Especially by a witch who refused to show their face.

The bell rang to dismiss school for the day, and Tara quickly washed the burn mark under running water to numb the pain and tugged her sleeves down again just as Daphne burst into the bathroom with both of their book bags.

"Are you okay?" she asked. "You left so fast. . . ."

Tara put on a genuine smile. "Thanks for thinking about me. I'm fine—I just felt nauseous for a m-moment."

"And you're better now?" Daphne didn't seem too convinced.

"I am. But . . ." She cut off the faucet and turned to her directly. The burn under her sleeve pulsed. "About homecoming tonight . . ."

Things had changed.

She was worried that her father wouldn't approve, but she was afraid of the warning on her hand, too—and the dream last night. Whenever she looked at Daphne, she couldn't get her milky, unseeing eyes out of her head.

The witch was watching them. She didn't know what their goal was, who they were, what they wanted, and it scared her.

What if Daphne found the witch at homecoming? Tara was sure the witch *had* turned to dark magic, but she wanted to know why. There was something missing from Daphne's murder board, but she wanted to keep her suspicions to herself for the moment.

Just like the mark on her hand. If Daphne found it, she wouldn't let her help anymore. Tara was sure of that.

"I'll come with you," she said, "to homecoming."

Daphne's eyes widened. "Are you sure?"

She nodded. "My dad should let me," she lied.

Daphne grinned, and it made her eyes sparkle. "It's a date, then, cupcake."

CHAPTER TWENTY-ONE
HOMECOMING

"**O**kay, *so*," Daphne said as she sank down in the bleachers beside Tara. The night was frigid, and everyone in the stands huddled in clusters, wrapping their warmest fall coats around them tightly. The football stadium was bare bones, with only a field and two sets of aluminum bleachers on either side, a scoreboard at the top. The team from across the river— the public high school—was *decimating* the Hellborne Devils in a loss the likes of which, apparently, hadn't been seen in fifty years.

It was almost halftime and the score read *DEVILS 7, HURRICANES 34.*

"What we've learned so far," Daphne went on, teeth chattering, "is that it's cold as *shit* and Hellborne Academy's really bad at football. Even during homecoming."

"I don't know when to clap," Tara admitted, putting her frozen fingers under her arms.

This was not the kind of date she'd expected. She knew

Daphne had just said it as a joke, but ever since, Tara could think of little else. What if this *was* a date? Was this Daphne's kind of date?

No. That was silly. One look at Daphne and anyone could see she'd rather be anywhere else.

The Devils struggled their way across the field as the game clock counted down to zero. There were three minutes left. Tara knew almost as much about football as she did about water polo, and that was surprisingly little.

Daphne laughed. "You went to school in the Midwest, and you didn't pick up on *football*?"

"I was a horse girl growing up," Tara admitted.

"Rodeo or dressage?"

"Show jumping. I w-wasn't very good."

"You're just full of surprises," Daphne said with a grin, and then put her elbows on her knees. She pointed to the field, at Baz settling into his position. "Your friend there? He's what you call a tight end."

"Um . . ."

"Both because he has one and he is one. The guy holding the ball is the quarterback. He snaps it—like that, and then the guy who catches the ball is the receiver, and— *Oof.*" She winced. "Well, he *would* have been the receiver if he didn't just get knocked into next week."

"You know a lot about football."

"I'm in a house full of males. At least one of them had to be tempted by the pigskin," Daphne replied. "And really? All you need to know about this game is that we *suck* and— Oh, wait, is that Hailey?" She nudged her chin toward the other end of the stands, where Hailey was standing by the stairs, shaking her head, as Elaine spoke to her. They both had on matching white earmuffs. "They look like they're having a fight. Oh, there goes Elaine. . . . Did you vote for her during lunch this week?"

Tara shook her head. "I didn't vote."

"Ha! I voted for me. Not like I'm going to win," Daphne added with a shrug. "Thought that counts, though, right?"

Fifteen seconds before halftime, Baz tripped over his own shoestrings and knocked his head against an opposing player's helmet. They both went down hard. Tara tensed. Daphne scooted to the edge of her seat. Was this the witch? Was this another accident waiting to happen?

But then Baz shook it off, stood, and thrust a thumbs-up into the air. The crowd cheered.

Tara breathed a sigh of relief despite herself. She'd grown to like Baz.

The other player didn't move again until Baz stooped down and patted him on the shoulder. He helped him up, and they wobbled off the field together.

"He's got a friggin' hard head," Daphne muttered.

"Baz?"

"Yeah. I really thought he'd snapped his neck or something."

"Me too," Tara agreed.

The teams ran the fifteen seconds down until the buzzer went off for halftime, and then they left the field for the locker rooms. At least Baz still seemed in good spirits as he smacked the quarterback's butt. Hailey had left Elaine on the stairs at the bottom of the bleachers. Harris and a few of the other populars were sitting in the stands, huddled together sipping coffee (that they poured something else into), while everyone else trickled down toward the concessions at the south side of the field, or the bathrooms on the north.

Tara shivered all the way from her toes to her scalp. It was cold, her breath coming out in puffs of frost. She tried to warm up her hands, rubbing them together—and winced when the back of her right hand flared with pain. She'd forgotten about the mark.

Daphne gave her a concerned look. "Are you okay?"

"F-fine."

Her eyes narrowed. "A spider *did* bite you, didn't it?"

"No." Then, quieter, under Daphne's serious gaze: "Y-yes. It hurts a little, but it should be okay."

"I think one of my dads has some good salve if you want to come over to my house after this and get some? I got bit by a brown recluse years ago and I thought the air conditioner was going to eat me, and I swear that shit works wonders."

Tara couldn't help but laugh. "An air conditioner?"

"I thought I was going to die."

"I don't think those spiders were venomous," she said. They weren't even real—they were magic. "But thank you. It means a lot."

"As long as you're sure."

"I am."

She felt bad for lying to Daphne and not telling her about the burn on her hand, but she wasn't sure what Daphne would do if she found out. Or worse yet, what sort of questions it'd lead to—why didn't the witch just mark her like the guys? Why did the witch warn her? And that would only lead to Tara weaving more lies, like a spider herself.

Just lie over lie over lie, a web of them.

Below them, near the concessions, Harris and Cory reemerged from the crowd and went to lean against the chain-link fence that surrounded the stadium. Harris offered Cory a cigarette, laughing at something. Then a tall guy with blond hair sauntered up to them from the other side of the fence, and they handed him a smoke. Tara's spine straightened with icy fear.

"Do you want anything to drink?" she asked Daphne. "I'm thinking of getting a hot chocolate."

Daphne gave her a puzzled look. "Hailey's about to go on the field, though."

"We both don't n-need to."

And Tara needed to know why he was here. What he wanted. *You know what he wants*, she thought, her fingers curling into fists.

"Also, Harris and Cory are down there." Tara pointed toward the concessions.

"Oh, good point, we need to keep an eye on them—something warm?" Daphne wrapped her coat around herself tightly, though her leather jacket didn't tend to offer much in the way of insulation against the Vermont cold.

"Hot chocolate? Or coffee?"

"Whichever's hotter."

"Noted. I'll be back." Tara stood, gathering her purse and looping it over her shoulder, and made her way down the steps. There were still students in the bleachers who whispered as she passed. It was better to just let them settle on their own and not cause much of a stir.

With *him* here . . . that was a little of what she was worried

145

about. What if Harris or Cory mentioned the rumors? And he went home to tell . . .

Her brother noticed her the moment she pushed her way through the crowd. He grinned and held up his hand with the cigarette. "Oh, hey! It's my sister!"

She swallowed the lump in her throat and came up to the fence. Cory and Harris exchanged a look. She studied her brother's face, trying to guess if they'd slipped up and said anything—but it didn't seem like they knew he was her brother.

Donny said, "You two know my sister, right? I think she's in your grade."

"Yeah, we know her . . ." Cory muttered.

Tara lowered her gaze to the ground. *Please, please, please don't say anything—*

"She's one of Baz's friends," Harris said. "He's a cool dude."

"Cool, *sure*," Cory replied pointedly, and then nudged his head toward the field. "Let's go cheer Elaine? She'll be pissed if we aren't there."

"Oh, heck yeah," Harris replied, mashing his cigarette under his toe. "I'm excited!"

"That's one of us," Cory deadpanned.

"Don't be a tool, dude—and hey, nice meeting you . . . ?"

"Donny," Tara's brother replied from the other side of the fence, and held up his cigarette. "Thanks for the smoke. And the chat."

The boys waved as they left for the field, and Tara was left in the shadows of the bleachers with her brother. A cold silence settled between them. Donny hung on to the metal fence and took another long drag of his cigarette. The end burned a bright orange.

"Smoking's bad for you," Tara said quietly.

"I wouldn't be smoking if I didn't have to come find you, so whose fault is it, really?" he replied, and blew a lungful into her face.

She flinched away, coughing. "It's n-not that big a deal."

"Isn't it? You told Dad you were going to a friend's to help with a project." His eyes flicked up to the bleachers. To Daphne. A sneer curved across his lips. "Some *project*."

"I a-am here to help with a p-project," she forced out.

"And that's what you're sticking with?"

"It's the truth."

This was a project. She wasn't lying about that. She never said it was a *school* project. Hunting down a killer was just as valid as debating *Macbeth*.

Donny sighed and put his cigarette out on the fence pole. "Whatever, Tara. I guess I'll have to tell Dad—"

"Please d-don't."

"What'll you do for me?"

". . . What?"

"What. Will. You. Do. For. Me?" he enunciated.

She pursed her lips. "What do you want?"

"Easy. Dad's got me applying to Dartmouth, right? I want you to do my essay. It's boring. I don't feel like it."

That's it? She was surprised. "O-okay."

He grinned. "Thanks, sis." Then he slid his gaze up to Daphne, oblivious, one last time before he gave Tara a wink and shoved away from the metal fence, back toward the station wagon.

Tara called after her brother, "How d-did you know I was here?"

He scoffed and tossed over his shoulder, "It's a Friday and there's nothing else to do in this shitty town. Where *else* would you be? Conducting a séance in the middle of the woods?"

Half of the school would believe that.

She didn't move a muscle until he climbed into the car and drove away.

Once he was gone, she got into line for the concessions and ordered two hot chocolates, since the coffeepot was already switched off. While she waited for her order, she turned to observe what she could of the field. Hailey was framed by the twenty-three-person marching band, Marissa's colorful hair spilling out of one of the hats.

Baz was leaning against the far goalpost, his arms over his chest as he watched, the rest of the team behind him as they looked on. Harris and Cory had found Elaine again in the bleachers.

The oiled and dappered Principal Greaves was at Hailey's side, holding the ballot box that everyone had voted in today at lunch.

All of their suspects were here.

Which one of you is the witch? Tara thought. *And which one of you is the next victim?*

"Thank you, everyone, for voting on our Red Witch this year," Hailey began.

Tara dropped the change the concessions worker gave her into the tip jar and moved through the crowd with her two cups of hot chocolate to make it back to Daphne.

"We received an outstanding number of votes, and we have worked very hard to tally up all of them into a fair and efficient election."

Hailey opened a sealed letter. "Our new Red Witch this year is . . ." Her face faltered, but then she smiled and said, "Tara Maclay!"

Somewhere in the stands, Elaine screamed in horror.

Tara stood there in the crowd, stunned. Her mouth dropped open.

"Holy shit, Elaine lost!" someone cried.

"Rigged!" someone else shouted.

"Heck yeah!"

Around her, students began to point and whisper to each other. How did she win? Who voted for her? Was this a trick?

Was it a trick? A horrid joke? Even Tara didn't understand who'd vote for *her*.

"Congratulations to Tara Maclay, our Red Witch for this year! She is *also* the recipient of our scholarship! Hurrah, Tara!" Hailey said enthusiastically into the bullhorn. "And now, a special show from our Fighting Devils Marching Band!"

Tara ducked her head and pushed her way up the steps to the bleachers. She could feel Elaine's death glare on her even from half a stand away. She'd never felt so mortified in her life. She wanted to melt into the bleachers and never be human again.

When she finally returned to Daphne, the witch hunter was smiling like Tara had done something. *Had* she done something? "Congrats on winning!"

Tara sat down. "I n-never want to be perceived e-ever again."

"It's not that bad, is it?" Daphne laughed, and Tara suddenly got a sinking suspicion.

"You . . . *you* . . ."

"Don't look at me like that," she said, and sipped on her hot chocolate. "*I* didn't cheat the votes or anything. What do you take me for?"

Someone who would have, obviously. Tara frowned, squirming at the looks people gave her as they went by. "Who, then?"

"Maybe Hellborne just voted for you."

"As a joke?"

"With a scholarship," Daphne reminded her.

College? Tara hadn't dared to think about it. She wasn't even sure where she'd want to go, or what she'd want to major in. She muttered, "I feel bad for Elaine. . . ."

"Don't. She wouldn't feel bad for you."

It didn't make her feel any better.

The marching band moved across the field as they did their halftime performance, the tuba blaring out the "Imperial March" a whole beat behind the trombones. As they cleared the field and the football players came back on to warm up, Daphne leaned back in her seat, frowning.

"So," Daphne sighed, "I guess the witch isn't showing their face tonight. . . . I doubt anyone else will be cursed here. And I can't think who'd be next."

"Baz? Harris? Cory?" Tara counted on her fingers. "There's only three guys left of the popular crowd."

"And we still have too many suspects," Daphne replied grimly, and gave a hard sigh. "*God*, why won't Giles get back to me? I swear if we knew where that stupid mark came from, it'd narrow down the search. I'm sure of it."

"I'll keep looking. M-maybe we'll luck out."

Daphne set her jaw. "No." Then she stood, hot chocolate in hand. "I have an idea."

CHAPTER TWENTY-TWO
GRIEVOUS SINS

What Daphne didn't tell Tara was that her idea included sneaking into the school and snooping in their lockers.

"Won't w-we get in trouble?" Tara mumbled nervously, darting her eyes down the hallway, looking for a security guard or a teacher working late or someone. Hellborne's halls were dark and deserted, and reminded her that Chad had died after the school had closed for the evening. The lights from the football stadium streaked in through the classroom windows, illuminating the halls that weren't already lit with the ominous red of the exit signs.

Daphne scoffed. "Do you *see* anyone?"

"N-no, but . . ."

"Then we're good, cupcake," she said a little too smoothly. Smooth enough for Tara to be very, very suspicious.

"You've done this before, haven't you?"

In reply, Daphne took out a bolt cutter from her bag. "I have no idea what you're talking about," she replied, and snipped through the lock belonging to Elaine's locker.

"Have you gotten caught before?"

"Not on purpose. Just keep watching the halls and tell me if you see anything?" She pulled the locker open. Tara glanced into it, but the locker was just how she'd imagined Elaine's locker to look. Frilled with pinks, the back of the door collaged with cutouts of Paul Rudd, Leo DiCaprio, Nick Carter, and a whole host of boy bands. There were also cute photo booth pictures of her and Cory, him showing a goofy side that surprised Tara. She had a cardigan, a spare pair of loafers, a mirror—and the more Daphne rummaged, the less she found.

"Damn," she murmured, and closed the door. "Next one—I think Baz's is down two, right?"

Tara nodded. "What are you hoping to find?"

"Anything, really. Witches usually have some sort of tell. They might have a note written in gibberish, or a string of knots or herbs, wildflowers—something. It's easy to differentiate wannabe Wiccans from real witchcraft."

"It is?"

"Obviously." She took the bolt cutters to Baz's locker.

Tara hesitated. "Are we really suspecting Baz?"

Daphne gave her a deadpan look. "A witch can be anyone."

Even the person standing right in front of her. That quieted Tara, and she went back to staring down the hall.

At least until Daphne said, "Now, what do we have here?" She reached up into the top level of the locker and pulled out a sprig of herb, its tiny flowers dried and withered, some of them missing. As if Baz had plucked them off, one by one, starting at the top.

Tara muttered, "I think that's rue."

"A plant used to ward off evil."

Yes, but it was also used medicinally—well, before studies found it to be more *dangerous* than helpful. But still, it was used in some herbal potions, some spells, but eaten raw . . . she wondered why he'd do *that*. It was like constantly dosing himself with a mild mutagenic poison, and when applied to the skin it could produce phytophotodermatitis. But "It's poisonous" was all she ended up saying.

Daphne frowned. "Huh." She thought for a moment before placing it back on the shelf. "The idiot probably just liked the way it looked and some flowers fell off it."

"Likely," Tara agreed.

"Damn, and everything is just"—she waved her hand at his locker, bare-bones as it was—"*boring*. Never took Bastion Leto to be this gray."

"Maybe he just doesn't use his locker much?"

"Probably." Daphne closed it again and went on to Hailey's. She scrubbed the back of her neck, almost agitatedly. "Argh! I thought we'd find *something* by now, you know? Anything! Where else can we—"

There was a clatter at the end of the hall.

Daphne and Tara whirled around, clicking off their flashlight. Then there were footsteps. They exchanged a look and focused their attention. The sounds came from an adjacent hall.

"Another student?" Tara whispered.

Daphne shook her head. "Why'd they be here? Unless . . ."

"It's the witch."

"It's the witch," Daphne agreed, then moved in front of Tara. "Stay behind me."

And together, they crept to the end of the hall. It was so dark, only the red neon exit signs gave them any light at all, and it wasn't enough to cut through the darkness. Daphne held the bolt cutter up as a weapon. The footsteps came closer.

Tara wanted to tell Daphne they should run—that they were no match for a witch. Daphne didn't have any weapons, and Tara couldn't do anything without giving herself away as a witch.

Never mind she wasn't all that sure her magic would answer her again.

But she didn't want the witch to kill Daphne. She wanted to protect her. As if the magic knew, her fingertips began to warm, magic teasing across her skin.

They whipped around the corner—and came face-to-face with Principal Greaves.

The magic on her fingers died with a sudden *pop*.

The principal stood tall, a box of things underneath one of his long arms. He narrowed his eyes at them. "Pray tell, Miss Maclay and Miss Frost, what are you doing here?"

"Nothing." Daphne quickly tried to hide the bolt cutter behind her back, but the principal only *tsk*ed.

"I've seen it, Miss Frost. It's very late for you two to be around the school."

"We could say the same of you, sir," Daphne replied.

He adjusted the lapels of his suit. The cuff links on his sleeves glistened in the light of the emergency exit to his left.

"Children have died at night in these halls. I'd rather not find another one."

Tara's gaze drifted down to the box under his arm. She recognized the letterman jacket—and the baggie of weed. "You w-went through my locker?"

"I thought it was time to give Chad's parents back his things. It was an oversight that it hadn't been cleaned out beforehand." Principal Greaves looked between the box and the girls. "I'll tell you what, if you two leave this second, we don't have to tell anyone about tonight."

Daphne narrowed her eyes.

He quirked an eyebrow at her. "Do you have a problem with that, Miss Frost? Or I could get your parents involved."

"We'll l-leave," Tara quickly said, grabbing Daphne by the arm. What he hadn't said was they'd get expelled if they didn't leave, but that was pretty evident.

"Good," the principal said, and held out his hand. "Now, the bolt cutters."

"What?" Daphne cried. "No—"

"Daphne," Tara whispered, almost pleadingly.

The anger unwound from Daphne's shoulders, and she pulled the bolt cutters out of her bag and handed them to him with a glare. "*Fine.* Can we go now?"

He inclined his head. His eyes almost glowed in the exit lights. "Don't come exploring the high school at night again, Miss Frost. And you, too, Miss Maclay. It might sound fun, but I assure you, it is not."

"W-we promise," Tara said before Daphne could so much as breathe, and pulled her down the hall, toward the main doors of the school. She felt the principal's eyes on them until they left down the stairs, and even then she didn't stop until they were out of the front entrance and Daphne finally wrenched her arm out of her grip.

"The *hell*?" Daphne snarled, and jabbed a finger back inside. "He's suspect number one now! He's suspect as hell!"

"I know."

"Then why did we *leave*?"

"Because if we get kicked out of this school, then we'll be in an even worse place to investigate the murders," Tara replied evenly. *And*, she thought, *if I get kicked out then my father will ship me off to that awful school.*

Tara's calming voice, along with her logic, seemed to dampen Daphne's anger down to a simmer. "God, you're right. And I went through the two lockers I wanted to, anyway." Then a small smile spread across her mouth. "You're pretty good at keeping cool under pressure, Maclay."

Tara quickly looked down, embarrassed. "I wasn't always."

"How'd you practice?"

Have you ever had dinner with my father? she wanted to reply, but she knew she couldn't without introducing Daphne to her home life, and that was something she . . . didn't particularly want to do. "Speech class."

"I think you're lying," Daphne said, and leaned in a little closer, squinting. So close Tara could smell the soft scent of citrus and fresh laundry that clung gently to her skin.

They froze there for a moment too long.

But despite her best efforts, her heart still pounded. During halftime, her brother had smirked and looked up at Daphne—was it that obvious? It felt obvious, her heart in her throat.

This is bad, she thought. *This is horrible. This is—*

A blur of white caught her eye at the edge of the parking lot. It stood at the edge of the line of firs, the shape familiar from the day she hid from the cops in the woods. She stepped aside to get a better look. "Is that . . . ?"

Daphne glanced over her shoulder, and her eyes widened. "Oh, hey, that must be the horse that escaped the barn— Tara?"

Tara moved past Daphne and hurried across the parking lot.

"Tara! What are you doing?"

In the distance, the end-of-game buzzer sounded to the riotous cheers of the opposing team.

Tara replied over her shoulder, "The horse'll die if we don't get it back to the barn. Or at least get hurt. They aren't the smartest."

And it was a reason to get away from Daphne, quickly, so her heart could catch up with her head. She did *not* need to fall for her. It was a bad idea—no, *worse* than bad. She'd had bad ideas before. She'd ridden bad ideas in the form of untrained horses in the past. They bucked her off quicker than she could blink.

This was a *disastrous* idea.

She'd had those, too. But those ideas ended up with books turned to ash and moving across the country.

No, it was best not to entertain disastrous ideas. No matter how beautiful they were.

The horse was nibbling on some grass by the trunk of a fir as Tara approached. The glossy white of her coat matched the moon, almost. She must've gotten out when someone tried to handle her, because the bit was still in, and the reins were draped over one side of her neck.

Her ears twitched as Tara got close.

"Tara, maybe we should call the coach of the equast—equestri—*the horse people.*"

"Equestrian," she suggested calmly, and moved her hand back to motion for Daphne to stop. The horse looked up and shook her mane. She stepped back, and Tara paused. "Shh. It's okay. I'm not going to hurt you."

Then she stooped to pluck a few blades of grass and offered it out to the horse. The mare whinnied and shifted on her front legs a bit in hesitation, until she smelled the grass and crept toward them. Nostrils flared as she sniffed Tara's hand. Then she nibbled at the grass.

"See? No harm here," Tara said softly, and patted the mare gently on the muzzle.

Daphne stood behind her, agog. "What are you, an animal whisperer?"

"Nothing so special," she replied, scratching the horse around the ears. "Horses are very sensitive. They know when you're anxious or scared. She's probably been very lonely out here by herself."

For a long moment, Daphne stood silently and watched. "You keep surprising me."

Tara smiled at her. "I hope in a good way."

"The best—"

Suddenly, there was a crunch behind them. The horse reared back with a cry, kicking out. Tara stepped backward to not get hit by her hooves, throwing her hands up to try to calm the mare down—but the mare's eyes were wide and afraid. Her nostrils flared.

No, not afraid.

The horse was *terrified*.

Daphne spun around toward the sound, reaching for something in her leather jacket, there between the trees. And before Tara could grab the reins, the horse darted off into the dark woods, too fast for either of them to catch.

Tara's father was waiting for her again tonight. She closed the door, her arms full of last-minute groceries. She'd stopped by the store, running down each aisle like a madwoman. After breaking and entering with Daphne, she wasn't sure if the principal would call home, and she wasn't even sure how to tell him about winning that college scholarship *or* the Burning. . . .

"I l-lost track of time," she said. "I'm s-sorry, Daddy."

He snapped his book shut. "Did you finish your project, at least?"

She winced. "Yes . . ."

"We were worried sick," her father went on. His voice was cold. Colder than usual. Tara felt a knot of fear form in her throat. "Donny went out *looking* for you. He came back alone. He said you were nowhere to be found!"

"I—I'm sorry."

"I thought you respected me a little more than to leave me like this, Tara."

She held the groceries tightly to her chest. Although Donny hadn't told on her, he hadn't lied for her, either. She wasn't sure which one she preferred now, honestly. Her brother watched from the end of the hall, his arms over his chest, a smirk curling across his mouth as he admired his handiwork.

"I lost track of time," she repeated weakly. She squeezed

the bag so tightly, a few oranges rolled out and thudded on the hardwood floor. "I—I was so involved in the project that I didn't notice how late it'd g-g-gotten and—and—"

He put his hand up, and she instantly went silent. "I'm sorry, Tara, but I need to trust you, and I can't. You will not hang out with any of these new friends until you can prove to me that you're trustworthy."

"At a-all? But th-that's—"

"Reasonable," he interrupted. "It's *reasonable* for the worry you put us through. You're a girl in a strange town. And with those mysterious deaths? I won't chance it."

She swallowed the lump in her throat. "Yes, Daddy. I'm s-sorry."

Her father clenched his fist and then placed it down at his side. "So am I," he replied, narrowing his eyes. "Now put up those groceries and go to bed. I don't want to have another conversation like this ever again, do you understand?"

She nodded and quietly put up the food she had bought, including the fallen oranges, and quickly left for her room, passing her brother in the hall.

"Don't forget our deal," he whispered to her.

"I won't," she muttered, even though she had a chance now to submit her own applications. Maybe there were other scholarships out there.

No, that was silly. Her father would never let her leave, anyway. It would've been best if Elaine had won the scholarship and the title of Red Witch. Not someone like Tara who didn't deserve it.

She didn't have to wonder anymore if everyone's families were like hers. Daphne's wasn't. She knew that at least—she could feel it. The kinds of people they were. Their auras. How soft and yellow they were, full of happiness, shimmering with orange and pink love.

She also knew the kinds of people her family were, too. Her father was the kind of person who would follow his only daughter down the hall to her room and close the door behind her.

And lock it with a click.

CHAPTER TWENTY-THREE
HIS STORY

Over the weekend, the maple trees turned yellow and orange with autumn, and the brisk wind that had caught the evergreens blew in cold, bulbous gray clouds that clotted the skies. Vermont grew brisk a lot quicker than Omaha. It was startling, and Tara had to dig out an old plaid coat to take to school with her to fight off the chill that hung in the daylight.

That Monday morning, she stopped by the herb garden behind the school just to see if her magic had lasted. It had, and Marissa had pruned more basil and planted some seeds near the back. Tara wasn't sure what they were until she placed her fingers over one of the mounds and muttered a soft word. A shoot of green erupted from the earth, and she plucked out a garlic bulb.

Her magic *had* returned, though she hadn't tried casting anything more than simple nature spells. She was a little afraid to, actually. Whenever she thought about casting from her mother's book, she heard her father calling her a demon and it withered her resolve.

But out here, she thought about her mother, and their garden, and those good memories, and she felt safe to let go.

She was so wrapped up in the garden, she almost missed the bus to the museum, and once she climbed aboard, she was glad she'd brought her plaid coat. The leather seats were so cold and hard, it felt like sitting on a block of ice. It was only the senior class going on the field trip today. Apparently, Hellborne Academy had the outing staggered between the different grades, and it was one of those field trips that every grade went on every year. At her old school, that would've taken four—five buses? And more than one day. But here the senior class was so small, it only took two buses.

She recognized a good many of her classmates, but there were some she'd never seen before, and they were all still talking about the big upset from the homecoming game—Elaine losing the Red Witch election to Tara. It was alienating, to say the least, and when Daphne went to go sit with the group of black-clad kids at the back of the bus, Tara felt more alone than ever. One of them had a Discman and headphones they hung around their neck, blaring Green Day's *Dookie*.

It was fine, she told herself. They didn't have to sit together. But Tara had kind of been looking forward to it—sitting with Daphne. It was silly, but still.

The museum was little more than a small parking lot set into the side of the mountains with evergreens—as always— towering around them, a two-story building boasting artifacts from the era before the town burned, and to the left, a slightly wilted wooden cabin. The museum was just off Main Street, but Tara hadn't even noticed the dilapidated wooden sign the dozen times she'd walked past it.

The wooden cabin was held together with rotted wood and stubbornness. Over the years, it'd apparently been refurbished, but Tara couldn't tell. It had kept its creepy, almost-burned charm, and yet stood as a testament to time—or, rather, that time couldn't erase it. Even if it wanted.

The buses parked in the almost-empty parking lot, and the homeroom teachers handed everyone a worksheet as they got off the bus.

"I'll be collecting these when you're done!" Miss Aberhorn, Tara's homeroom teacher, shouted to everyone. She handed Tara a worksheet and moved on. It was just a simple question-and-answer sheet, reminding her a lot of a scavenger hunt.

What color did the Red Witch wear?

Who was the mayor of the town in 1693?

What was the town's name before it became Hellborne?

Most people already knew those things, she supposed. Heck, Hailey and Elaine had answered almost all of them in history the other day.

"Whose house survived?" she murmured, reading one of the questions.

"The Grey House." Daphne came up beside her. "The Red Witch's house."

"I do remember that from the story Hailey told in class," she admitted. "Though I might've forgotten a bit."

"That's why I'm here," Daphne replied with a wink.

Tara smiled. "My hero."

"Obviously."

A thought suddenly occurred to Tara. "Isn't it a bit strange that another witch is here in a town that *burned* a previous witch?"

"I'd say the opposite. Witches are attracted to powerful points in the earth. Ley lines. Hellmouths. What have you," Daphne replied with a shrug.

". . . A *hellmouth*?" Tara wondered.

"Yeah, not important. Hellborne's on a ley line. You know, a place of power—"

"Class! Class! Quiet now!" Miss Aberhorn called, clapping her hands together. Beside her was the museum attendant, a small and freckled woman with short brown hair and large circular glasses.

"Welcome to the Hellborne Museum! I've seen a good many of you before . . . so you know the drill. No climbing on the rocks. No getting on the roof. No licking the displays," she added with a look in Baz's direction, and Tara didn't even want to imagine why. "The main building here is where you will find a lot of the archives from the town's history, as well as the bathroom and the gift shop, and to your left is the Grey House itself, home of Adelaide Grey, the witch who burned our town to the ground. Almost everything in her house is a replica of what was in there at the time, though we do have her original journal. Adelaide Grey was responsible for countless deaths, or so the stories go. . . ."

Hailey rolled her eyes. "Miss Aberhorn, if we wanted to hear a ghost story, we'd just watch *Hocus Pocus*."

Baz joked, "I got a lighter if anyone wants to light the Black Flame Candle!"

"Why would you need a volunteer?" Daphne asked loudly.

He gasped and pressed his hand against his heart. "You wound me, Icy Hot! New Girl, I get around, you know. I'm a lover to be *experienced*—"

Miss Aberhorn cleared her throat. "All right, all right, students, *enough*! Baz, calm down. Hailey, I would've expected better from the senior class president."

Hailey bit back a smile. "Sorry, Miss Aberhorn."

Then the homeroom teachers dismissed them to go on their field trip scavenger hunt, and reminded them very loudly, "NO LICKING THE CASES!"

As everyone dispersed, Tara jotted down a few of the answers she knew onto her sheet of paper, but she kept having trouble as her pencil punctured the sheet—repeatedly. Daphne rolled her eyes and slipped off her backpack.

"Write on me," she said.

So Tara did. She pressed the sheet against the middle of Daphne's back and filled in the answers, and then turned so Daphne could do the same. She tried not to concentrate on Daphne's long and looping script as it crossed her back, the way she dotted her *i*'s and crossed her *t*'s with a vengeance. "Where did your friends go?" she asked hesitantly, remembering the other punk kids at the back of the bus.

"My friends?"

"On the bus."

Daphne glanced over her shoulder to give her a strange look and then said, "*Oh*, them. I was just asking around about some stuff. They knew some dirt on Chad—the guy who died before Moss—so I wanted to see what it was."

"Dirt?"

She nodded. "Apparently—"

Miss Aberhorn interrupted them. "Go in and explore the museum, you two! Hellborne has some really fascinating history. You never know what you might find."

Tara had some idea, but she only nodded and put her pencil into her bag. Daphne shrugged her book bag back over her shoulders. "I'll tell you the rest later," she muttered. "You take house, I take museum, we'll compare notes?"

Tara nodded. "Okay. This worksheet looks easy, anyway."

Daphne departed for the museum, while Tara slipped into the decrepit cabin.

Most of her classmates had gone into the Grey House, too, joking about the butter churn and throwing their chewing gum into the cauldron. For a history that was revered, they sure didn't seem like they cared a lot about it.

The cabin was dark and damp, lit by a few directional lights in the ceiling that shone on the big pieces in the room—the antique bed, the witch's workstation, the mantel . . . all of it draped in what Tara could only describe as a *hexing* aesthetic. Everything a moviegoer would think witches of the eighteenth century had in their houses—animal bones and tinctures and strange torture devices and broomsticks, though most of what was in the house wouldn't be useful in any sort of real spell or ritual.

Well, except for maybe the bag of chalk.

As she moved around the house, opposite of most of the other seniors, she kept an eye on the populars, wondering who would be next. Harris? Cory? *Hailey?* Just because it had only been men to begin with didn't mean the killer would *only* target men.

A strange feeling shivered over her skin. Electric almost, and she rubbed her arms absently—until she realized what that feeling was. *Magic.* In the house of a witch who had been dead for two hundred years. She would've thought all Adelaide Grey's energies would've subsided by now. Lost to time.

But it felt new.

Raw.

As if the Red Witch had just been here.

"She wasn't *that* pretty," Elaine was saying on the other side of the house. She stood with her friends in front of the mantel, where the portrait of a beautiful woman hung. She was lovely and soft, with dark russet hair and a heart-shaped face, in a simple red dress faded a little with the sun. "I guess I get why everyone voted for that new girl now."

"Babe, she's ugly," Cory said.

"The new girl or the witch?"

He laughed and pulled her into his arms. "Both."

Elaine rolled her eyes and then said, "It should've been *me*. My family's been here since the founding. My eighth-great grandfather set the torch to the pyre that *burned* the witch!" She huffed. "Maybe I can ask Principal Greaves for his role this year instead . . . and actually *light* the pyre."

"Elaine, that's not funny," Baz warned.

"Do I look like I'm joking, Bastion? What're you doing over here anyway? Go and lick that case of yours. It'll be the only action you'll get this year."

A few of his friends laughed.

He groaned. "Hey, c'mon, you know you dared me to. . . ."

Tara stood on the other side of the museum, by re-creations of a cauldron and a spindle, garlic hanging from the rafters. Also, peculiarly, there were ropes draped from beam to beam, filled with knots. She reached up and touched one, and an aura blurred her vision—soft and warm and . . . loved?

Not the feeling of a witch two hundred years burned.

"She used to tie knots for power."

At the sound of Hailey's voice, Tara gave a start. She turned to her. "P-power?"

"That's the story," she said, looking up at the ancient knots of rope. "She tied one for each bit of magic she cast. For Mathilda's cow to milk again. For little Aisling's fever to break." She touched one for each magic. "For love. For health. For truth. And revenge . . ." The last knot she lingered on. "Did you know that in the sixteenth century if you were a woman with no want for a man, a woman who might have lived beside a family who caught a fever or a farm whose cows had died, they would storm your house and look for knots to see if you were a witch—a spool of thread that had gotten mangled, a length of rope in your attic . . . a ribbon in your hair? Then they would hang you, or burn you, or drag you through the streets behind the mayor's horse."

Tara had heard stories like that before, obviously, but they still made her skin crawl when she thought about those witches being like her. Girls with mothers and fathers and brothers. "That's horrible."

"Is it?" Hailey inclined her head. "The town said that Adelaide Grey welcomed devils into her house. Maybe she did. Maybe she danced with them and made a pact to live forever, so when the townsfolk came upon her door, she wasn't afraid to die."

"That's dark magic."

A troubled look furrowed Hailey's brow. She turned to Tara and asked quietly, "And who decides that?"

Unsure of what to say, Tara shook her head. Her mother had told her what was right and wrong, dark and light, but beyond that . . . who made the rules? The people who wrote the spell-books, who traversed through the magics of lore?

Those same spellbooks that were mostly penned and mostly attributed to men?

"They're just stories," Hailey said solemnly, "but I'm afraid that some people think it might be real."

Elaine? Tara thought, turning her gaze to the redhead in question.

"And I think maybe sometimes they take it too far."

Was—was Hailey trying to tell her that she thought *Elaine* was the one cursing her friends? Her mind reeled. She wanted to ask her outright, but then would Elaine hear? It might not be safe—Hailey might've been putting her in danger by just saying *this*.

Tara felt a bone-deep chill. "Wh-why are you telling me this?"

Hailey smiled and tapped her sheet of paper. "The knots. They're one of the questions, Tara. Least I can do to make up for one—or a few—of my friends being rude to you."

Tara began to thank her, but Elaine called to Hailey from the other side of the house, "Hey! We're leaving!"

"Coming!" Hailey replied, and gave Tara a wink before she slipped out of the cabin with her friends toward the museum building, leaving Tara alone with the rotting garlic and dusty cauldron.

This was a possibility that neither she nor Daphne had actually thought about—it was oversight on her part. What if someone was using the Red Witch's spells? It made sense when she thought about it. The strange markings on the guys' hands weren't from any curse she knew of, but if it was one *created* specifically by a witch . . .

A terrifying thought.

She glanced down at the worksheet, at the tenth question—
What is the witch's book made of?

So, it was here in the cabin. She hadn't seen it, but she hadn't really been looking for a *book*, either, or anything involving the Red Witch. Searching, she started from the door and revisited every station in the house—the cauldron, the mantel, the bed, until she came to a stop at the rotten workbench, and a cloth draped over something beside it. *NO TOUCHING!* a sign atop it read, and in neat handwriting beneath it was added (*AND NO LICKING!*).

So, the infamously licked case in question. She leaned over the rope guard and pulled off the velvet cloth, and it puddled at the feet of the glass case.

The golden plaque read *THE BOOK OF BLOOD.*

The book in question was bound in crimson leather. It looked more like a journal than a spellbook, sitting in that case so simply, a strange symbol burned into the leather cover. She could feel its magic, having seeped into the wooden podium, the glass case—all of it. It was faint, but it was there, like an almost-invisible layer of dust.

And, to her horror, she recognized that aura—that feeling. If a spellbook was strong enough, and tied close enough to the witch it came from, their auras bled together. So even though the witch was two hundred years dead, her aura remained wreathed around this crimson-bound tome.

It was the same magic she'd felt in the library before Moss died.

The murderer, whoever it was, had used the Red Witch's spellbook—somehow.

Things had just become a lot more complicated.

She had to tell Daphne.

Quickly, she pulled the velvet back over the case and hurried out of the Grey House. Maybe Daphne was at the bus already?

Miss Aberhorn sat on the steps of the main building and looked up from her Nora Roberts novel. "Is there something wrong?"

"D-do you know where Daphne is?"

The teacher frowned. "She's somewhere around here! By the way, congrats on being the Red Witch! It's such an honor, you know?"

It didn't feel like one.

"Are you finished already?" the teacher added.

Tara handed her the worksheet. "I th-think so."

Miss Aberhorn scanned her answers—Tara hated when teachers did that in front of her, expecting her to wait while she was judged—before nodding and putting the piece of paper into her folder. "I wouldn't expect anything less from you, Miss Maclay. But are you sure you don't want to go visit the gift shop or anything?"

"I might." She just wanted to find Daphne. First she'd check the bus, then the museum. She quickly left across the parking lot to the buses—the drivers were taking a smoke break by the sign at the entrance—and climbed up the steps. "Daphne?"

There wasn't a response.

She frowned. Maybe she was in the gift shop—

Mid-turn, she froze.

A shiver up her spine. A tingle across her skin, like a wave of electricity.

Magic.

She dumped her book bag into her seat and took her pencil from behind her ear. Holding it like a weapon. She thought of the wooden stakes at Daphne's house. It'd be nice to have one of those right now. Not that she could do much with it, but—it was the thought that counted.

"Daphne?" she called, taking a step down the aisle.

There wasn't a response.

Then she saw a red Converse sticking out from underneath one of the seats. And then the other. Someone was on the *ground*? Why? Were they sleeping or something? *Don't be foolish.* She knew they weren't.

The bus reeked of magic.

She lowered herself onto her knees to see if they were okay, but when she bent down and looked beneath the seat, she came face-to-face with Cory—eyes wide, mouth frozen open. He was contorted in such a weird way, he looked broken. Because he was. There was a burn mark on his outstretched, grasping hand. The same rune that was on Moss's hand. The same rune from the spellbook in the cottage.

The longer she looked, the more she realized that his neck was twisted at a strange angle. A fly landed on his eye.

He didn't blink.

He didn't move.

She screamed and scrambled out of the bus, forgetting her backpack. She tripped on the last step and fell—hard—into the one person she wanted to see.

Daphne.

They both went tumbling to the ground. Tara quickly tried to shove herself off Daphne, but she'd bitten her lip on the fall and her mouth tasted like blood. It stained her teeth as she fumbled for words. About the body. About Cory.

"T-th-there's a-a-a—"

"S-s-s-sp-sp-spit it out, Maclay," mocked Elaine, coming up with her group, who had just turned in their worksheets, too.

Tara looked at her. *You already know. Because you did it. You killed your own boyfriend*, she thought, and said one simple word: "Dead."

That seemed to have the exact effect that she'd been hoping for. Miss Aberhorn quickly abandoned her book and rushed up into the bus.

A moment later, she let out an ear-piercing shriek.

Harris dropped his backpack, hurried onto the bus after the teacher, and helped her down the steps. He closed the door, shaking his head at his friends.

Elaine turned to Tara with rage. "You killed him! You—you *witch*!" Elaine shrieked and lunged at Tara.

Baz full-body caught her. "Whoa, Elaine."

"LET GO! SHE KILLED HIM! SHE KILLED HIM!" Elaine's shrieks turned into a sob. "They *both* did!"

Daphne snapped, "Don't be stupid! We came to Hellborne after the murders started, *idiot*. And Tara couldn't hurt a fly."

"HE WAS MY BOYFRIEND!" Elaine screamed. Tears brimmed at her eyes. Poured down her cheeks. Elaine's aura pulsed with agony. Waves of it, a riptide of anguish. It threatened to pull Tara in. It prickled at the edge of her soul.

"I—I'm sorry," Tara murmured, even though she hadn't done anything.

"You *admit* it?" Elaine asked in horror.

"N-no, that's n-not what I—"

Daphne put a hand on her shoulder. "It's okay. Breathe."

Tara's shoulders slumped, and she nodded. How could she have ever thought it could be Elaine? How could *Hailey*?

The other students who had quietly gathered around them cautiously looked between Baz and Elaine, and Daphne and Tara, until Daphne snapped, "What're you looking at?" and took Tara gently by the arm and led her away from the bus. She sat her down on the curb.

Tara was shaking. She couldn't quite stop. She'd never seen a dead body before. Even when her mother died, she hadn't been in the room. She had gone for some snacks, and all she remembered was the glow and hum of the vending machines and the soft murmur of beeps and whispers and ventilators. It had been almost midnight.

She hadn't even felt it when her mother passed. She'd been choosing between Snickers and Runts, and the next thing she knew, her brother was in the vending machine alcove, shaking his head, saying, "She's gone."

Tara had imagined what it might have been like if she'd just stayed in the room. Her mother's eyes slowly losing their knowing, becoming marbles set into a gaunt mask. But she'd never seen dead eyes before.

Not until just then, and Cory's eyes were nothing like she'd imagined.

They weren't marbles—they were still eyes, and they were still fixed somewhere. But it was somewhere she couldn't see. On some*one* she couldn't see. Frozen there.

Frozen there forever.

And that magic . . .

This *was* the same magic that killed Moss. And presumably Chad and Brian, too.

"Hey." She heard Daphne's voice near her ear, and she jerked herself out of her thoughts. Daphne was rubbing circles on her back. "Hey, breathe, yeah? It's tough, I know, but breathe."

But all she could see were Cory's dead eyes as he stared at her. She leaned against Daphne and pressed her face into Daphne's shoulder, her familiar citrus scent soothing, and cried.

CHAPTER TWENTY-FOUR
PRINCIPALED

The next morning, Tara cracked an egg on the side of the frying pan and watched it sizzle.

Last night, after she'd talked to the police one too many times, she came home and ended up falling asleep on *Maths and the Modern Magic* and woke up with indentations of pages on her cheek. She couldn't recall a single thing she read. Which irritated her, because normally she was unparalleled at absorbing information. All of yesterday was a blur, from the cops questioning them to getting a ride home from Daphne.

"I was going to tell you earlier," Daphne had said in the minivan, "but those guys I was talking to on the bus? They said Brian and Hailey broke up a week before he died, and apparently he wasn't very happy about it. He started spreading some nasty rumors about her and his friends helped."

Tara was baffled. "How do they know?"

"Guy I was talking to works at the car wash in town. Brian

went to get his car detailed and he was ranting *all* day about Hailey. He was furious, apparently."

"So, you think *Hailey* is our prime suspect?"

"Yeah, I do. Or Elaine."

She thought back to what Hailey had told her in the Grey House about Elaine. "Why would she kill her own boyfriend? And with Hailey—why would she jeopardize her future over some boy? She's the senior class president. She wouldn't."

Because Tara knew now what a *little* of that possibility felt like, to be able to leave—to go anywhere else. The Red Witch scholarship was an awful way to collect five thousand dollars, but that was enough money to get her out from underneath her father. It was the kind of hope, small and fragile, that she didn't want to mess up. She thought Hailey might feel the same.

Daphne threw up her arms. "Then we're back at square one?"

"I guess so," Tara muttered.

And her head *still* felt like a tangled ball of yarn. There was something she needed to tell Daphne, but she couldn't for the life of her think of what it was. She'd spent all night trying to think of it, and well into the next morning, when she cooked breakfast for her father.

"Your cousin Beth's coming this weekend," her father said as he sat down at the kitchen table. "Clean out the spare bedroom for her, please?"

Tara set his and Donny's plates down in front of them, scrambled eggs, bacon, and toast, and slid into the air between them. "Oh, right. Of course."

"She's looking forward to her visit," he said happily. "She'll be with you while Donny and I take a tour of Dartmouth."

Her brother turned his gaze up from his Game Boy to Tara. "And I gotta have my *essay* done by then, too."

Right, his essay.

"I told you not to procrastinate on that," his father said.

"It'll be done." Donny gave her a look.

Tara gave the briefest nod, and he went back to his boss battle. She shifted in her chair. This was her chance—it was a question she'd been thinking over since she heard her name announced over the loudspeakers as this year's Red Witch. It was a question laced with hope, and a little more fear: "May I apply?"

Her father gave her a strange look. "To *Dartmouth*? Oh, sweetheart, no. I couldn't afford both you and Donny."

"I can try a scholarship? Or two. There's one the school gives out—"

He looked at her over his newspaper. "We can talk about it later, Tara. Let's get through Donny's process first."

Tara bit the inside of her cheek and broke off the corner piece of her Pop-Tart. Her brother didn't even *want* to go to college. He told her himself. She would've done anything to go.

Well, almost anything.

She couldn't imagine her life away from her family. She couldn't imagine them ever letting her go. Maybe that was why she didn't suspect Hailey, because with so much going for her, why would she mess it up? Be trapped in a small, nowhere town on the edge of a dark wood, while the world was at her fingertips just beyond the interstate?

She wouldn't. No one would.

Tara broke off another corner of her Pop-Tart and nibbled on it.

Her father turned a page of his newspaper. "It seems there are no leads in that Cory Bouvard boy's case. Too bad, he seemed to be a good boy. Isn't your high school doing anything to protect their students?"

"Nah, it's a public school, Dad," Donny said. "You get what you pay for."

"It must be frightening," her father added. "Tara, are you okay at the school?"

"Yes, I'm fine," she quickly replied, a flash of the brochure from that private all-girls school in Ohio in her head.

She forced down the rest of her Pop-Tart before asking if she could be excused for school, and with a wave of his hand he dismissed her. As she stood from the table to clear all their plates, she glanced over at the newspaper and the headline, "Principal Greaves Reports 'We Will Not Let Fear Get in the Way of Learning.'"

Tara frowned at that.

In a lot of ways, she realized, it was the *lack* of fear at Hellborne Academy that was the problem.

CHAPTER TWENTY-FIVE
CONSOLATION PRIZE

"Here's the books back." Tara offered Daphne the stack she had borrowed. They met at the west side of the school, near the garden, Daphne's longboard tucked under her arm. The morning was gray, and it made her feel sleepy and useless—talking with her father always made her feel useless. "I read them. There's nothing there we can use."

"Is everything okay?" Daphne asked, taking the books. Confusion knitted her thick black eyebrows together. "After . . . you know. Everything with Cory."

"Yes," she lied. She'd picked a lavender sprig earlier and now spun it between her fingers. She didn't want to worry Daphne with the knowledge that she'd spent last night half-afraid she'd see Cory's dead face in her dreams, and then the other half doing just that.

"You sure? You have that look like you're lying to me."

She gave a start. "Wh-what? You can tell?"

Daphne pointed at her. "Ha! See! You *are* lying to me!"

"That was a horrible trick," she muttered, wilting, only for Daphne to slide up beside her and knock their shoulders together.

"C'mon, you can tell me. I promise I won't judge."

"I don't think my dad is going to let me go to college," she admitted, deciding that her nightmares were her own problem. "My brother is applying to Dartmouth. No, I'm applying to Dartmouth for him. And we don't really have money for both of us to go to college. . . ."

Daphne frowned. "Does he know about that Red Witch scholarship?"

Tara shook her head.

"Well, my parents can totally help you with scholarship stuff. And we can talk to the guidance counselor. They usually have a list of scholarships you can apply to, and can answer questions about student loans and applications and stuff."

"You know a lot about it all."

Daphne shrugged. "I can't take education for granted."

It struck Tara, then, how different their lives really were. Daphne was a Black teen who moved around more often than not. She remembered their English teacher's comment about catching up together on *Macbeth*, even though Daphne had been at the school for a few weeks already, and had read the entire thing. She wondered what other microaggressions happened that she didn't notice. Didn't even think about.

Their lives, their lived experiences, were so different—and yet, in other ways, as they glanced around to make sure no one was watching before they held hands, a little bit the same.

"And once you turn eighteen and graduate high school, your

dad won't have any power over you," Daphne went on, holding her hand tightly. "When's your eighteenth birthday?"

"A week or so ago."

"See? That means—" Daphne froze. Then she turned an accusing gaze on Tara. "You just had a *birthday* and you didn't *tell me?*"

She winced. "It was the sixteenth. . . ."

"And we didn't *celebrate?*"

"You kind of suspected me of being the murderer, I think."

The fight left Daphne as she sighed. "Oh, right. Well, mine's January first, by the way, and I *do* expect a cake."

Tara laughed. "Noted."

Daphne opened the west doors into the freshman hallway, and they cut into the stairwell up toward the third floor and their homeroom together. Tara tried not to think about their hands, but it felt like her fingertips were filled with Pop Rocks. Daphne's grip was solid, the calluses on her hands rough against Tara's soft palm. It was all she could think about.

Them. Holding hands.

And how wonderful it felt.

After Cory's death yesterday, a letter had been sent home detailing what had happened, the principal's promise to get to the bottom of these deaths, and that counselors were available if anyone needed one. But school went on as normal. After all, Cory's death hadn't happened on school grounds. And the other grades hadn't seen it, been a part of it. The murders, at least, had been limited to the senior class.

Students flowed around them, a few glancing over, whispering behind their hands that *she* was the one who found Cory. It only made it more plausible that she was the killer.

No, she was just unlucky, on a lot of different fronts. Her hand slid out of Daphne's, and she pulled her sleeves down over her fingers.

"Oh," Daphne went on, unbothered by everyone's looks, "I requested a used copy of *Writings of Dramius*, so that should get here today."

"You think something useful is in there?"

"I don't know. It's got some things about powerful words, so maybe? We're grasping at straws. Our suspect list has dwindled to Harris, Baz, and Principal Greaves."

"So not Hailey or Elaine?"

"Yeah, we can't ignore their alibis—and I thought a lot last night, and I agree with you. Why would Hailey ruin what she has? Elaine, too, at that. Harris flies so far under the radar that it *could* be him, and yesterday he was so quick to blame you. . . . Then again, Baz is so universally liked that no one would ever suspect him. . . . Ugh! Why is this so *hard*? TV shows make this seem so easy. You find a clue and BAM! You've got your culprit." Daphne sighed and rubbed her face. "I get a headache just thinking about this."

"I'm sorry."

As they sat down in homeroom, Tara noted that Baz looked a little more jumpy than usual, tapping the rubber of his pencil against his desk. He caught Tara looking at him and gave a half shrug with a smile.

There weren't many guys left in that friend group.

Four had already been axed. Of course he'd be jumpy.

"Hey, did you hear me?" Daphne asked, drumming her fingers on her desk impatiently. She frowned and scooted her desk closer. "Tara?"

"What? Oh, yes."

"Then what was I saying?"

"I . . . Hmmm." Tara cringed. "I'm sorry."

Daphne laughed. "I was asking if you'd like to eat lunch together. I usually go to the library. Miss Starino doesn't mind if I eat in there if I'm discreet about it. I was thinking we could do more work then?"

"Lunch?"

"I mean, unless you like eating alone."

"N-no," Tara replied. "I actually kind of hate it."

"Yeah, I do, too," Daphne said as someone walked into the classroom with Miss Aberhorn. He was a tall and gray-haired Latino man in a long trench coat, and when he put his hands into his pockets, he showed the class his badge clipped to his waistband and a handgun in its holster.

Daphne sank back into her chair. She narrowed her eyes.

"Morning, students," said the man, and flipped out his badge. "I'm Ryan Lopez, a homicide detective, and I'd like everyone's cooperation, if possible."

"Homicide?" the students whispered between each other. Baz stiffened in his seat, glancing at his friends, who all looked equally uncomfortable.

One of the students raised his hand, and the detective pointed to him. "Yes?"

"You're here about Cory?"

"And the others," he replied, and another student raised their hand. "Yes?"

"They weren't accidents?"

"That's yet to be confirmed."

"Is it a serial killer?"

"Dude, that'd be gnarly," said another student.

"Scary."

"Like in *Scream*?"

"Or *I Know What You Did Last Summer*?"

"Are we in, like, a *real-life* horror movie?"

The detective cleared his throat. "This is not a movie. It's not something to take lightly. Four of your fellow students are dead—"

"You think it's a *student*?" Hailey asked, incredulous.

"No one here would kill Cory," Elaine added, and then turned a sharp glare to Tara. "Except maybe . . ."

Daphne growled, "Watch it," as Tara sank down in her seat.

"I'm not saying the suspect goes to the school," the detective replied in a calming voice. He held his hands up as if to try and physically calm the mounting anxiety. "This is just an investigation, and I'd appreciate any and all information you have. I'll be in the principal's office today if you would like to come by. Thank you for your time."

Then he nodded to the homeroom teacher, handing her his card, before he ducked out of the room. Tara and Daphne exchanged a look. Now the authorities were involved. That would make their investigation ten times harder.

As it turned out, the library was a much better place to have lunch.

It was quiet, and Miss Starino didn't mind in the slightest when Tara shuffled in after Daphne, peanut butter and jelly sandwiches from the lunchroom in tow. They sequestered themselves in a back corner of the sun-drenched library students didn't often visit voluntarily—the nonfiction section—and Daphne took a stack full of books out of her bag and spread them out over the table. And they got to work.

"I doubt it's a karmic spell," Tara muttered, scanning the counterfeit copy of *The Study of Demonic Arrays: Ancient Lore and Modern Management.* "Why are there so many footnotes?" Frowning, she closed the book and took up another one off the stack.

Daphne nibbled on the crust of her sandwich. "Lan Stroud's translator loves footnotes apparently."

"*Loves?*"

"The translator is a demon. Still alive."

That gave her a shock. "A *demon*? Translating things?"

"Oh, yeah. Why not?"

Because they're evil. She turned her gaze back down to the footnotes, and the few tongue-in-cheek notes she'd chuckled at. In her head, they'd always been sharp-toothed, horned monsters, not translators and researchers and academics.

She was a part of those people, that community, but she knew so little about it.

She wanted to know more. Everything. And she could start through these books, a new lifeline, to learn and absorb and not be so *useless*—

The bell rang, and they'd gathered up their books and set off toward biology together when Baz stopped them at Tara's locker and took a flyer out of his back pocket. "Heeeey, New Girl, Icy Hot," he added, nodding to Daphne, "we're having a party. You should come. Celebrate winning Red Witch!"

"I'm sorry," Daphne deadpanned, "but we don't participate in Neanderthal mating rituals."

ASHLEY POSTON

"And half your friends probably want to kill me," Tara added under her breath, taking a flyer. She smoothed it out, skimming down the information—which admittedly was scant.

"I . . . know," he replied, a little uncomfortable, "and I know that one of my friends just passed. His funeral's in the morning. So we all decided to push through; it's what Cory would've wanted. I *would* do it on Halloween weekend, but you know, the Burning. Can't interfere with that, so why not on my birthday instead? Right?"

"Tonight?"

"It *is* October twenty-seventh, if I remember correctly."

"It's a weeknight," Daphne added, frowning. "And a bit last minute, isn't it?"

He winked at her. "I trust I'll see both of you there? Wear your best costumes and BYOB, bros!" he added as he retreated backward, and then spun on his heel and left down the hall.

Tara turned her gaze down to the flyer again. *BAZ'S BIG HALLOWEEN BASH!* it read. *BOOZE, BEER, AND BABES. (Parental discretion advised.)* "Aren't booze and beer the same thing?"

"I think he meant liquor and beer."

"Ah."

Daphne took it from her hands and crumpled it up. "They're all idiots." She tossed the crumpled ball of paper into the nearest trash bin and left for biology, and Tara caught up to her.

"But we sh-should go."

"You're kidding. I know Baz is your friend, but—"

"No, to clear him. If he has anything to do with the curse killing his friends, then his house might have some clues. Some residues of spells—something."

188

The realization slowly crossed Daphne's face. Then she dove into the trash can for the flyer and flattened it out against her binder. "But how're you going to get out of your house? With your dad having you on lockdown?"

"The window."

"That easy?"

Tara shook her head. "No, but I th-think I can risk it. As long as we go together," she added, her ears burning red.

Daphne bit her lip to keep from grinning. "Yeah, I think we can do that. I'll pick you up at eight? Around the block so your old man doesn't see?"

It was as good an idea as any, and Tara figured that she could retire to her room early, lock the door, and darken her room so that even if her father *did* peek in, he'd assume she'd gone to bed. She did sometimes, so why not tonight?

The bell rang, and Daphne cursed under her breath. They were a few seconds late to biology, enough to both get written up for being tardy. Daphne already had two other write-ups, so she went silently to the principal's office while Tara sat down and opened up her textbook.

Underneath her desk she flipped through the rest of *The Study of Demonic Arrays: Ancient Lore and Modern Management*, while her biology teacher taught them how to slit open a frog.

CHAPTER TWENTY-SIX
HELL OF A PARTY

"Going to bed early?"

"I'm a bit tired," Tara replied, facing the hall so she didn't have to lie to her father's face. Lies were getting easier, weirdly enough. Especially with him. "I feel like I might be catching a cold."

"The weather is different here than it is in Omaha," he replied, licking his thumb to turn the page in his novel. It was a different book every night, but they all looked the same. "Be sure to bundle up."

"I will," she replied softly, and left down the hall. The moment she closed her door, she pressed her hands, fingers splayed, against the wood and closed her eyes.

Her mother would frown upon this. She would tell Tara, "Magic isn't used in this manner," with that gentle disapproval.

But Tara wasn't her mother, and she didn't want anyone else to die by this witch. Besides, she wasn't even sure if magic would answer when she called. She had only been able to do spells in the garden, and every time she tried in the quiet of her room, the energies around her would slosh away, leaving the air empty.

Maybe this time magic would answer.

She pulled the sprig of lavender she'd picked from the garden, held it between her fingers, and closed her eyes. Pulled the energy around her into her fingertips like her mother taught her. And more than that—she concentrated on the *feeling* of magic. Of creating something. Of borrowing and replacing and blooming into something new.

The air around her vibrated—and then the familiar pull began to draw in the energy from around her, sharpening it into pinpricks—points at the tips of her fingers.

She whispered, hopeful, daring, *"Somnum."*

Sleep.

Like a firework, the energy dispersed from her fingers into the house, shrouding it. She felt the pull, heavy, dragging the house downward, the quiet becoming silence, the silence becoming sleep. Her father in his chair. Her brother at his computer in his room, face sinking onto his keyboard.

The air was thick with lavender.

As the spell dissipated, her eyes flew open with a gasp.

She'd *done* it. Outside the garden! She could still feel it in her veins, rushing through her blood and bones like warm honey.

"Thank you," she murmured, though she wasn't sure to whom or what—the world around her, the universe, her mother perhaps, as she put the lavender on her dresser and changed into jeans and a heavy multicolored sweater and—just in case her spell wore off before she came back—stuffed a few pillows under her covers to make it look like she was in bed. Then she pulled out a box from the closet and dug inside for the few pieces of Halloween costumes that she managed to scrounge up. Cat ears and a tail, and she added a black dot to the tip of her nose and drew whiskers on her cheeks. That was good enough. She'd never been to a costume party before, but she wasn't going to enjoy the festivities.

If students were there, then that meant the killer probably was, too, and she was going to hunt the killer.

And make sure they couldn't hurt anyone else.

The headlights broke through the darkness as Daphne's blue minivan pulled up to the corner of the street. Tara crawled out of her window and hurried over to it.

Daphne leaned out the window as Tara came up to the van. "Hey, cupcake," she greeted, "need a ride?"

Tara climbed into the passenger seat. The van smelled like Daphne, her jacket folded on the middle console, a silver cross necklace hanging from the rearview mirror. Then she looked behind her into the rest of the van. It looked half–lived in, pillows piled in the back, snack wrappers everywhere. Almost normal-looking, if not for the two-way radio set up against the back of her seat.

"There's probably a decade-old Snickers somewhere back there." Daphne adjusted the rearview mirror. She was dressed completely in black, with a shot glass hanging around her neck. "You sure your dad won't find out?"

Tara glanced back at the small, unassuming house that was more a prison than a home. She could feel her magic vibrating around it, strong and sure. "I'm sure."

"Okay, then, here we go. I think I know where this place is," Daphne said, pulling the flyer out of the glove compartment. "I asked the guy at the gas station—he said you can't miss Baz's house. We'll see if he's right."

Then she put the van in gear, and the vehicle hiccuped forward down the road.

Cars were parked for a quarter of a mile down the road from Baz's house, and after looking for a parking spot, Daphne settled for the end of the line down by a stop sign.

"Jesus, I didn't know there were this many people *at* Hellborne," Daphne muttered, grabbing her keys and mini backpack from the middle seat. She climbed out of the driver's seat, and Tara met her around back.

"Maybe they're from neighboring schools, too?" Tara supposed.

"I hate crowds."

"I don't mind them," Tara said. Daphne gave her a disbelieving look. "I like to people-watch. You can learn a lot about a person just by whether they choose the punch or a beer."

"Oh?" Daphne asked as they set off down the sidewalk toward the loud house. The night was chilly, and the wind that swept through the trees picked at the leaves still left on the maples that lined the neighborhood. "Lemme guess, punch people are chaotic and beer people are cautious?"

"Beer people distrust more," Tara replied. "Which are you?"

"Neither. I don't drink. Do you?"

"Not much."

Daphne barked a laugh. "We're *such* buzzkills." Then she added, sticking her hands into her leather jacket, "I've actually . . . never been to a house party."

"Me neither."

"It's hard always being the new kid, never mind it's a crap-shoot depending on *where* you go. . . . Besides, I train so much I don't have time, anyway. I'm scared of disappointing my dads. After last time . . ."

Tara frowned. "Last time?"

Daphne opened her mouth, then frowned and shook her head. "Don't worry about it."

"But—"

"We're here," Daphne interrupted, motioning up the steps to the two-story house. Baz's house was, in fact, what the cool kids called *da bomb*. Maybe a little literally, because with the fake fire flickering in the windows and the red wiggly air dancers set in the lawn out front, it kind of looked like hell had exploded.

A few drunken students mingled in the front yard. Well, *mingled* was a polite word for it. They were in a heap. Tara wasn't sure if the heap was passed out on purpose there together or by accident, but they seemed to be perfectly fine with it either way.

It wasn't even that *late*—when had the party started?

"Lightweights," Daphne sighed, shaking her head, and rang the doorbell.

A demonic gong reverberated through the house, almost covered up by the pulsing sound of the Backstreet Boys scream-ing, "*QUIT PLAYING GAMES WITH MY HEART!*" Huh, maybe Baz really *did* like that music. They waited at the front door, standing on the *BOO TO YOU!* doormat that was quite charming, really, if you ignored everything else.

Baz threw the door open with a cry of delight. "FRIENDS!"

He was dressed like a devil, which was pretty apt for the cloth fire in the windows and the noodle-y blow-up creatures on the lawn. But he looked especially imposing with beautiful ram horns that curved from his forehead and nested almost perfectly in his hair, which wasn't spiked tonight but left in soft curls, and prosthetic pointed ears. He smiled, showing off fake fangs. The red of his shirt and dress trousers made him look a lot bigger in the doorway than he otherwise would have. Just so loud and *there*.

He must've *really* liked Halloween.

His eyes glittered when he realized it was Tara and Daphne. "You made it! What are you, a Luna? Are you here to lead the Sailor Scouts?"

"U-um . . ." Tara hesitated, not sure what the heck he was referencing.

Daphne, thank god, did. "Yeah, and if you don't let us in, we'll moon-crystal-power your ass to oblivion. It's freezing out here."

"And what're *you* supposed to be?"

She rolled her eyes and pointed to the shot glass hanging from her neck. "A shot in the dark? *Duh.*"

"Well, I can't say that's not creative," Baz muttered.

"I'll take that as a compliment," Daphne replied nobly. "What're you supposed to be? Beelzebub?"

"Just a lowly demon, at your service," he replied with a mock bow. "Come in! Come in! The party's just getting started."

"Tell that to the guys passed out on the lawn." Tara motioned to the pile of bodies, and it seemed like the first time Baz noticed them.

"Oh! I was wondering where Jonathan went. Nice to see he made some friends. Don't worry about them—they partied too hard too fast." And then he bent toward Tara and mock-whispered, "If you know what I mean."

Tara absolutely did not, and her cheeks prickled red just *thinking* about it. Daphne grabbed her by the hand and pulled her inside, and her heart fluttered as they laced their fingers together, all the while Baz grinned after them, as if he knew a secret.

But he couldn't.

No one could.

Because there isn't a secret. We aren't a secret, this isn't a secret, she thought to herself.

"Enjoy!" he called after them.

Daphne raised her hand to wave, signaling that they heard him, and wandered deeper into the house.

The party was everything Tara was not. Loud. Obnoxious. Claustrophobic. There were bowls with candy on every available surface that wasn't taken up by expensive-looking artwork and Solo cups, and people dancing together in the living room where the sound system was. Someone was DJ'ing, but she couldn't tell who.

She felt like a fish out of water—everything was so chaotic and jumbled, she almost instantly regretted suggesting that she and Daphne come. How could a witch even think in this sort of environment? And she had to wonder—if a witch couldn't even hear herself think, would her spells work?

It was a little quieter in the kitchen, where Daphne decided they should set up shop. She seemed comfortable, her mind on her mission as she glanced around each room, noting the people, the songs, the costume choices. There were vampires and Frankenstein monsters and werewolves and *Scream* killers. Axe murderers, sexy nurses and sexy maids and sexy witches. There was even a group of friends dressed up as the *Scooby-Doo* gang. Daphne dropped her hand almost the moment they found a spot in the kitchen to roost, and Tara's fingers tingled from her touch—and the sudden lack of it.

You're reading too much into it, she told herself. *You always do.*

Daphne had agreed to her help solely because she needed to find the witch. They both did, and Tara knew that she could help. There weren't any ulterior motives. She had to remind herself of that.

"Okay, I'll go upstairs to scope out those rooms and snoop around a bit. Will you keep a lookout here?" Daphne asked.

"Sure."

"Scream if anything happens—or if Baz goes upstairs," she added, and when Tara nodded that she understood, Daphne elbowed her way through the crowd—How were people still arriving? How did they all fit into this house?—and soon she disappeared into the pulse of bodies and music.

Tara found herself alone at the corner of the counter, near the refrigerator and the half-empty punch bowl. By the smell of it, the punch was a mix of Kool-Aid, vodka, and regret. Tara frowned as she watched classmates come into the kitchen, refill their cups without so much as noticing her, and slink away again into the throbbing masses.

Anyone could be a witch, with enough training and knowledge. They didn't have green skin. They didn't wear pointy hats—unless they wanted to. They didn't all dress in black with spiderweb cloaks. They didn't tie their souls to Black Flame

Candles and come back from the dead when virgins lit them. (Well, *maybe* there was a spell for that, but Tara hadn't come across that one yet.) The closest depiction Tara could think of to witches was, well, that one book with the moody wizard who changed his hair color and bargained his heart to a fire demon, but even that was strictly fantasy.

Which was to say, Tara felt completely and utterly useless.

Witches didn't *look* like any one kind of person. Did demons look like any one kind of demon? Did vampires all look the same? Werewolves? There was so much about the world she suddenly realized she didn't know. Everyone had a mask they wore, even regular people. Some of them wore masks they wanted you to see; others were so good at hiding that somewhere along the way they themselves forgot they were wearing a mask in the first place.

Trying to find the witch by just looking was useless, but lucky for her there were other ways to find sources of power. If the witch was someone close to Baz's friend group, then they were here.

Tara closed her eyes and concentrated. Tuned out the blaring music that had somehow drifted from *NSYNC to a new song Tara had only heard a few times on the radio. It was peppy, the lead vocalist sharp and cute.

Tara shut out everything. The sound. The smell of the kitchen. The hot bodies that kept jostling against her, even as she stood stagnant at the corner of the kitchen counter. And she concentrated—on the feel of the room. The soft ebb and flow. The lingering traces of energy all around her.

A witch who could curse someone had to be powerful. She

remembered the feeling from the library. Their magic would feel like a bright flare—

"Oh, *look*, it's the Red Witch."

Tara opened her eyes and glanced toward the voice. It was Elaine, dressed as a very sexy witch, in a wide-brimmed pointy hat and a gauzy dress with cobweb leggings. Her eyeshadow glimmered purple in the kitchen light.

Elaine asked, "Drink?"

"O-oh, no, I don't—"

Elaine scooped up a cupful of punch and shoved the sticky cup into Tara's hand. "You'll look less weird if you just hold it."

Tara frowned. "Thanks . . ."

"Whatever. I can't believe Baz actually invited you. Ugh, he's such a softie," Elaine muttered, crossing her arms over her chest.

There was a shout from the other side of the kitchen as one group of guys won a round of beer pong. Tara thought she recognized a few guys from her classes—including Harris. He was taking every drink handed to him.

Elaine narrowed her eyes. "How did you win, anyway?"

"I don't . . . I don't know."

"Hmph. Well, that makes two of us." Elaine swirled her drink in her Solo cup. "Baz is really good at taking in strays. I guess because he *was* one. He used to follow Hailey around like a puppy before she started dating Brian, and then I guess he just started tagging along. Cory thinks—" She abruptly stopped and corrected herself: "Always *thought* he was weird. Guess that's why he chose you."

Over at the beer pong table, Harris slammed back a beer

and threw his hands into the air with a shout—and then fell backward directly into a planter. Elaine cursed and excused herself, hurrying over to save him.

Baz used to be a loner? Charismatic, smooth-talking Bastion Leto? She couldn't imagine that. Then again, maybe he was good at wearing many faces.

Tara settled back into the corner of the kitchen again and closed her eyes. The air held nothing, just the gentle steady rhythm of bodies in motion and lives being lived and laughter and music and kissing in the corners—

Until suddenly that wasn't all that was there.

Suddenly, there was something else. An energy she didn't recognize. One that Tara, abandoning her drink at the punch bowl, pursued.

CHAPTER TWENTY-SEVEN
MARK OF THE WITCH

Tara followed the energy to the backyard.

She should've grabbed a knife on her way out. She'd passed the entire butcher block, but she hadn't even thought about grabbing something to defend herself with. Despite the crowd in the house, the backyard was almost deserted. There were a few couples making out on the deck, but she hadn't felt the energy so close. She'd felt it a bit farther. In the dark yard.

She slowly walked down the steps to the grass. It was turning brown with fall, and piles of leaves sat waiting to be scooped up into bags. The pulse of the pop music inside was dulled the farther she crept into the darkness. Maybe if she got in trouble, Daphne would come and look for her soon, anyway. There was a swing set toward the back of the yard, with someone sitting in it.

Baz.

Her heart jumped into her throat. The magic had emanated from here. She was sure of it. Then that could only mean . . .

Was it *Baz*? Had he tricked her the whole time, been nice to her to—to what? Throw her off his scent? Or had he given her a warning because he didn't want to hurt her?

Baz rocked back and forth on the swing set, leaning his head against one of the chains. As she got closer, the distinct smell of liquor punctured the air. His eyes were blurry. "Mmh, New Girl. Fancy hearing you meet— I mean, oh, you know."

"Is everything . . . ?" She was going to ask *okay* until her gaze settled on the bandages wrapped sloppily around his left hand.

"What happened to your hand?"

"Oh, this? Worried about little old me?" he drawled, giving her an easy smile. "I was just a little clumsy with a bottle opener. Cut the hell out of my hand."

She swallowed the lump in her throat and asked, "Did you use some rue for it?"

He gave her a strange look at first, and then his eyes widened. "Oh. *You* went into my locker. Huh. Nah, rue's no good for me. Put it on my tongue, and it blisters."

"It shouldn't. . . ."

A wry grin curled across his lips. "You think I did it, don't you?" he asked, abruptly changing the subject.

She gave a start. "I . . ." She *had* followed the flare of magic out here only to find Baz, but . . . something didn't feel right. Deep down in her gut. And her mother had always told her to listen to that feeling. "No," she admitted, "I don't."

His large shoulders visibly sagged with relief. Then he rallied himself and asked, "How're you liking the party?"

"Um—it's loud." She hesitantly sat down on the swing beside him. Now that she was closer, and in a quieter place, she decided that he was very good at putting on his horns. They looked almost real. So did the barbed tail that scraped the sandy ground behind him. "Is the cut bad? I can take you to the ER. I didn't—I don't really drink."

He waved her off. "It'll sort itself out eventually. Where's Icy Hot?"

"D-Daphne?"

"Yeah, Icy Hot."

"Why do you call her that?"

He tilted his head. "Nicknames make it easier."

"Make what easier?" *Killing friends?*

"Remembering them."

Oh. "So . . . I'm most memorable as the new girl?"

He tilted his head and squinted at her. "No, because I think you're going to be new again, after all this. Brand-new."

She didn't understand. "And Daphne?"

He laughed at that one. "You know, she's icy one minute, but then the moment *you* walk in the room she gets all warm and gooey."

"She . . . *doesn't*. . . ."

"Mm-hmm, she does. Why don't you go inside, have some fun, dance with her, live your one wild life? Human lives are always so short. They're there and then gone in a blink. *Poof,*" he added, miming a blast with his free hand. "Oh, what I would give for a life like that."

Tara didn't have time to try and guess what he was talking about. "Baz, you're drunk."

"And you're in love."

Her eyes widened. "I—I don't— I'm not—"

"Oh, come on, Tara, you *reek* of it."

She bristled.

"Love always smells so good."

"What?"

"Bastion Leto, accosting another girl already?" asked a voice from the house.

He quickly shot to his feet—and swayed, catching himself on the side of the swing set. "Hailey. N-no, I'm—I don't. I'm not. I'm not, right, Tara?"

"We were just talking," Tara replied as Hailey stepped into the silver moonlight that surrounded the swing set.

Baz rubbed his hands on his red costume and winced, shaking his wounded hand. "I'll, um, go inside."

Hailey inclined her head. "Perhaps that'd be for the best, Bastion. Go inside. Hydrate. Take a few Tylenol."

"Y-yeah. You're right, Hailey," he agreed, and put his mouth against Tara's ear and whispered, "Ruh-roh, I'm in trouble." Then he gave her a wink, Hailey a salute, and stumbled through the yard to the treacherous stairs, clinging to the railing as if he was afraid it'd escape him. Which it did, a few times, before he found his way inside.

Then Tara was alone with the senior class president. The last time they were alone together was in the Grey House. That felt like eons ago. Tara's palms began to sweat, but she didn't understand why. It was frigid outside—why was she nervous around the other girl?

Hailey flipped back her hair. She was dressed like a princess, in a flowing Renaissance gown and a brown corset cinching her waist. She looked perfectly . . . perfect, not a single hair out of place. Perfect makeup, perfect smile, perfectly sharp eyeliner.

Perfect timing, too.

"Sometimes Baz doesn't know when to stop. He parties

with the best of them. A real devil when it comes to it," Hailey added, tongue in cheek.

"He . . . wasn't really doing anything. We were just talking—"

"Of course not. He's a *gentleman*," Hailey interrupted, though the edges of her words were barbed. "And you look like you need a drink—you're so tense. Is something wrong?"

Tara shook her head. "No. I just . . . I've never been to a party like this before."

"Out of choice? Or because you were told not to?" Hailey asked, cocking her head. "Baz was saying a few days ago how you go straight home. You must have a pretty strict family."

"They're . . . fine."

"Do they know you're here?"

Tara shook her head.

And Hailey smiled, but it was all teeth and trouble. *"Good."*

Suddenly, Daphne called her name and came down the deck steps and into the dark of the yard. "Tara! I've been looking *everywhere* for you. I now remember why I *hate* house parties. I don't think the witch is gonna show up here— Oh, Hailey. Nice to see you," she added, though Tara knew full well that Daphne had seen Hailey from the very beginning. She knew because when Daphne folded her arm through Tara's, she pulled her closer, tighter. Too tight. "What're you doing out here?"

Hailey said, "Same as Tara, I suppose. Getting some fresh air."

"Well, I think we're going to leave—what do you think? I have a headache," Daphne added, and when Tara nodded, she said, "Tell Baz this was a . . . *party*."

It seemed like a compliment coming from Daphne.

"It was indeed," Hailey replied as Daphne pulled Tara away

from the swing set and through the side gate, into the front yard. Tara glanced over her shoulder, waiting for Hailey to go back inside, but she simply sat down on the swing set herself, alone in the darkness, the moonlight bathing her in silver and shadow. She looked . . . sad, and so small in that harsh light. Someone who had lost a lot of her friends, and for what?

Then the backyard gate closed, and Tara looked ahead. "You talked about the witch in front of Hailey. Aren't you worried she'll . . . ?"

"I did it on purpose."

Tara was alarmed. "To put a target on your back? Daphne—"

"I'm a witch hunter, aren't I? I think I'm equipped to handle this," Daphne retorted. "And better me than anyone else."

Yes, but there's already one on mine, she wanted to say. *And I care about you*, she wanted to say even more.

The realization was so loud it made her trip. Baz had been right—he'd told her as much, after all. About Daphne. About *liking* Daphne. Maybe even something more. But that feeling felt too big, and too loud, and the night was too quiet.

Love was too encompassing of a word. It considered too many things that Tara was unfamiliar with. Too many things uncharted. Unknown.

No, she couldn't *love* Daphne.

She didn't even know what love was.

And besides, it wasn't like Daphne would reciprocate. She couldn't—not in any lifetime, in any scenario, because Tara was who she was, and so was Daphne, and magic did not mix with matches.

Just as witches did not kiss their hunters.

It was a good fairy tale, but she was grounded enough to know that fairy tales were best told on paper, and love was best given without lies.

"I think he really likes you," Daphne said as they got back to the van.

Tara opened the door and climbed in, fastening her seat belt. "Who?"

"Bastion Leto." Saying his full name sounded a little mocking.

"Oh."

Daphne had seen her with Baz at the party? Probably from an upstairs window. So she *had* been looking out for her. Tara's heart skipped at the thought.

"How can you *not* see it?" Daphne went on. They pulled away from the curb.

Night in Hellborne was almost like driving through a movie set—nothing moved, all the doors were locked, all the people in their nice little houses, cozy and warm. The autumn wind rolled through the trees, picking off leaves and swirling them across the street.

I didn't see it because I've been looking at you.

She wanted to explain Newton's law of gravity, how the moment Daphne first looked at her she inevitably fell an impossible distance, down and down and down. It wasn't that Baz wasn't attractive—he absolutely *was*, and he was also nice and thoughtful, and there was something so magnetic about him it pulled everyone in—but there was something about Daphne that overrode everything else. It was fiery and passionate and bright, so bright Tara felt like a moth to a flame, and the moment Daphne came to her rescue in the backyard, looping their arms together, she decided just then that it would be a good death, burning in her embers.

But that was the kind of thing she couldn't say to her. For a *multitude* of reasons. Tara wasn't even sure what a relationship like the one she wanted looked like. She'd never seen it before—not really—only in the periphery of heterosexual couples and their romantic-comedy lives.

And that was what she wanted, with Daphne, without the trauma of wondering if she deserved it.

"I didn't notice," she muttered finally.

"Not your type?"

"No."

Daphne shrugged. "I get it. He's not my type, either."

"What is your type?"

To that, Daphne gave a one-shouldered shrug. "I never had a lot of luck in that department. All of my crushes have been one-sided, and then they just don't understand."

"Don't understand what?" Tara didn't know why she was prying, why she was flying so close to the sun on her wax wings, knowing they'd melt and Newton's law would send her crashing down.

Daphne glanced over to her and said, "That love doesn't choose sides."

Her breath caught in her throat. "A-and if—um—if someone—if someone did? Understand? And—um—if they—I mean—if . . . if . . . ?"

Silence swelled between them, and Tara suddenly thought that she'd made a mistake, that she'd read the words wrong, that she was foolish and stupid and—

Daphne squirmed in her seat. "Do you . . . wanna go get some food with me?"

It was late, pushing one a.m., and she wasn't particularly hungry—or was she? Not for food, not really, but for time. For moments.

She was ravenous for those.

"I—I could use a bite," she said hopefully, and for the first time since she met Daphne, the witch hunter smiled—really and truly smiled, bright and electric and lovely—and it made Tara's terrible liar of a heart flutter.

"I know just the place."

CHAPTER TWENTY-EIGHT
THE SPELL

Daphne took her to a small diner at the edge of the town, where the only road into and out of Hellborne met the interstate. One way, you went straight to Canada, the other down, down, down, into the belly of the country.

There was only one waitress and one cook working, but neither Tara nor Daphne minded the wait. Tara knew that because Daphne kept laughing even at things that weren't funny, and she—for the record—hadn't stopped smiling since Daphne asked her out to eat. Her heart was full of cotton candy, and she was just waiting for the hidden razor blades to cut this moment to shreds.

That was what hope felt like to her—something she never deserved.

And yet here she was sitting across from this girl with beautiful ink-black hair and soft brown eyes, and if this was what happiness felt like, talking about terrible pop songs and *Sailor Moon* and the horror movies that were never quite scary enough—then she would gladly sink into this happiness and drown in it.

"I wonder why that is," Daphne mused. "It's not like we're different from anyone else. We scare just as easily. Probably."

Tara gave it some thought, rubbing her thumbs along the outside edges of her warm coffee mug. "Maybe because we've seen things that are actually scary, so the movies just feel like . . . a fantasy."

"Yeah. Are you okay, by the way? I mean, the whole Cory thing . . ."

Tara's throat tightened. "Yeah."

"It never gets easier," Daphne replied. The waitress came by with a pot of coffee and topped them both up, asking if they wanted more hash browns or bacon before she sauntered off again to go flirt with the line cook. When she was gone, Daphne said, "My younger brother died at the hands of a witch five years ago."

Tara's eyes widened. "Oh."

"Yeah. Apparently, Fred killed the witch's husband—a warlock—and so she wanted to take revenge." Daphne's eyes settled on her cup of coffee, though her gaze looked a thousand miles away. "I didn't even hear the door open. I was supposed to be watching him, right? While my parents were at work and Gabe and Mike were doing some reconnaissance at the library. Danny—Daniel—was eight. He liked cartoons—*Batman* and *Goof Troop*, and always played them so loud. I was trying to perfect some stupid judo kick so I could show my dads that I could handle a hunt and help out. I was twelve. No one in their right mind would take a twelve-year-old out on a *job*. The next thing I knew . . . Danny was gone." She shrugged and sat back. "It's funny, right? One minute everything is normal and the next the world turns upside down."

She wanted to ask how Daphne's brother died, and how her family had taken revenge, but she wasn't sure if she wanted to know how the witch died—or if the witch had died at all. Hadn't Daphne's dads said that she'd failed once before? Was that the time? And worse yet, here *she* was sitting down in a midnight diner with her, the same kind of monster who murdered her younger brother.

Maybe my dad is right, Tara thought. *Maybe we're all monsters.*

Daphne blinked her eyes rapidly, clearing away the tears, and said, "Wow, that was *deep*. I'm sorry about that."

"It's okay," Tara replied softly. And then she took a deep breath and said something she never had aloud before—"I killed my mother."

Daphne's eyes widened.

"I mean, not in the way you think," Tara amended quickly. "My mother was dying, and I should have been able to save her. But I couldn't. And my dad got angry." She swallowed the knot in her throat. "Sometimes, I think my family has a curse. One that makes sure that we can never be happy, and the moment we are—the *second* we are—it takes that away from us the only way it knows how."

She remembered her mother tending to her garden in the backyard, golden afternoon sunlight bright in her graying hair. Tears burned in her eyes as she remembered how perfect that memory was. How pristine. She remembered the smell of the flowers, and the soft spring breeze that toyed with lavender and myrrh.

"For a second, we were happy, and then . . ." Tears slid down her cheeks. She wiped them away with the back of her sweater, and with it smeared the whiskers from her costume makeup. "I—I'm sorry. I'm usually not this . . ."

This open.

This trusting.

This human.

Daphne reached over and laced her fingers through Tara's. "I'm sorry," she whispered.

And so was Tara. Her lips wobbled. "I wish we could stay like this forever."

"Okay."

"We can't."

"Why not?"

Tara couldn't answer. *Because I'm not who you think I am. Because I'm a monster. A name on your list.* She couldn't tell Daphne the truth because she was too scared. All her life she'd hated the demon blood that coursed through her veins, that gave her magic, but now she just hated herself. Why did she ruin everything she touched?

Suddenly, Daphne leaned forward and waved a hand over Tara's face.

"What are you doing?" Tara laughed, pushing her free hand over her other cheek to wipe away the rest of the tears—and smeared her whiskers again.

"I have a power," Daphne said conspiratorially. "I can see your future, Tara Maclay."

"You can't—"

"Shh. Didn't I tell you I believed in fate?" Daphne closed her eyes and hummed. A smile flitted over her mouth. "I see happiness."

Tara looked away. "Impossible."

"Oh?"

A spark lit in Daphne's eyes, and she held up a finger. "Give me a minute." Then she slid out of her booth, leaving Tara alone, as she sprinted out of the diner and to her van.

She's not going to leave, is she? Tara thought with a pang of fear—but it quickly turned to surprise, and then confusion, when Daphne returned with a plastic Tupperware container and slid back into the booth.

"Close your eyes," Daphne told her.

"Why?"

"Just *do* it, cupcake."

So Tara did, and she heard the pop of the Tupperware container. The flick of something—a lighter? Then—

"Okay, open your eyes."

Tara did.

In front of her, sitting on a saucer plate, was a single white-frosted cupcake with blue sprinkles, and sticking out of the top was a single birthday candle, flame flickering in a dance. Daphne was grinning from ear to ear.

"Happy belated birthday!" she cried.

Tara just stared at the cupcake, mouth open, her heart hammering so loud and so fast she was afraid her chest would crack open and spill all her love onto the table. Because no one had ever done this before. After her mom died, she'd thought no one else would care.

Daphne's smile faltered. "Do . . . you not like vanilla?"

"I love it," Tara croaked in reply, her eyes brimming with tears. "I love it very much."

"And the sprinkles match your eyes, cupcake," Daphne added. "Well? Are you going to make a wish?"

Tara closed her eyes, but everything that she could possibly want—and possibly get at the moment—was already here sitting across from her. So she wished for the one thing she could, and blew out the candle.

"Did you wish for happiness?" Daphne asked.

"I can't tell you, or it won't come true," Tara replied, averting her gaze, and the girl with daring in her smile leaned forward, gently grabbing Tara's chin to get her to meet her eyes, and kissed her.

Daphne kissed her like she was the dessert, and not the cupcake forgotten between them. It was soft and playful. The kind of kiss that sent electric currents racing all the way down to her toes. The kind of kiss that made magic.

The kind of kiss that *was* magic.

The jukebox in the corner of the midnight diner began to play "Hungry Heart," though no one had touched it.

Finally, they came up for air, but Daphne's lips lingered against hers. "How about now?"

"I might need a little more convincing," Tara replied, and Daphne laughed against her mouth and kissed her again, and it felt like home. Warm and welcoming in a way nothing had ever been before.

It reminded her of that golden afternoon, of a perfect moment.

Her blood sang with the hope that it could last a little longer, because for the first time since her mother died, she felt *alive*.

And suddenly she realized the true tragedy of this story—

It wasn't just her life that Daphne could take, but her heart, too.

CHAPTER TWENTY-NINE
ILLUSTRIOUS ACTIVITIES

On the walk to school the next day, Tara forgot her umbrella. Thunder crackled overhead. A raindrop plopped on her nose. Another on her cheek. Oh *no*. What was the forecast? She was already halfway to school. If she walked briskly, she might make it before—

The downpour started.

It drenched her in a matter of moments. But even so, she couldn't hate her predicament too much. There was still a buoyancy in her heart from last night, the taste of the hash browns and the coffee and Daphne's lips—

They'd *kissed*.

They'd actually *kissed*, and after Tara got home and lay on her bed, she stared at the ceiling until sleep finally claimed her, as she thought about how they had *kissed*.

Even as the chilly autumn morning shivered goose bumps up her skin, she felt warm. And giddy. She pulled her plaid coat around her tighter, though it hung heavy and wet, and marched on in squelching loafers.

Daphne had kissed her, the rain sang, and it was good.

As she passed the town bookstore, a blue van pulled up beside her on the road. Tara's eyelids fluttered as she blinked the rainwater out of her eyes. It was like she'd summoned her out of thin air. Daphne rolled the passenger window down and asked, "What has four wheels and a roof over her head?"

Tara opened her mouth. Closed it. Frowned. "I'm not sure?"

"Your girlfriend. Now get in."

Girlfriend. It was still strange to think about it. When Daphne dropped her off last night at her house, she'd asked quietly, "Do you . . . I mean, want to date? I—I don't know how long we'll be here after we nab the witch, but—"

"Yes." Tara had replied so quickly, it startled Daphne.

"O-oh. *Oh!*" And then Daphne had smiled. "I'll see you tomorrow?"

"Tomorrow," Tara had promised, and they had leaned in for another kiss, and it was long and perfect and sweet at the ends from all the creamer they used in their coffees. It wrapped a ribbon around her heart. It helped it stay together, beating soft and sure, instead of the rattle she always heard, the sound of broken things.

Daphne leaned over to peck Tara on the cheek as she climbed in, when a familiar station wagon pulled out onto the main drag behind them. Tara quickly sank down low in the seat. The station wagon came to a stop behind the van and put on the horn.

Daphne scowled. "The hell?" She leaned out the side, gave the man the finger. "Go around, asshole!"

Oh no.

The station wagon backed up and then swerved around them. Tara sank lower in her seat, as far as she could go. She'd melt into the floorboards if she could.

"Idiot . . ." Daphne muttered as the station wagon disappeared down the road in front of them before she noticed Tara practically fusing with the seat. "Uh, what's this?"

"Is he gone?"

"Who?"

She motioned in the air. To the vehicle that wasn't there anymore.

"Oh, the car? Yeah. Dumbass didn't think to go around. Is everything okay?"

Slowly, Tara sat back up in the seat and peered out over the dashboard to make sure the coast was, in fact, clear, before she sat up and buckled herself in.

"Tara, use your words," Daphne deadpanned.

"That was m-my father," she replied softly.

"Your—what? *That* asshole?"

Tara pursed her lips and gave a single certain nod. Her hair hung wet in her face, and she pushed it back behind her ears. "He, um—it was good he didn't see me."

"You should've told me that was him! I would've gotten out and slit his tires here and now."

"Oh, no, he wouldn't like that."

"No, but I would—and you would, too. Admit it."

Tara pursed her lips. "You'd get in trouble."

"It'd be worth it."

"Probably not."

"It *would*," Daphne insisted, "because even from the few things you've told me about that man, he's shitty. You're scared to even talk bad about him when he's not around!"

Tara shook her head. "I'm not—"

"You are."

"It doesn't matter."

Daphne rolled her eyes. Another few cars passed them. She put on her hazards and turned to look her directly in the eyes. "It *does* matter, Tara. It matters a lot because you matter," she added vehemently. Then, as if mustering up the courage, she added, "especially to me."

Oh.

Oh.

Was this what love in the movies felt like? What poets waxed on about for centuries?

It was seven thirty in the morning. Tara had been up for maybe an hour after barely four hours of sleep, but her brain suddenly felt in a fog again. She couldn't think. The words rendered her speechless. She opened her mouth, but only a squeak came out.

She *mattered*?

What a novel concept.

Daphne reached over and braided her fingers through Tara's. Her nails were painted black, chipped at the edges. Her fingertips were calloused. And all Tara could think about was the taste of Daphne's lips, and the way they had lingered against hers for longer than Tara had ever dared to linger anywhere before, and how she wanted to drink Daphne in. How she wanted to run her hands across her cheeks, kiss the birthmark behind her ear, bend into her sharp edges.

"You're in love," Baz had said. How had he known before either of them?

Love was this bright thing on wings that she could never quite look directly at because she was afraid of what she'd find.

She was afraid it would look like home.

And when Daphne squeezed her hand tightly, she looked up into her girlfriend's eyes, and yeah, there it was.

There it was.

"I care," Daphne repeated, picking up their held hands and kissing the back of Tara's hand. "A lot."

Yes, Tara thought, *but would you care if you knew the monster that lurked under my skin?* Or would Daphne just take out a dagger and stick it through the ribs, between her lungs, straight to her heart?

And feel no remorse even after all these pretty words?

Truth be told, Tara thought she would still feel the same for Daphne, even as the witch hunter turned her to dust. And that was probably the most frightening part of all of this. How little she actually cared about herself, as long as she could lie in Daphne's shade just a little while longer.

"Let's stop by my house so you can change into something dry," Daphne decided, turning off her hazards. She made a U-turn on Main Street, heading back for her house.

"But—we'll be late for school."

"Cory's funeral's this morning, so half the senior class will be out anyway. And besides, I'm not letting you go to school soaking wet, and you don't want to be walking around in damp socks all day, do you?"

"No, I don't. . . ."

"Case closed."

A few minutes later, Daphne pulled into the driveway and jumped out with an umbrella. She hurried over to Tara's side and, even though Tara was soaking wet, guided her over the stone pathway to the front porch, where she unlocked the door and shouted to Gabe and Mike that she was home.

"You're playing hooky!" Gabe teased before Daphne gave him a glare and they both laughed. "I knew it—pay up, Mike. It took less than a month for Daph to skip school."

"Ugh, fine, fine," the other brother sighed. They were at the table reading through what looked like a film script. As soon as one brother read the page, he would give it to the other, who would then put it on another stack. They had separate markers to circle different things, and sticky notes littered the table. It was for their movie, Tara figured.

"Don't listen to them," Daphne advised. "I haven't skipped school in at least six months."

"Half of that time was summer vacation," Tara pointed out.

Daphne gave her a wounded look. "Et tu, Brute?" She elbowed Tara in the side and guided her to her room upstairs, though Tara hadn't been very sure what kind of room Daphne had. She imagined band posters on the wall, and maybe anarchy posters. Some sort of witch hunter motif maybe?

But it looked a lot like Tara's room did—barren. Daphne hadn't hung anything on the walls, and her clothes were folded and put up neatly into the cheap dresser. Her makeup was on top of her vanity, along with a few books—her personal library, Tara gathered. *Frankenstein* by Mary Shelley. *Interview with the Vampire* by Anne Rice. A good many Anne McCaffreys.

"Here, you can wear some of my clothes today so we don't become *super* late. I have some things that will probably fit you. . . ." Daphne shuffled through her closet. "Then we can come back, grab your clothes, and your asshole dad'll be none the wiser. Hmm, I don't think you wear much black. . . . How about this?" When she turned back around, she presented Tara with a simple button-down white blouse.

"Um . . ."

"And I think my spare skirt might fit . . ." Daphne added, handing it to Tara, and going over to her dresser.

Quietly, trying to be as inconspicuous as possible, Tara lifted the blouse to her face and smelled it. Citrus and fresh laundry. Just like how Daphne smelled. She was going to be walking around all day in this? She wasn't sure she could handle it.

But she had to.

Daphne showed her to the bathroom where Tara buttoned up the blouse—it was a little big, but she didn't mind—and the borrowed skirt. They were a bit more ill-fitting than she normally wore, so she hoped no one would be able to tell that they were Daphne's clothes—

Why don't you?

She should want that, shouldn't she? Because every time she thought about Daphne, her heart fluttered.

Yes, Tara thought. *I do want everyone to know.*

She tucked her blouse into her skirt, and when she stepped out of the bathroom, Daphne gave her a once-over with a nod and said, "I'm trying to play it cool and, like, I know we all wear the same uniform, but knowing you're in *my* clothes really makes me want to kiss you."

Tara bit back a smile. "Then why don't you?"

"If you insist . . ." Daphne kissed her in the hallway. It was rough and hungry, and Tara found herself holding on to the lapels on Daphne's jacket just to stay anchored. Daphne broke it off after a moment, leaving them both breathless.

"We should . . ." Tara began, her head spinning. "We should probably . . ."

"Probably," Daphne agreed, but prying apart from each other felt like they were two sides of Velcro.

Mike and Gabe kept their heads down toward their scripts when they returned to the living room, but when Daphne wasn't looking, Gabe gave Tara a thumbs-up with a wink.

She blushed ten shades of red.

"Oh! Before we go, I wanted to grab another book from the workshop anyway," Daphne said, and pulled Tara into the garage. The murder board was still there, filled with more papers somehow, impossibly.

But the first thing Tara noticed was the list of suspects. Marissa's name had been crossed out.

Daphne pulled a few more books off the shelves, rustling through some stacks for one last one.

Then the newspaper caught Tara's eye. She meandered over to it and picked it up off the coffee table. Today's paper. And there, in bold letters, read "The Story of the Red Witch!" With a photo of the portrait she'd seen in the Grey House beside a familiar-looking spellbook.

Her blood ran cold.

Oh—*oh*, she'd forgotten all about the spellbook in the aftermath of Cory's death. She wasn't sure how she had—it'd been there right on the tip of her tongue and then suddenly . . . gone.

As if by magic.

But she remembered now. "Daphne—Daph?"

Daphne had five books in her arms, and she was balancing precariously on a stepstool to get a sixth. "What?"

"This." Tara showed Daphne the newspaper. Pointed at a picture beside the article. At the book.

Daphne wrinkled her nose. "Yeah, I think they run the story every year?"

"No—the book. The Red Witch's spellbook."

"What about it?"

Tara hesitated, setting down the newspaper. If she told Daphne what she'd felt, she'd have to explain how she could sense auras, but if she didn't, then there might be another dead kid on their hands. "Do . . . you trust me?"

Daphne gave her a strange look and then got down from the stepstool, pushed the books in her arms onto the coffee table, and took Tara by the hands. She squeezed them tightly. "With my life, cupcake."

"I think the witch is using that book, and I think we'll find the curse the witch is using to kill people in that book, too."

There it was—that look of confusion. "How are you sure?"

"Trust me?" she repeated.

Questions warred on Daphne's face. She wanted answers, but she did say that she trusted Tara. So she nodded. "Okay. Then we need that book."

"We need that book," Tara agreed. "But I doubt the police will see it that way. . . ."

"*Psshhhh*, you're already ten steps ahead. *If* we get caught—"

"*When* we get caught—"

"We won't. Shit," Daphne added, looking at the clock above

the doorway, "we have to get to school—and then steal that spellbook."

"But—"

"Now *you* have to trust *me*."

Tara went to point out that it wasn't so much as not *trusting* Daphne, but not trusting herself to steal a book from a museum and not get caught, but instead she let Daphne pull her out of the workshop and pushed the foreboding feeling deep down into her gut.

She trusted Daphne, like Daphne trusted her.

What could go wrong?

CHAPTER THIRTY
CRUEL INTENTIONS

No one noticed Tara wasn't wearing her own uniform. She wasn't sure if she was excited about that or bummed—but then again, there were bigger things to think about than her clothes. Apparently after they left Baz's party last night, Baz got so drunk he climbed onto the rooftop and shouted to all the onlookers that he was a demon, that he couldn't be trusted, that what happened was *his* fault, of course it was his fault, who else's fault could it be?—before he promptly slipped off the roofing and fell two stories into the shrubbery on the front lawn.

"It's a miracle he's okay," a student Tara passed muttered. The girl closed her locker door, cocking her head. "Like, do you think it's true?"

"That *Bastion Leto* murdered his friends? No," her friend scoffed.

Tara stopped at her locker and opened it to grab a textbook for class.

"But rumors say he *was* gunning for Hailey, and now that her boyfriend and all his close friends are dead . . ."

"They were his friends, too."

"Yeah, that's what makes him most likely, isn't it? He's the only one who could get close enough. And overpower someone like Brian—and even Chad. They say alcohol makes a liar tell the truth. . . ."

Tara spun her locker combination closed. *That is silly*, she thought. She agreed that Baz was hiding *something*, but killing his friends? She thought about how nice he'd been to her since the beginning, and how open and honest, and that was something that was hard to fake—and Tara had grown up with a man who faked it often.

"Coulda been him *and* the girl Elaine saw in the library. . . ." someone else muttered.

"The new girl?"

"They *have* been pretty buddy-buddy together. . . ."

Rumors caught like wildfire, and by lunch, Tara was swimming in half-whispered conjectures and lies about the both of them. Maybe her gut was wrong, and maybe Baz *did* have something to do with it . . . in the same way that there was some truth to her having a hand in Moss's accident.

"You've got that thousand-yard stare again," Daphne said, chewing on a Fruit Roll-Up. They were sequestered in the library, the books Daphne borrowed from her parents' workshop piled between them. "Did you think of something?"

No . . . Yes . . . She debated how to phrase it. "What if the murderer is doing it for a good reason?" she asked, closing *A History of Herbology.*

Daphne gave her a look. "*Murdering* people for a good reason? Tara."

"Aren't you going to murder the witch?"

"That's different. Look—I know you don't really understand, but I'm not the same as the witch going around using her powers to hurt people. We stop that. It's like the Slayer staking vamps—they're not *good*. They deserve to die."

Oh. She felt her throat constrict. And if Daphne found out about her? Tara wondered how Daphne would kill her. Tie her to a pyre? Watch her burn?

She won't find out if you stick to being the daughter your dad wants, a little voice in her head reasoned. If she just shut the other part of her away and locked it up tight.

And that meant blotting out the parts of her that were her mom. She curled her fingers into fists. That was something she could *not* do.

The bell rang for next period, startling Tara out of her thoughts. Daphne stood, slinging her satchel over her shoulder, and gathered half the books to stash in their lockers. "Pick you up tonight around midnight?"

"To . . . break in?"

Daphne rolled her eyes. "No, to sit in the parking lot and play chess—*yes* to break in. It's just a small break, promise."

Like last time? she wanted to ask, but thought better of it. "Sure."

"Perfect!"

"Maybe after class we can— Wait, where are you going? We have biology."

Daphne shrugged. "I've got a dentist appointment, so I'm

skipping the rest of the day. Besides, gotta prepare for our heist, don't I?"

Tara hesitated. "But what about your clothes?"

"You can give them to me tonight—and I'll bring yours, too."

"Oh . . . okay."

"I can also pick you up in the mornings?" Daphne ventured on. "Like, every morning? So you don't have to walk anymore. It's getting *way* too cold. I don't even skate here anymore."

"Please," Tara replied, relieved, "though pick me up on the corner? So my father doesn't find out."

"Say the word and I'll slash his tires," Daphne deadpanned.

Tara laughed. "I'll keep that in mind."

"That's all I ask. See you tonight, then, babe." Daphne kissed her on the cheek—in front of everyone in the hall, just as easily as breathing, and turned in the direction of the student lot. "Let me know if you find out anything else!"

A few students whispered behind their hands, but Tara told herself not to worry. The only way for her father or brother to find out about Daphne was if someone told them—and neither her brother nor father seemed very keen on getting to know the locals. She put the rest of her books in her locker and departed for biology.

True to her word, Daphne was gone for the rest of her afternoon classes. In biology, most of the other groups were working on their frog dissections, and she stared at Mr. Ribbit—the name Tara had given him—a bit woefully, apologizing to him as she sliced down his belly.

After class, she made her way to her locker to put the rest

of her books away before PE. She glanced around to make sure there wasn't anyone else watching her, but most everyone else was leaving the hall for whatever they did after class, so she pushed her shoulder up and smelled Daphne's scent on her blouse again. It mingled with hers now.

You're so idiotic, that little voice inside her whispered. *You threw yourself off a cliff, and you're happy about it.*

Maybe she had.

But maybe the trick was not to care.

A tingling feeling filled her blood—*magic*. She sensed it. In the hall?

The witch? she thought, frantic. Then, with a bolt of fear—*Baz?*

Quickly closing the locker, she followed the feeling down the hall toward the stairwell. It was close. Just inside the door. She quietly dug her house key out of her backpack and put it between her fingers as she crept toward the door to the stairwell. The magic pulsed gently. Pressing her back against the wall, she leaned in to spy through the door window into the stairwell.

Blond hair. Pulled back with a chunky black band. Hailey?

Tara leaned a little farther and saw that standing beside Hailey was exactly who she expected—Baz. She'd tried to avoid him all day, but the few times she had seen him, he looked the worse for wear. Dark circles under his eyes. Slicked-back hair from the funeral this morning. Crumpled dress shirt. He still had a bandage around his hand from last night. Had the bottle opener accident been that bad?

They were arguing, it looked like. She pressed her ear against the metal door to try to make out their words. Although it was muffled, she caught most of it.

". . . I don't know what to tell you, Bastion," Hailey snapped, her voice echoing in the stairwell. "I'm not who you think I am anymore."

Then she left down the stairs. Baz cursed and kicked the bottom step, pulling his hands through his hair. He turned and—in the worst possible moment—saw Tara through the window. His eyes widened.

Oh no.

Tara's heart was lodged in her throat. She took a step back. He stepped toward her. His mouth formed her name.

No, no, no, no—

She spun on her heel and hurried back to her locker, entering the code. 6-22-4—

"Tara—"

She froze. Her heart slammed into her chest. "I d-d-didn't see anything."

"You . . . believe them, don't you? That I—everyone's saying that I . . ." His voice faltered. He bit the inside of his cheek and slumped heavily against the lockers. "I don't know what to do, Tara."

She cautiously looked over at him.

"I—I kind of remember last night, but not much. Nothing after . . ." He lifted his bandaged hand. His left hand. The same hand that held her almost-healed warning.

"Was it really a bottle opener?" she asked quietly.

He looked surprised and then pulled his hand into his letterman jacket. "It's nothing."

Tara pulled up her shirt cuff and let him see the warning. *LEAVE IT ALONE.*

For a long moment, he stared at her hand, his eyes widening. They were the only ones left in the hall, as if the entire school had abandoned them. "Mine . . . doesn't look like that," he finally admitted.

Oh no, she thought.

"Mine is . . ." He gingerly unwrapped his hand. The bandages were speckled with blood, and unlike the marks on his late friends' hands, they hadn't tried to scratch it away. But it was very evident that Baz had. Maybe he'd even taken a bottle opener to it, like he'd said last night.

Recognition flickered across her face.

"You know what this is." It wasn't a question.

She nodded. "When did you get it?"

"Last night at the party, before I saw you by the swing set. I remember that a bit, but everything else is a blur."

"You drank a lot," she confirmed, wrapping her hand up again.

He barked a cold laugh. "Of course I did. I'm gonna die."

"So . . . you know?"

"I could sense something was up with my friends before they died," he said bitterly, looking at the mark. "But now I know why. I'm not as good at sensing magic as you."

She jerked away. "How do you . . . ?"

"You're a witch," he said simply.

"I'm—I'm not—"

"It's okay."

No, it *wasn't*. She took another step back. "How do you know? Are you a warlock?"

"Man, wouldn't that be easier?" he sighed, shaking his head. "You're the magic person here. I'm just the good-looking himbo from hell."

From . . . *hell*.

She remembered back to his party last night. What he said at the swing set. About humans and their lives. The way his horns looked a little too real, and his tail a little too lifelike. She narrowed her eyes at him, to see if his face was a mask—some sort of Buffalo Bill skin suit. She thought for sure that she'd be able to see the monster underneath. Her father made it so *certain* that it would be so *clear*.

But all she saw was a young man in a letterman jacket with fear in his eyes, trying to look calm and cool, and for the first time failing miserably at it.

"You're . . . a demon?" she finally asked.

"In the flesh."

It didn't make sense. Demons were evil. They murdered, they stole, they committed horrendous acts of violence. They weren't spiky-haired tight ends of losing football teams. And of all the people at Hellborne, he was one of the few who actually treated her like a person. He hadn't been nice to her to get something; he'd been nice just because he *was*.

But demons . . .

"Demons are evil," she said, her voice tight. She should know. She was one, too. Her dad told her as much.

In reply he said, "And witch hunters are hired assassins. How do you know Icy Hot won't kill you the moment she learns who you are?"

Who. Not *what*. It was such a little thing, such a small detail that shouldn't have held any weight, but it did. Because of that one word, that one change in vernacular, it was the difference between someone and some*thing*.

Her mother always gave everyone the benefit of the doubt. She said that people deserved empathy, and not suspicion. Besides, Baz hadn't done anything wrong as far as Tara knew, and even if he did—he didn't deserve to die because of it.

That wasn't her choice to make.

He started wrapping his hand again, but she reached out and stopped him, because he was doing it wrong, anyway. As she rewrapped his injured hand properly, she asked, "What kind of demon are you?"

"Wow, going into my *breeding* at school?" he asked with fake outrage. "Tara, I thought you witches were taught better."

She ignored that. "You can smell love and you heal quickly . . . maybe I can find something in *Beasts of*—"

"I'm an incubus," he interrupted. "Or at least partly. My mom was a succubus. My father? Not sure. I was adopted."

"How did you find that out?"

"Traumatically."

"I'm sorry." She turned his hand over to make sure the wrapping didn't twist. "Daphne and I are investigating the murders. We think it's a witch cursing you."

"Do you know who?"

She shook her head. "But we're sure we know where this mark comes from now. The Book of Blood."

"The Red Witch's spellbook?"

"That one." She tucked the excess bandage underneath the wrapping and looked up at him. "How do you feel about breaking and entering?"

"Not great . . ." he replied hesitantly. "I'm not really very sneaky."

"Neither am I," she admitted, and told him about Daphne's plan to steal the spellbook. It was going to be a nightmare. But . . . not as big of a nightmare as having to tell Daphne that she may have just added another member to their witch-hunting team.

And an incubus, at that.

CHAPTER THIRTY-ONE
SPELLBINDING

Midnight in Hellborne was cold as hell.

But not as cold as the glare Daphne gave Tara as she rolled up in her blue van and saw Bastion Leto was standing beside her. She leaned over and rolled down the passenger window. She didn't even invite them in.

"What is *he* doing here?" Daphne asked frigidly.

Baz unwrapped his hand and showed her his burn.

Her eyebrows jerked up. "Oh, shit, dude."

"Yeah, dude."

"I think he can help us," Tara added. Partly because of the demon thing, and partly because of the fight he had with Hailey in the stairwell. She hadn't brought that up to him yet, but she tucked the information in the back of her head for later. They'd been fighting about something—something unforgivable. Maybe it was that Hailey believed the rumors about Baz and the murders? Or maybe it was something else. . . .

Daphne looked between the two of them; then she gave a sigh and pushed open the passenger-side door. "Fine, get in."

"Yes, ma'am," Baz muttered, making a fist and pumping it in the air. He followed Tara into the van, and because it was a bench seat, she found herself pressed against Daphne, as Baz was such a broad guy he filled up a good portion of the cab. It was a tight ride, to say the least.

Tara wasn't worried about her father or brother finding her missing. She'd used that sleeping spell on them again. Magic was easy now. It came when she called. Maybe it was a bit too easy, really, but she promised herself that she wouldn't use it too often. That she would keep herself in check.

When they got to the museum, Daphne parked a block away and took a bag out of the back of the van, and they headed up the street to the museum. A lone flashlight flickered in the main building as they hunkered behind the sign, watching for any movement on the property. By the looks of it, there was only that lone security guy, and he had an office in the main building.

"He'll probably walk the perimeter a few times tonight," Daphne guessed.

Baz shook his head. "Nah, Nate's lazy as hell. He only got the job because of his dad. He'll probably just lock himself in the office and plan out his next Dungeons and Dragons game."

"Dungeons and Dragons . . . ?" Tara asked.

"It's a really intricate role-playing game that you play with a few different kinds of dice and—"

"Lemme know when you nerds are done talking," Daphne interrupted, dipping out from behind the signage, and headed toward the witch's cottage.

"Rude," Baz muttered.

"She's very business oriented," Tara apologized.

"And I'm not-dying oriented, so we should probably follow her."

"That's a good idea."

Though the Grey House was a lot darker than it had any right to be. It was like shadows coagulated around the cottage, so thick even the light from Main Street didn't quite reach it. Not even the moonlight wanted to shine on the cottage. It was foreboding.

The front door was bolted closed, but Daphne produced bolt cutters from her black duffel and cut them open.

Tara whispered, "I thought the principal took those. . . ."

Daphne scoffed. "I *always* have a spare." She pushed the door, and it creaked open. Then she took out two flashlights, handing one to Tara, and told Baz, "Sorry, didn't know you were gonna be here."

"I can see just fine," he replied, and then added quickly, "I've got, uh, sensitive eyes."

"Uh-huh, stick close, Letterman," she said, and crept into the house.

Tara patted his shoulder and mouthed, "Good save."

He sighed, shaking his head.

Everything looked exactly as it had the day they came to tour the museum. There were a few cloths draped over the older pieces of furniture. Baz lifted the closest cloth, revealing a mirror with a wardrobe.

"This place always skeeves me out," he said. "Where's this book of bodily juices at?"

"The Book of Blood," Daphne corrected, lifting another

piece of cloth. It was a display box, showing the witch's comb and some other odds and ends, but not the book that they were looking for. "It should be over there by the cauldron, right, Maclay?"

"Was that just Monday?" Baz asked, surprised. "It doesn't feel like it was Monday."

Daphne gave him a look. "Days running together like your friends' deaths?"

"Daphne," Tara hissed, but she simply gave a shrug.

Baz dropped the cloth, and with it his reflection in the mirror. "You think I don't mourn them?"

"Hard to mourn shitty people," Daphne replied coldly, and Tara winced.

"Yeah, they were a little shitty," he agreed, "and they weren't always good people, yeah? But they were Hailey's friends. So, they were mine. I dunno why she ever wanted to be their friend—none of 'em deserved her, but she really liked Brian."

"But she broke up with Brian," Daphne said.

"Yeah, I know. Is that it?" he asked, pointing to the square-shaped box draped in cloth.

Tara nodded. "Yeah, I think so." She reached over the guard rope and pulled the cloth off it. The velvet puddled at the foot of the glass case.

And there it sat. It looked like any other old book, bound in crimson leather, crinkled and yellowed with age. The Book of Blood.

"Brilliant," Daphne muttered. "Okay, let's get this over with." Then she went to slam her elbow into the box to break the glass, when Tara stopped her.

"Maybe it's unlocked?" she murmured.

"It wouldn't be."

But then Tara lifted the glass case.

"See? Told you. The people at this museum are lax as *hell*," Baz said matter-of-factly.

But something was off. Something Tara couldn't place until she took the book out of its case. It didn't feel the way a spellbook should feel.

This book didn't feel magical at all.

Dreading what she'd find, she opened the book, and the pages fell open silently. It didn't creak or crack or groan in its old age. Because it wasn't old at all. A library stamp greeted her on its first page. *Property of Hellborne Academy.*

And just under that was the title of the book—*Macbeth.*

It wasn't the witch's spellbook at all, just made to look like it, dressed in fake leather and with distressed edges. And Tara had a feeling she'd finally found the book that was missing from the school library.

"Daphne . . ." she whispered, and the witch hunter looked over.

"Is that . . . ?"

"Fake."

Which meant there were no clues on how to remove the curse from Baz, either. He turned away, pulling his hands through his hair as he paced back and forth across the witch's cottage. "What're we going to do now?" he asked, his voice tight.

"We'll figure it out. Just let us think," Tara said, trying to calm him down, but he was going the opposite way.

And increasingly quickly.

He turned on his heel again. He clenched and unclenched

his hands, trying desperately to control his mounting fear. "I'm going to die, aren't I?"

"Maybe it'll affect you differently."

"We all bleed, Tara," he snapped, and pressed the heels of his palms against his eyes. "I'm going to die. I'm—"

He abruptly stopped.

Daphne asked her, "Why would he bleed differently?"

"Because he's—"

Suddenly, he looked up, and his eyes were completely white. Like Moss's had been when he'd been chased through the library. Baz's face stretched in a scream, like Cory's fear-stricken frozen face under the bus seats.

And it clicked—what the burn mark did.

It didn't paint them with bad luck or misfortune. It was something much more sinister.

It scared them to death.

It frightened them so terribly that accidents befell them trying to get away from it.

What could have scared Cory so much, he contorted himself under a bus seat? What would run Moss into a bookcase? Make Chad reel backward into a locker? Chase Brian up rickety old bleachers?

Make a grown demon begin to cry?

Baz's face scrunched in terror, and he backed away, his breath coming in short gasps, tears pooling in his eyes. "No, no, no, n—"

And he screamed.

CHAPTER THIRTY-TWO
INCUBYE

"Shut up, you big *idiot*! You'll attract the guard!" Daphne cried.

It was no use. There was no getting through to him. His panic was like a wall that shut out everything, and he was left alone in his own nightmare. It was the kind of nightmare that light couldn't chase away, even as Tara found the switch and flipped it on. The bulbs in the circular chandelier above them flickered to life, and it only stretched the shadows on Baz's face longer.

He was staring toward the wardrobe, pleading with it. "Th-they already know, they already know," he repeated to himself, stumbling backward into the spellbook's glass case.

Tara caught him by his arm. "Baz, snap out of it," she begged.

"No—stop. I'm not a—" He choked on his own words and flinched away.

Daphne grabbed his arm tightly. "He's going to hurt himself if he keeps this up," she said.

That was Tara's fear.

"No," he begged, "stop it—"

Tara curled her fingernails into his arm. "Listen to me, Baz."

"What do you see?" Daphne asked. *"Bastion!"*

"I'm not a monster," he whispered, whimpering, squeezing his eyes closed. "I'm not a monster, I'm not a monster."

Tara watched helplessly as Bastion saw something that didn't exist. Like Moss had. She remembered Cory, twisted into a pretzel in sheer fear. And that fear had killed him. She glanced around the witch's cottage, and there were too many accidents waiting. Hooks that could wobble off the walls. Furniture that could fall over and crush your skull at just the right angle. Pencils that could stab you in the ear. Fire pokers, iron chains—a *cauldron*, for god's sake.

Baz bent in on himself, crouching down, curling into a ball.

The rafters above them began to rattle.

She didn't know what kind of demon Baz was, but if they didn't do something soon, then she was sure she'd find out. His fingernails had already sharpened into claws as he pressed his hands over his face, scraping his skin. The burn on the back of his left hand bubbled—

That's it.

"Baz, where is your lighter?" she asked, but he was too far gone, whispering, *"I am not a monster, I am not a monster, I am not a monster,"* as if saying the words would ensure it was true. Maybe it would. Words had that sort of power, but Tara already knew he wasn't a monster.

Daphne said, "Why do you need a lighter?"

"We need to burn the mark off."

"What?"

"Trust me!"

"Fine, fine! Baz, I'm sorry, dude, but I hope you don't have anything weird in your pockets," Daphne prayed, and dove into his pockets as Tara held his hands. His fingers curled tightly around her fingers, grinding them together. She sucked in a painful breath. He was *strong*.

And she was afraid he'd break her fingers.

He gasped for breath and squeezed tighter. She heard a snap. Pain shot through her pinkie finger.

"Found it!" Daphne cried, and flicked the Zippo open. The flame flickered between their faces. "Hold him still, yeah?"

Tara nodded, not trusting herself to speak, afraid that her voice might give away her pain.

"Now, this is gonna hurt a bit. . . ." Then Daphne set the lighter against the burn. His skin began to redden and blister— and then turn black. He tried to jerk away, but it was Tara's turn to hold on to his hands tightly. Her pinkie finger screamed in pain.

But finally, the skin around the burn began to bubble, too, obscuring the mark just a little—

Just enough to break the curse. Tara felt it. The sudden release. The mark couldn't be marred; it had to be erased—and fire was the best way to do that. The magic in the mark burst out, releasing with a rush of wind, and dissipated.

Baz jerked forward with a gasp. His eyelids fluttered, and the white film disappeared. He dropped his gaze to his and Tara's hands. And the welts coming up on his skin. Tara could already tell that they were beginning to disappear. Was that because he was a demon?

"Did I . . . ?" His voice shook.

She let go of his hands, her pinkie finger throbbing but probably not broken, and hugged him tightly. "You're okay."

His shoulders drooped, and he pressed his face into her shoulder. "Thank you," he said, though it was almost inaudible. A sob nibbled at the edges of his words. She rubbed circles on his back, wondering what could have scared Bastion Leto so terribly.

Suddenly, a flashlight blared through the windows of the cottage, pinning them in place.

CHAPTER THIRTY-THREE
UNDER PRESSURE

"I think we overstayed our welcome," Daphne said, looping Baz's arm over her shoulder to hoist him back on his feet. "Let's go—*now.*"

The jingle of the security guard's keys came closer. "If it's the raccoons again . . ."

Tara quickly flipped off the lights again, plunging the house into darkness.

The security guard froze. "H-hello . . . ?"

Tara crept over to the other side of Baz and helped heave him to his feet. He was a lot heavier than he looked, and his feet kept wanting to slip out from underneath him, so she and Daphne had to take the brunt of his weight. But before they left, Tara took one last look at the stamp on the first page, claiming it as property of Hellborne Academy's library, and closed the case with it inside again, determined to find out who had checked it out last.

Daphne hissed, "Why aren't we taking it with us?"

"If we steal it, whoever else stole it'll know we know."

"Oh." Daphne paused. "Good point."

The security guard toed open the front door. He shone his flashlight into the cottage, the beam trembling. "H-hello?" he called again. His other hand was fastened on something at his hip, something Tara sorely hoped was a Taser instead of a gun. "Who's there? Show yourself!"

Absolutely *not*.

As the security guard moved around one side of the cottage, the three of them kept to the shadows. The security guard's flashlight shook more the deeper he stepped into the cottage; he was scared out of his wits.

"Th-this is p-p-private property!" he warned.

Baz's feet slipped out from underneath him, and one of his shoes hit a table leg. The candles on it rattled.

The security guard whipped around. They ducked as he shone his flashlight over their heads, illuminating the wardrobe, the bed, the cauldron. Then, slowly, he crept around toward them. Daphne quietly reached up for one of the fake tea candles on the table, nabbed one, and as the security guard came around the large fireplace in the middle of the room, she tossed it back toward the kitchen. It clanked against the pots and pans.

The security guard screamed, jumping clean out of his skin, and whipped around toward the kitchen. And drew what Tara saw was, to her immense relief—

A *Taser*.

"Go, go, go, *go*," Daphne whispered, pulling Baz along as they crept toward the open front door. They couldn't get out of there quick enough, but they couldn't go any faster, either. Small steps. Creeping. Shuffling.

Go, go, go—

"Hey!" the security guard shouted, whipping back around as he heard them escape. "You there! Stop!"

They cleared the Grey House. Still half carrying Baz, Daphne and Tara broke out into a run toward the wooded area that separated the museum from Main Street's buildings. They ducked down beside the thick shrubbery, the cold air sharp in their lungs. Baz slumped down between them.

"Hey! Hey, you! Stop!" the guard cried as he ran toward them.

Tara tensed. Held her breath . . .

. . . as the guard passed them. Through the woods to the other side. But there was no one there. He lingered only a few minutes, his flashlight scanning the trees, before he muttered, "I'm not paid enough for this," and quickly moved back toward the main building, holstering his weapon as he went.

It felt like an eternity before Tara breathed again.

"Holy *shit*," Daphne said, slumping back onto the ground. Baz went down right along with her, still a bit in a daze. "That was close."

"He had a Taser," Tara fretted. "We could've gotten *hurt*."

But Baz dismissed her with his hand. "It's never charged. Just for show."

"That would've been nice to know *before*," Daphne deadpanned.

"Is the ground spinning to you?" he went on, wholeheartedly ignoring her. "It's spinning. Round and round and . . ."

Daphne rolled her eyes and forced herself back to her feet before grabbing Baz by the jacket collar and hauling him up, too. He stumbled a little, swaying, but he stayed upright for the most part. Tara let him lean a bit on her shoulder as they trudged through the thicket to the back of a cafe, and into an alley to cut over to Main Street.

"That was quick thinking to burn the mark," Daphne said after a moment, giving Tara a look, but because it was so dark, she felt it more than she saw it. Not accusing and not suspicious—unreadable.

Maybe not in a good way.

"It was a hunch," Tara replied, which was true.

"You were so sure it'd work."

"I mean, the curse works because the victim is branded, so it would make sense if, you know, that branding was destroyed."

"And it hurt like hell," Baz added, slurring his words a little. He pulled the gauze out of his jacket pocket and began to wrap his burned hand up in it again, but in the moonlight cast between the tall buildings, she could tell that it was almost already entirely healed. "Thank you."

"This still didn't get us anywhere closer to the witch," Daphne sighed, a little frustrated. "We almost died for nothing."

"That's a bit of a stretch, Icy Hot."

"Okay, *you* almost died."

". . . I see your point."

Tara went ahead of them, the wheels in her head turning. Daphne was wrong; they *didn't* almost die for nothing. In fact, finding out about the fake spellbook might've been the second-best thing that could've happened tonight. "If we figure out who took out that library book," she mused, "it might point us to the person who took the spellbook."

Daphne seemed suspicious. "You think?"

"Yes," she replied.

"It's not Leelee, it can't be Leelee," Baz mumbled, and then added, pointing to the left, "My car's that way—"

"Oh, no, you don't, tiger." Daphne grabbed him by his coat to keep him from going anywhere. "You rode with us, remember?"

Baz frowned. "Oh, right. My car's at Maclay's. You can drop me off there, and I'll—"

"No way, you're too out of it. I'm taking you home."

"Aw, shucks, ma'am, you care that much?"

"Don't push it," she added, making their way back to the blue van. She and Daphne tried to get Baz into the cab but realized their folly, because he was about to melt right into the pavement where he stood. So they gently eased him into the rear of the van, where he flopped onto a tarp and rolled over onto his back.

"Are you okay?" Tara whispered as Daphne went around to the driver's side to start the van.

He gave a thumbs-up. "Body good. Body healing. Hand no hurt."

"So, this is . . . *normal*?"

In reply, he turned his hand to her, the flesh almost fully healed. "See? And I don't mix with magic. Oil, water, whatever. Makes everything spin."

"Okay." She hesitated and then left him in the backseat.

As Tara climbed into the front passenger seat, he started singing the Hellborne fight song. Which was less endearing than it sounded. He was a terrible singer.

He was even worse at navigating the brick stairs up to his front door.

"We probably should've taken him to the hospital," Tara muttered, chewing on her lip nervously as they watched.

"Pff, he'll be fine," Daphne replied.

Baz tripped over his own feet and kissed the brick steps—hard. Then he stuck a hand up, thumb raised. "I'm okay!" he cried, and peeled himself off the pavement. He managed to get inside, and as far as Daphne was concerned, that was the end of their duties.

"He'll be *fine*," she reiterated when Tara gave her a skeptical look. "He will!"

Then she jammed her van into gear, and the vehicle puttered down the road. She drove a few blocks before coming to a stop at one of the only two red lights in town. She reached over and gently took Tara's hand. She rubbed her thumb over Tara's thumb joint in slow, calming circles.

"I was really worried there for a second," Daphne said in the silence. The radio didn't work, so it was even quieter than normal quiet rides.

Tara nodded, though the comfort of Daphne's hand was enough to drive any fear she had away. "We ended up fine. But I need to tell you something—"

"We make a good team," Daphne blurted instead. "Your brains, my brawn— Oh, sorry. What do you want to tell me?"

"I . . ." *I'm a witch.* "I think we make a good team, too," Tara echoed, a bit weakly. She was a coward.

A soft, terrible coward who couldn't even tell the person she liked the truth.

And soon, she wouldn't get the chance.

CHAPTER THIRTY-FOUR
BOOK SMARTS

T hat Friday, Tara tapped the bell at the school library's help desk. "Hello?" she called. "Miss Starino?"

"Coming!" the librarian called from the back.

At the end of the counter, Daphne nosed through a few of the books on the cart ready to be shelved again, picking up the *Iliad* before putting it back, muttering to herself about the injustices of Patroclus.

The librarian shimmied out from the back room with a handful of books and set them on the counter, before fixing her glasses. "Oh, Miss Maclay, Miss Frost, what a pleasant surprise. Do you two need anything?"

"We're actually looking for a book," Tara replied. "Um, *Macbeth*?"

"Your teacher should be able to give you one of her class copies."

"There aren't any left. And I can't find the one here at the library. Can you tell me who checked it out last?"

"Oh! Well, that is a pickle." Miss Starino pushed her glasses up the bridge of her nose. "We should have one in . . ." She shuffled over to the card catalog, pulled out a drawer, and began to riffle through the papers. She hummed as she went, "Thriller." Tomorrow was Halloween, and it felt like it had come both too suddenly and wouldn't come at all. Daphne came up to stand beside her, drumming her fingers on the counter impatiently, standing so close Tara could smell the fresh scent of laundry and the cinnamon from her breakfast on her tongue. Their elbows brushed, and it was a comfort.

"Hmm," Miss Starino said as she came back, frowning at a card in her hand, "it *says* that book was last checked out a month or so ago by Miss O'Toole."

Elaine.

"I suppose you can talk to her about when she'll be returning it."

Tara winced, remembering. "Yes, I will. Thank you."

"Of course. It always warms my heart to see young folk find love in the Bard. He's truly a master of the poetic arts—and he is very naughty, you know. Scandalous when it comes to innuendos. Why, even in *Hamlet*—"

"I think I hear the bell, oh, look at that," Daphne interrupted loudly, hooking her arm through Tara's. "Sorry, Miss Starino, don't want to be late for class!"

"Oh, I didn't even hear it!" the librarian fretted. "Have a good Halloween, you two!"

"You as well!" Daphne cried over her shoulder as she tugged Tara out of the library. She asked out of the corner of her mouth, "Halloween's *tomorrow*?"

"Um, yes," Tara replied.

"Speaking of which," Daphne said with a frown, letting go of Tara's arm in the hallway. She turned to her, and there was a troubled look on her face. "Elaine."

"Elaine," she agreed.

"And," said a voice behind them, "we've got a quiz in English."

They gave a shriek and spun around, only to find Baz towering over them. He looked absolutely horrid, dark circles under his eyes, his right hand still wrapped in a bandage. He laughed a little self-consciously, rubbing the back of his neck. "Sorry, didn't mean to startle you two."

"Warn us next time!" Daphne snapped, punching him in the pectoral. He winced but barely moved. Then she paused. Frowned. And asked, "Did you say a quiz? In English?"

"Yeah. About the final act of *Macbeth*—"

"*Shit!*" she cursed, spinning around on her heel. "My book's still in my locker. I haven't read it—I'll meet you in class!" she added, waving over her shoulder as she hurried down the hall before Tara could so much as say that she could *tell* her what happened at the end of *Macbeth*.

Everyone died.

Tara eyed Baz's bandaged hand. "Is it . . . ?"

"For show," he replied, flexing his hand. "Don't worry, the curse didn't come back. Sorry I was a bit out of it last night. When my body heals itself, it also makes me more susceptible to my own *demon-ness*," he added softer, darting his eyes around.

"The incubus part," she inferred, and then realized: "Like being love drunk?"

"It's embarrassing, yeah. And I kept thinking last night—if we foiled *my* death, then who is the witch coming for instead?"

"You know who the witch is, don't you?" she asked.

He shook his head. "But I think I have an idea."

"I do, too," she agreed. "The last person to check out that book was Elaine."

Baz's expression soured. "Yeah, that's my thought."

"Right? She's obsessed with the Burning; she— I don't know. Maybe she stole the book as a good-luck charm, and maybe there was a spell in the book that turned her dark; I'm not sure. But she *did* take the book."

"And Icy Hot's going to kill her."

Tara reached out and squeezed his hand tightly. "I don't think Daphne's really that kind of person."

He gave her a disbelieving look. "You don't?"

"No."

"I guess we'll see soon enough, won't we, New Girl?" Then he flicked his gaze behind her. "Uh-oh, here comes trouble."

Not a moment later, Elaine grabbed Tara by the shoulder and spun her around. Her face was pinched, her lips pressed into a thin line. "You better not mess up the Burning. It's an *honor* to play the Red Witch, I hope you know. So don't go screwing it up."

Elaine turned to leave again, when Baz very quickly slid in front of her. "You know," he began, "Tara would be a lot better in the role if she had a . . . mentor."

Tara stared at him like he'd grown a second head.

Elaine glared. "A what?"

"Someone to show her the ropes. Someone who knows

exactly what to do—someone who will make sure she doesn't crash and burn." And he stepped a little closer. Tara could sense when he used his powers now. It was a soft pulse, his aura turning bright. Shimmers of pink and orange crept into his mint-green eyes. "Someone like you, I'd guess."

The redhead hesitated. "I . . . *am* the only person who understands the role."

He smiled, and his aura dimmed. "Exactly! And everyone'll know you were the reason the Burning was saved this year when all these idiots elected a newbie—no offense," he added to Tara.

Tara shook her head. "N-none taken."

Elaine thought for a moment, looking between the two of them as she played with one of her ringlet curls. Then she turned to Tara and raised her chin. "Fine. I'll teach you the Red Witch's part. I don't want to. But I'm going to. Because it's important to me, and it was important to Chad, and Brian, and Cory, and—and because I'm a good person," she added, though it felt a bit too aggressive to be true. "And a better friend."

Tara swallowed the knot in her throat. "I— Um. Okay."

"Meet me at my house after school. I'm sure you can find it." Then she turned on her heel and marched off to their English class.

As she left, Baz stuck his hands in his jeans pockets, a shit-eating grin on his face. "You're welcome, by the way."

Tara was at a loss. "Have you . . . ever used that power on me?"

He rolled his eyes. "You fall head over heels all on your own," he replied as the bell rang, making them abysmally late to English.

CHAPTER THIRTY-FIVE
TRUTH BE TOLD

Elaine O'Toole lived in a brick two-story house on the same street as Baz. Ivy grew up the side of the house like delicate fingers, reaching up to the gutters and the pristine dark roof. There was an autumn wreath on the front door with a plaque that read *WELCOME!*, and worst of all, Tara didn't sense any ill auras. She didn't sense any magic at all.

Still, she smoothed down her jacket and rang the doorbell.

Daphne was camped out in her van half a block away, and if anything went south, then Tara would use the walkie-talkie tucked into her jacket pocket to call for backup. Tara had decided that she should go, simply because she was less conspicuous. After all, Elaine had told *her* to come. Not her and an entourage.

Still, Daphne hadn't wanted to let her go. She'd leaned close, pushing a lock of Tara's hair behind her ear, her palm cupping her cheek. "It'll be dangerous—"

"I'll be fine," Tara had said, leaning her face into Daphne's hand. She just wanted to close her eyes and stay there for a moment. "I'll ask for some tips about how to burn on a pyre and inquire about the *Macbeth* book. I'll be careful. I promise."

"You better be, or I'll be mad. You don't wanna see me mad."

Tara had grinned. "I'd hate that."

It wasn't like Daphne could *get* to Tara in time if anything happened. Magic was faster than bullets, faster than shooting stars. She knew that a simple well-said spell (or perhaps if the witch was *very* talented, a single thought) could turn her entrails into ex-trails in a blink. She really hoped she was dead before that happened.

And anyway, it was the thought that counted, and the walkie-talkie made her *feel* a little safer, at least.

That, and the white chrysanthemum in her pocket. A flower to help bring out the truth. She'd picked it from the school garden after class before she met up with Daphne to head over to Elaine's house. She hoped she wouldn't have to use it. She didn't want to rely on magic, but there was little other choice.

She pressed the doorbell. A happy, bright chime rang through the house. Then the sound of footsteps down a set of stairs.

And then—

Elaine, opening the door, rolled her eyes. "You absolutely took your time, didn't you?"

Tara gave her the smallest smile. "Sorry, I had to stay after school for a bit."

"Well, come on," the redhead said, stepping away from the door. "I don't have a lot of time."

Tara hesitated, reaching into her pocket. She closed her fingers around the chrysanthemum. And stepped inside. Elaine's house was large and cluttered with—stuff. A lot of stuff. Vases and picture frames, trophies displayed on curio cabinets, fine porcelain plates and stacks of newspapers. Elaine shifted uncomfortably in the foyer as Tara looked around.

"My mom likes to collect things. Ignore all of it, okay? So, the Red Witch needs to be at the museum by five thirty at the *latest*, okay? The museum director should have the costume and everything laid out for you. If *I* had been chosen, I had a different costume picked out but—like—whatever, right?"

Tara winced. "I . . . am sorry that I took this away from you."

"You didn't," Elaine replied sharply, and took something out of a drawer in the hallway table. A binder. "You won it, so it's yours. The public has spoken."

Still. It felt awful.

Elaine handed her the binder. It had, in cutout sparkly letters, *THE BURNING*. "You'll stay in the Grey House until the mob comes to get you, they'll lead you to the pyre, and you'll have to pretend to be tied up—and like, you need to actually *pretend*, okay? The mayor will come out and say a few things . . . or is it the principal this year? Whatever. It doesn't matter. Then it's over! And you get to go back to the Grey House, change into your clothes, and go on with your lovely little life."

Tara flipped through the binder. It really was a wealth of information. "Will you be there?"

"No. I won't—"

From somewhere in the back of the house, an elderly voice called, "Elly? Is that a friend of yours?"

"No, Grandma. They were just leaving," she called back, and then looked at Tara expectantly, waiting for her to leave.

Tara tightened her fingers around the chrysanthemum. "Actually—I have some more questions. They aren't about the Burning."

Elaine put on a hollow smile. "Then I don't care to answer them; now if you'll leave, I've got a load of things to do tonight that *don't* deal with the Burning." And she led Tara back out the door.

It was now or never. Elaine wasn't going to be truthful. Tara knew that for a fact. If no one would talk to her honestly, then this was how to catch the killer. Muttering under her breath the spell—*"Veritas"*—she turned back to Elaine with her last bit of courage, on the front steps of her house, and asked, "Are you trying to protect Hailey?"

Elaine blinked. "Why would I—" She cut herself off, eyebrows furrowing, and then she touched her lips. "Weird."

"Answer the question, please," Tara commanded.

Elaine shook her head, but her face paled as she fought against the spell. "N-no, I don't know what you're talking about."

"I heard that Brian and Hailey were together. You didn't like how it ended."

Elaine's hand grew white-knuckled as she gripped the door-knob tighter and tighter. "And?"

"And, as her best friend, wouldn't you hate that? If it ended bad and you could do something about it?"

Elaine's brow furrowed. "What would I do?"

"What *wouldn't* you do?" Because Tara knew Elaine was mean and cruel and she looked down at everyone who couldn't do something for her.

And so Elaine answered truthfully, surprising them both—"Nothing. I would do anything for Hailey."

"And you did, didn't you? You—"

"Brian and Hailey had a fight, okay?" Elaine snapped, suddenly unable to stop herself, like a dam breaking and rushing over her tongue, something she couldn't control. Tara stood there, as still as a statue, horror growing in the pit of her stomach at what she'd unleashed. "He said he'd waited long enough. That Hailey wanted it, too; she was just scared. You know, *sex*. And when he wouldn't take no for an answer? She dumped him! Of *course* she did! She didn't want to take another person telling her what to do. When to do it.

"And then that *bastard* started spreading all these rumors—that Hailey got around. That she slept with college guys. That she wasn't who she said she was—that she was *poor*. And you know what the principal said? That they couldn't *prove* it was him. That Brian was a *good kid*. But, like, what about her? He ruined her reputation at school because he couldn't control her. Because she wasn't *his*. Hailey—Hailey deserved *none* of that! Brian? He didn't care. So yes, I'd do anything if I could. If I had the power. You know what I think? I think he *deserved* what he g—" Suddenly, she slammed her hands over her mouth. She swallowed thickly, took a step back into her house, and then another.

Tara tried to reach out, her mind reeling. Elaine *wasn't* the witch? "It's okay—"

Elaine's voice shook as she said, "I want you to leave, Tara Maclay." Then she slammed the door in her face. From behind it, she heard Elaine whispering, "Stupid, stupid—she'll know, she'll *know*," to herself.

Well, she *did* know. Now, at least. And Tara had a new suspicion, and a terrible feeling brewing in her bones.

As she left down the front steps, Elaine's words echoed in her head, that Brian was a bright student. He was a good kid. And Hailey wasn't? Senior class president. Early acceptance to Yale. Full scholarships—*control over her own life.*

Brian couldn't control her, so he wanted to ruin her.

Tara knew what anger felt like, but this brimmed with something more. She wasn't angry. She was livid because she wasn't surprised, and worse yet—she *identified* with her. Tara understood. As someone who didn't have her own life, trapped on the leash her family used to lead her . . .

God, she understood.

Did that make her wicked, too?

Crossing the street toward the van, she took her walkie-talkie out of her jacket pocket and decided then and there what she had to do.

"Elaine doesn't know anything," she lied, hugging the binder tightly.

She didn't know why at first, but as she walked back toward the blue van, she figured it out. Because if what Elaine said was true—and it had to be—then there was a point in time when Hailey wasn't a murderer.

When she just wanted revenge.

That meant that maybe . . . she could be talked out of it, too. Before she murdered someone else.

Maybe Tara was thinking about herself when she made the call to lie to Daphne, but she needed to know the truth. If a witch went dark because witches were destined to, no matter how good or how bright they were, she wanted to see for herself.

If she was destined to, as well. If magic was really a pull to the shadows, or if it could be used entirely for light.

"What? *Seriously?*" Daphne's voice crackled through the speaker. "Are you sure she wasn't lying?"

"I don't think she was."

"Shit. Then we're at another dead end." There was a long pause. "And there was nothing else? Nothing you picked up on?"

Yes, but I can't tell you. Not yet.

Yes, because I need to sort this part out myself.

Yes, because you'll be in danger.

"No," Tara finally replied as she saw the blue van in the distance. Daphne came up and pushed open the passenger-side door. Tara climbed in silently, and they made their way back toward the center of town. She reached for the radio only to realize that it was broken. Maybe it was for the best. Not even a saccharine pop song could salvage her mood.

Daphne drummed her fingers on the steering wheel. "Then what next? If not Baz, who's their next victim?"

Tara didn't know. But maybe she could find out. Find answers. Something. She put the binder in the seat between them.

Something began to ring from the glove compartment, and Daphne cursed as she leaned over, opened the door, and took out a chunky Nokia cell phone. Tara was surprised Daphne had one, but this was her parents' car, and they were in the business of demon slaying, so it sort of made sense. Daphne answered it. "Yeah? O-oh. He called? You? Okay, but—yes, sir. Yes, sir." She cursed as she hung up and threw the phone into her lap. "*Speaking* of what's next. The guy I told you about—the Watcher in Sunnydale? He just called my parents. They want me home. Probably to tell me this is too big a job for me."

"Maybe they're right," Tara suggested timidly, earning the sharpest look from Daphne she'd ever gotten.

"What's that supposed to mean?"

"This is getting dangerous."

"And?"

"And what if we're wrong?" Tara added, because she had to, because it was gnawing at her. "What if the witch is doing a good thing—"

"What's with the change of heart, suddenly?"

"It's not a change of heart—I just—" Tara bit the inside of her cheek and looked into her lap. "I'm scared."

Which was the truth, as much as she could admit.

Daphne reached over and took her hand, and squeezed it tightly. "Hey, I won't let anything happen to you, okay? I won't fail again. Not this time. I'll take you home—"

"I can get out here." Tara pulled her hand out of Daphne's, and it felt like trying to pry apart Velcro. She didn't want to let go.

"What? No way, at least let me take you home. Cupcake," she added, and Tara froze as she went to open the van door. She asked softly, "Are you sure you're okay?"

"I just need some fresh air," Tara replied, and gathered her book bag. She slid out of the van at the stop sign and closed the door.

With a belch of black smoke, the vehicle rolled through the intersection and sped off down the road. She stood there for a moment longer and then checked her watch. Thirty minutes until her father got home. Maybe that gave her time to visit Hailey.

She didn't know where Hailey lived.

She did, however, know where Hailey *worked*. The bookstore was right down the street, so she headed for it when she recognized someone in the coffee shop window.

Baz.

Even better.

He was sitting at a corner table, head propped up on his hand, elbow on the table, his eyes closed as if he were soaking in the sun. But it was overcast. A few tables away, however, there were two lovestruck goth boys leaning into each other, their hands touching, giggling over autumn lattes.

Baz cracked an eye open when the bell above the door chimed. She sat down opposite him.

"You don't smell as nice this afternoon," he noted, studying her. "Did something happen between you and Icy Hot?"

"No," she replied a little too quickly. "It's creepy, telling me how I smell."

He scrunched his nose. "Sorry. I usually can't tell other people."

"And you can tell me?"

"Well, neither of us are normal, are we?"

No, they weren't. She chanced a look at the goth boys in the corner, too wrapped up in each other to notice if an atomic bomb detonated at the table next to them. He followed her gaze and said quietly, "I absorb happy emotions. Good ones. Love, like, *pleasure*. I can hear how quick someone's heart beats for someone else, I can smell how sweet their feelings are—like being in a cotton candy store."

"How about bad emotions?" she asked, noting that he *did*

look a bit healthier than he had at school today. Less run-down from last night's terrifying ordeal. The dark circles under his eyes were almost gone.

"They smell rancid. I can't eat those. Makes me sick." Then he turned his gaze back to her, thoughtful. "What happened?"

"I lied to her."

"Haven't you been lying this whole time?"

She cast her eyes down, ashamed. "I need to do this part without her."

"And what part is that?"

"The part where I talk to Hailey," she replied, and then took a deep breath and added, "witch to witch."

CHAPTER THIRTY-SIX
WITCH TO WITCH

Baz's face went through a range of emotions. From confusion, to acknowledgment, and finally to frustration. He sat back in his chair with a long, dejected sigh. As if the last hope he'd clung to had just come unraveled.

"Not Leelee," he muttered, shaking his head. "No. No—not her."

"You said you could sense magic. Was that a lie?"

"No."

"Then you could sense her—"

"I couldn't!" he snapped. The couple on the other side of the coffee shop glanced over before lowering their voices. He clenched and unclenched his hands. "I . . . Something's not adding up. I've known Leelee since I could remember. I mean, we sorta grew apart these last few years because she was dating Brian, but I would've sensed something like that. She doesn't have magic. She doesn't *know* magic even exists."

Tara said gently, "It can't be anyone else."

"But . . . she . . . she *wouldn't*," he insisted, his voice cracking. He scrubbed his face with his hands and then finally asked, "How do you know?"

So Tara told him what Elaine had told her, and by the look on his face, he knew nothing about any of it. His aura, once soft and blue, was flickering into a red rage. When she finished, she added, "I think . . . I think she took the spellbook, and she used it. In some way."

"Fuck," he whispered, wiping his eyes with the back of his hands. She hadn't guessed him to be the type to cry when he got angry, but here he was. "She could've— I was right there. I didn't know Brian was spreading those rumors—and they were just that, *rumors*. I didn't know where they came from. God, this is my fault. If I'd just—if I'd paid more attention . . ."

Tara reached out and put her hand over his. "It's not your fault, Baz."

"Isn't it? I knew her best. Or I thought I did. We kinda grew distant after she started dating Brian—he didn't like me around. It was a territorial thing. Hailey doesn't like me like that."

"Would just what happened with Brian make her do this? It feels . . ."

Slowly, he shook his head. "I'm sure it was compounded. She's the golden girl, right? Yale-bound. Her parents put her in every extracurricular. Every club. She had to be perfect. The Brian thing—the rumors—they probably . . ." He ran his hands through his spiky hair. "I don't know. I didn't think she could kill people. Our *friends*."

She agreed. "Which is why I think we should talk to her."

"And Daphne?"

"I lied and told her that I didn't know anything. I want to make sure first."

His large shoulders wilted with relief. "She's going to be mad at you." She squeezed his hand tightly, telling him that she knew.

But perhaps she'd have enough time to figure out how to tell Daphne. How to brace for that look—the one her father had given her when her mother died. She didn't want Daphne to look at her like a monster, not yet.

Baz said, "I still don't know how she used magic—if she's not even a witch. How could she?"

"I don't know. But we're going to find out."

"Yeah." He sniffed, pulling his letterman jacket off the back of the chair and shoving his arms into it, before wiping his eyes. "Okay. Let's go."

"Thank you."

Baz drove a smooth black Mustang that purred like a kitten. It was a conspicuous car, but Tara really couldn't complain. They'd parked across the street from the unassuming log cabin on the outskirts of Hellborne. It was a cute little place, where summer flowers shriveled in painted pots and dying vines clung to the sides of the brick exterior with the last of their strength. There were piles of orange leaves and pumpkins sitting carved into funny faces on the steps.

"I thought it'd be . . . bigger," Tara decided. "A *lot* bigger."

"Nah, her mom's a nurse and her father works at the factory over near Dartmouth," Baz dismissed. "Not everyone in Hellborne is rich. Hellborne might look fancy, but a lot of kids aren't. Hailey's parents, though, they're pretty strict, least what I can remember. So, they might have an issue with you coming in all unannounced. . . ."

"I know what that's like," Tara muttered. How *had* Hailey found magic? And how had she gotten so strong in such a short amount of time? To be able to place curses that killed and put a warning on Tara's hand? And who knew what else she had done?

Could the Red Witch's book really be that powerful? she thought, afraid to find out the answer.

"Hey, I *can* go with you," he said.

She shook her head. "No. The only person who can talk to her is me, anyway. She'd suspect something was up with you, wouldn't she? And me . . . I don't think she wants to kill me." She motioned to the almost-healed burn on her hand. "But if something goes wrong . . ."

Baz waved his hand. "Gotcha. If you're not back in ten, I'll come knocking. Just . . . be careful?"

"I will," Tara replied. "I promise."

"You're probably the only person in Hellborne I trust."

"Likewise," she agreed, and she was glad that Baz had her back, because she wasn't sure what she was walking into at all.

But walk she did, up the cobblestone path to the front porch. The wood creaked under her weight as she climbed the short set of steps to the porch. There were two rocking chairs on either side of the door, one with a pumpkin in it, the other with a droopy-looking scarecrow. The closer she got to the house, the rottener everything looked.

It was all just a facade.

She didn't sense magic here, either, but it was odd in a way that put her even more on edge. Because the air was hollow, like something had pulled all the energy from it already.

Something was wrong.

She could feel it before the door even opened. Hailey smiled at her, bright and welcoming, and the forlorn feeling dissipated. Why had Tara been so nervous? She couldn't remember.

"Oh, Tara!" Hailey cried. "I didn't expect a visit! You should've told me you were coming—is something the matter?"

"No," Tara replied. "I just . . . I was . . ." She faltered. Furrowed her brows together.

Why was she here again?

"Darling," a voice called from the kitchen at the back of the house, "is someone here?"

"It's a friend from school, Mother!" Hailey shouted back to her, and then took Tara by the hand and pulled her inside.

The next few minutes were a blur.

Tara remembered looking at family photos on her way up the stairs to Hailey's room. She remembered telling her about the *Macbeth* book and looking for it. She remembered thinking how odd it was that she felt so safe here. Why had she come here alone? Daphne would have loved this place. The murders were a distant ember in her thoughts, and she really didn't care about them anymore.

She didn't know the guys. Why should she care?

"You should be glad you didn't know them," Hailey said, leading her to the kitchen where her mother sat quietly, reading the paper. "The world's better without them. Chamomile or Earl Grey?"

There was something in that statement that troubled Tara, that pushed at the edges of her thoughts, screaming.

Screaming so distantly she barely heard anything at all.

"Chamomile," she said, though she'd wanted to say something else. She couldn't remember what anymore, though.

"Good choice." Hailey took a packet from the tea rack and fixed two cups. "I know it's crass to say they're better off dead, but you didn't know them, and the people who really did didn't want to."

But what about Elaine sobbing in the parking lot of the museum? Amala's quiet move out of town, Harris's sadness—and Baz?

What about *Baz*?

Hailey's mother asked, "Dear, do you know when your father will be home?"

"Later, Mother," Hailey replied, handing Tara a mug of tea. "Let's go to my room?"

"Sure. It was nice to meet you," Tara added to Hailey's mother, and realized that she hadn't even stuttered to a new person. That was a strange feeling, because she always did, but it was like her mouth moved before she even thought about what to say.

Hailey's mother smiled. "It was nice to meet you, too." Then she turned the page in her newspaper. The date read *SEPT. 19*.

Strange, why was it—

A sharp pain sliced through Tara's thoughts, and suddenly she found herself back in the foyer again, following Hailey up the stairs. Her mom was nice. Why had Baz said she was controlling? She didn't seem that way at all.

Tara's father would have loved Hailey and their small house. He would approve of her. A lot more than he'd approve of Daphne and her family.

Daphne was a terrible person, anyway, wanting to kill people.

She was a murderer, too. Wasn't that why Tara wanted to come talk to Hailey in the first place? To tell her all of Daphne's secrets?

"You can tell me everything," Hailey said, leaning close to Tara.

They were sitting on her bed. How did they get here? Tara didn't remember. Weren't they just in the hall? Her brain felt fuzzy and numb, and every thought had to crawl through molasses.

Hailey went on. "Everything about those *mean* witch hunters and what they want. What is Daphne's weakness? Her biggest fear?"

Fear? "Daphne doesn't fear anything," she replied.

"She has to be afraid of something—losing her family? Herself? *Failing?*"

Tara frowned, thinking about the fight in the van. Daphne was afraid of failure, but not because she would *fail* anyone—she was afraid of it because she thought she already had failed with her brother. She wasn't afraid because she'd already lost the one thing she was terrified of losing. The words to say as much bubbled up in her throat, but she tried to keep them down because they weren't *for* Hailey. She shouldn't learn about Daphne's trauma from Tara. That was evil. It was wrong.

It was a betrayal.

Hailey leaned closer, her eyes wide as they stared into Tara's, and she asked, each word like a fishhook into Tara's belly, so sharp it hurt. "How close is she to figuring me out?"

The doorbell rang.

"Drat," Hailey muttered. "I'll be right back. Don't go anywhere."

The fishhooks released, and Tara slumped against the head-board. Hailey left and closed the door to a crack behind her. The farther she moved, the more Tara felt the molasses ooze out of her head. She blinked, steadying herself on one of the bed-posts. The doorbell had dissipated the warm haze between her thoughts, and she could think again. Baz had said he'd come to ring the doorbell in ten minutes. Had it been that long already?

She glanced around to get her bearings.

She was in Hailey's room? She vaguely remembered climb-ing the stairs. . . . She'd been bewitched. That much she knew. Controlled. Something so wicked and powerful it made Tara want to vomit once she realized.

Think. You know why you're here. Look around, she told her-self, steeling her courage.

The room was small, a large window on the far wall looking out to the thick and dark firs. The comforter was a soft pink; the posters on the wall were of *NSYNC and 98 Degrees. Hailey's dresser was full of awards for cheerleading and debate clubs. Tomorrow's Halloween costume was hung up on the back side of the door. It was a deep purple dress, the edges cobwebbed and whimsical.

Nothing was out of the ordinary.

Except the more Tara got her bearings, the hollower the feeling in the air grew. Like the air had been sucked out of the house. It was so heavy she didn't understand how she hadn't noticed the second she stepped into the house.

Something awful had gone on here. Something that had pried the magic from the air, stolen it, and burned it away.

The spellbook must've done this. It had to be somewhere in this room. She started going through the drawers in the nightstand, the books on the shelf, until she opened the top drawer of the dresser—and there it sat on top of a cable-knit sweater, like it was a diary instead of a terrible book. The edges were stained, newly, with blood. It pulsed gently like a heartbeat.

Tara was afraid to touch it, but she had to.

When she picked it up, the book felt heavier than it should have, and there was a hot-pink bookmark inside. She flipped to it. Had Hailey *bookmarked* where she found the spell to become so powerful? That seemed too easy.

But when she flipped to the page, her stomach twisted. It was blood-splattered, but the witch's writing was still readable. It wasn't a spell for knowledge, or magic, or power.

It was a summoning spell.

Why would Hailey bookmark that? Unless—

The strange hollowness in the air. She closed her eyes. Tried to trace where the feeling was the strongest, and stopped in the middle of the room. And looked down. She stood on a soft blue shaggy rug that didn't fit the rest of her decor.

Here.

She quickly dropped to her knees, unsure when Hailey would come back. She hoped Baz would keep her busy for a minute or two longer. She threw back the rug. Her body began to shiver. There was a marking on the hardwood floor. It was faint, but still there. She traced her fingers along the curving line of the sigil.

Hailey had drawn the summoning circle.

There were dark patches on the hardwood floor that could only be blood. It looked like someone had tried to clean it up, but blood was one of the hardest stains to remove—and blood used in magic?

Sometimes it left marks for centuries.

And not just on hardwood floors.

There was writing above one side of the summoning circle. She pulled back more of the rug until she bumped up against the four-poster bed, to be able to read the whole inscription.

To take revenge on my enemies. I call you.

She traced her fingers across the strange letters. They looked familiar, but only in passing. Perhaps from *A Study of Demonic Arrays*? But if so, what did this spell summon? And from where?

"So," interrupted the sweet voice of Hailey Conrad, "you broke out of my spell. You must be a stronger witch than I realized."

Tara froze.

Then slowly lifted her gaze.

Hailey stood in the doorway. "Your girlfriend came knocking. I told her you'd left. So, there will be no one here to save you."

"What did you summon?" Tara asked, trying to control her voice, but it shook anyway.

Hailey inclined her head, and the expression on her face looked so wrong, as if someone else was peering out of a mask. "Wrong question, darling."

Who.

Tara tried to scramble to her feet, holding the spellbook tightly to her chest. "Wh-what did you do with Hailey?"

"What she asked of me. She offered me her life in exchange for revenge. So I gave it to her. Or, at least, after tomorrow night I will have."

Tara narrowed her eyes. "Who a-are you?"

Hailey, who was not Hailey, sighed. "I warned you to stay away. I *asked* you."

"Are you a demon?"

"Some called me that, but no." She pointed to the spellbook in Tara's hand. "That is mine. I would like it back."

Surprised, Tara looked down at the spellbook, and then back to Hailey. The pieces clicked into place. Hailey had summoned the one person in the mythos of this entire town who had more hatred for Hellborne than she did. "You're the Red Witch."

"Adelaide, please."

"Let H-Hailey go."

The Red Witch *tsk*ed. "That's not how this works. She traded her soul so that I can give her vengeance." Then she spread her arms wide, and the air in the room began to shiver. "And that is what I will do."

What was happening—another spell?

But it felt different.

And Tara's hand, it was—

It *hurt*. She gave a cry and dropped the book. On the back of her left hand, a burn carved itself across her flesh. Not words this time, but the curse itself.

The deathmark.

"I gave you a choice, and you chose wrong," Adelaide said, and the air shimmered her away.

The room stretched. The walls turned pale. She was hallucinating—was this how Baz had seen his nightmare? Moss? Brian and Chad? The furniture faded, or twisted into uncomfortable chairs and hospital apparatuses, until she was no longer in Hailey's pastel bedroom but a florescent-lit hospital room.

A voice, one that she remembered from deep in her golden-soaked dreams, said, "Tara."

Her eyes widened. She turned toward the voice, even though she was already sure of who she'd see.

Not Adelaide.

Not Daphne.

Petite with blond hair laced with gray, knobby but caring hands, callused from years of gardening. She wore a simple soft pink cardigan that smelled like dumplings over a fluffy white blouse, and a long corduroy skirt. She smiled and said, "I should have killed you when you were born, sprout."

Tara's throat constricted in panic. *This isn't real*, she told herself.

But she *looked* real. So real that Tara could reach out and touch her, and that had been all she'd wanted to do for the last eight miserable months. She just wanted to hug her mother again, smell her sweet perfume she dabbed behind her ears, and tell her how much she missed her. How she was sorry.

How there weren't enough words to explain the emptiness she felt inside.

How nothing could have ever prepared her for losing her.

"Mom . . ."

"You used to be so obedient," her mother went on. "It's all your fault. You killed me—slowly."

The words felt like a slap in the face. Tara took a step back. Shook her head. "N—no . . ."

Her mother stepped forward. "You could have saved me if you were stronger. If you loved me more."

"I—I do love you. So, so much," Tara forced out as her

mother cupped her face in her hands, and oh, she looked just like Tara remembered, heart-shaped face and kind gray eyes, and Tara would give anything— *anything*—to see her again.

But this wasn't her.

"Come keep me company, sprout," her mother begged. "I'm so lonely."

And Tara was heartbroken as she grabbed her own left hand, nails digging deep into her flesh, and began to gouge scratches into the rune. She gritted her teeth against the pain. It was almost unbearable. Tears pooled in her eyes.

"I love you, Mom," she whispered, "but I want to stay."

And with a scream, she scratched her hand so deep across the burn she drew blood.

Her mother disappeared in a shimmer of air, revealing instead the witch with Hailey's face, who had wrapped her fingers around Tara's throat.

"Oh, aren't you smart?" Adelaide whispered, her eyes shimmering a terrible burning red. "I used to be like you. Right up until the end."

"Where's Hailey?" she whispered, choking as the witch tightened her grip on her throat.

"She sacrificed herself so that I can avenge her. So, vengeance I shall give her."

Suddenly magic pooled around her hands, burning the skin on Tara's neck.

No—no, wait—

"Discede."

An invisible wave of magic hit Tara in the chest. It knocked the air out of her so hard she felt something *pop*. The force sent her hurtling through the window behind her, Hailey standing perfectly framed, hair swimming around her in a sea of red magic, as Tara went plummeting to her death—

"Got you!"

Large arms wrapped around her, catching her in midair, and they landed without so much as a sound. Red-and-black jacket. Spiked hair. There were jagged points on Baz's forehead where—where *horns* were beginning to break through.

The next thing she heard was the sound of a crossbow firing with a sharp hiss. The bolt scraped Hailey's cheek and embedded itself in the dresser behind her.

Daphne pulled out another bolt and loaded it. Daphne, who came to her rescue. Daphne, who saw through her lies and came to Hailey's house. Daphne, who Tara had underestimated. Daphne, who Tara was happiest to see. The monster hunter aimed her crossbow and—

Hailey's mouth formed a spell.

One Tara recognized. She pushed herself out of Baz's arms. *"No!"* she cried.

Daphne fired.

The crossbow bolt streaked through the air. And then froze. And turned back, multiplying into ten. Hailey muttered another word—and sent them swirling down toward them.

Tara threw up her hands, squeezing her eyes tightly shut. And she murmured a spell, invoking Minerva, the goddess of war and wisdom, for protection.

A glimmer stretched across the air in front of them like a bubble, swirling with rainbow light.

The arrows hit the barrier and stuck fast.

Daphne reloaded her crossbow as the witch burst into smoke

and swirled out of the broken window. She fired another arrow, but it sailed right through the smoke as it disappeared into the woods.

"Shit!" Daphne snarled. "Shit, she got away!"

"She's not Hailey," Tara rasped, finally letting her barrier drop. The arrows dropped onto the autumn leaves. "She's the Red Witch. She's Adelaide. There—there was a summoning circle on the floor. And blood."

"Then where's Hailey?" Baz asked in alarm.

"I . . . I think . . . Hailey summoned her into her body, but I don't know if Hailey is trapped in there with her or . . . I didn't get a chance to look harder at the spellbook. I'm s-sorry."

His jaw worked back and forth, his brow furrowing. "I guess that's a good thing, then. I knew she wouldn't murder anyone. Whoa, are you okay?" Baz added gently when Tara tilted sideways, but he caught her and steadied her on her feet.

The witch hunter spun on her heel to face them. Her dark eyes lit with rage. "What *are* you?" she snarled at Baz.

"That's rude." He reached up to touch his horns, self-conscious. They had sprouted from his head, now curling back like ram's horns. "I'm me, obviously."

"You're a monster."

"Also true," he agreed, a little morosely.

Then her gaze dropped to Tara, so livid tears burned in her eyes. Tara reached out to her. "Daphne, I can explain—"

Daphne jerked away. Tara's heart fell, and fell, and fell. Daphne was so close, but suddenly so far away. Farther than the moon, the stars. And never coming back. Daphne gritted her teeth and spat, "You don't need to explain, Tara. I can't believe I was so stupid—you went to warn her, didn't you?"

Baz said, "Oh, come on, you know she didn't—" His words caught in his throat as the witch hunter reloaded her crossbow and leveled it at his face. "Hey, hey, watch where you aim that thing—"

She pulled the trigger.

The arrow *plinked* off his left horn. "*Ow!* Hey! That could've hit me!"

"If I wanted to, I could have."

Baz paled as the witch hunter spun toward Tara, lowering her weapon. "And you think I didn't *know* that you were a witch? Of course, I knew! I just *trusted* you!"

She . . . *knew*? Tara stared at the girl she'd kissed and wanted to kiss a thousand times over, and she realized the exact kind of fool she'd been. The kind who had underestimated Daphne Frost, the kind who had been so caught up in her own world and her own feelings that she hadn't paused to consider Daphne at all.

Come to think of it, of course Daphne knew. She'd probably known since that first day, at least, in her parents' study filled with witchy books and that murder board.

"We could have had her!" Daphne went on. "We could've killed her! Taken her by surprise—"

"N-no," Tara interrupted, remembering the spell the Red Witch had cast on her in the house. "She would've killed us first."

The witch hunter clenched her jaw. "So, you went behind my back?"

To that, Tara didn't have an answer.

The silence was damning.

With a growl, Daphne threw her crossbow to the ground. "We were a *team*!"

"I was a-afraid," Tara admitted, unable to meet her gaze, her tongue stumbling over itself as tears burned in her eyes. Her throat hurt from where the witch had grabbed her, and her chest felt so tight she could barely breathe. "I was afraid you'd . . . you'd find out what I was. I w-was afraid you'd h-hate me."

Daphne looked at her for a long moment. And then she said, quietly, "Tara, do you really think I would immediately assume the worst of someone? In *you*?"

A knot formed in Tara's throat. Because yes—she had. Because her father had. Because of the way he looked at her, because she was afraid Daphne would look at her the same but . . . now that seemed really silly.

Of course Daphne wouldn't. Daphne wasn't like her father.

But it was too late to realize that.

"I think I've had enough help—from either of you," Daphne snapped, glaring at Baz and Tara both, before she turned and left through the woods after the Red Witch. She didn't look back.

Not once.

Tara figured she never would again.

Tears burned against her eyes and fell down her cheeks in large, terrible drops. She tried to push them away with the backs of her hands, but they wouldn't stop no matter what she did. Her chest hurt from trying to keep her sobs in. Her heart hurt more. It was rendered useless. Twisted and torn and wicked.

She hadn't told Daphne who she was because she didn't want this exact thing to happen, and still she'd known it would. All paths led to this.

And it hurt so badly she wanted to tear out her heart, bury it, and never need it again.

"C-can you eat all of m-my emotions?" she begged Baz. "Can you take it a-all away?"

He gave her a sad sort of look and pulled her into a tight hug. His chest was warm, and his arms were comforting, and she cried into his letterman jacket. "I wish I could."

CHAPTER THIRTY-SEVEN
EVIL AT THE DOOR

"Are you sure you'll be okay?" Baz asked as he dropped her off at her house.

"I'll be fine," she replied. "Hailey doesn't know where I live, and I think there's some mint in the pantry so I can set up a warding spell—"

"No, I mean . . ."

She knew what he meant. She just didn't want to think about it. "I'm fine," she repeated. Her hand would be fine, though two injuries to it in the same number of weeks might leave a scar. But she knew what he meant. . . . Instead, because she didn't want to think about her own broken heart rattling in her rib cage anymore, she asked, "Are you okay?"

"No," he replied. "No, I'm not."

"I'm sorry, Baz. . . ."

"Hey, it's not you. We just gotta figure out what happened to Hailey now. And how to get her back."

"Yeah," she agreed, but it was half-hearted. She didn't want to think about it right now. She didn't want to think about anything.

The walk up the drive felt like it took eons, and as she slowly picked her way up the front path to the door, she just wanted to sink underneath the autumn leaves and never come out again.

Maybe Daphne would've understood if she had told her about Hailey, but in hindsight, that would've been too dangerous. They *both* could have been bespelled. Not just her. The acidic taste of the magic still curled around her molars.

Then again, Daphne must have known Tara was lying to her when she was dropped off at the corner, or Daphne was planning on going to Hailey's herself.

Without Tara.

She took out her keys from her bag and inserted them into the door and twisted—but nothing happened. She jiggled the key again. But it wouldn't turn.

Panic clawed up her throat.

Her father had changed the locks. She'd only been late a few times! And the times she snuck out, she'd put her father and brother to sleep. They couldn't possibly know. No one could. She'd been so careful.

Hadn't she?

Suddenly, there were footsteps on the other side of the door. The dead bolt unlocked, and the door opened.

But it wasn't her father or brother in the doorway.

It was her cousin Beth.

She looked as pristine as she always had, her red hair neatly combed into a curtain down her back, her mascara sparse, the gloss on her lips perfectly subtle. She was dressed in a simple button-down shirt and a pencil skirt that reached her knees, with nude hose and sensible flats.

Her gaze was sharp, though. It cut Tara to the bone.

"I warned your father that you would only get worse," her cousin said, her voice ringing with authority. Beth was only a few years older than Tara, but she'd become the matron of the family in the last few years with her sensible submission. She was a viper dressed like a mouse.

"H-hello, Beth," Tara greeted, and looked around inside the house. "It's been a while."

Her cousin smiled coldly. "Hasn't it. I see you haven't changed a bit. It's a good thing I've come to look out for you."

"Thank you, but I'm perfectly fine taking care of myself."

"Oh?" She stepped aside to let Tara in, and Tara slipped inside and put her book bag down on the couch.

"I'm going to bed—"

"I told your father that you would disgrace our family."

Tara froze in her footsteps. "I haven't done anything—" Her words caught in her throat when Beth produced her mother's spellbook. She made a move to grab it, but Beth stepped back, a look of triumph on her face. Tara gritted her teeth. "That's m-mine."

"Your father got rid of all of these," Beth said accusingly, "but you hid one! I told your father that it would be hard for you to change."

"It's h-harmless."

"Harmless?" Beth barked a laugh. "Oh, like you and your mother's *magic* was harmless? How it seduced my uncle? *Bewitched* him? How it bewitched *you*?"

"I don't d-do magic l-like that. N-neither did my m-mom."

"She was wicked—"

"She wasn't!" Tara snapped. She shook in anger.

"She was wicked, and she died because of it!"

"No."

"And it's a good thing I came," Beth went on, and opened the spellbook. Then she grabbed a fistful of pages, and Tara felt her heart stop. "If only to save you from yourself."

Beth began to tear the pages out. Tara gave a cry, reaching out to try to grab the spellbook from her, but she couldn't get a hold on it as pages and pages sloughed away, torn and fluttering to the ground like autumn leaves. She grabbed at Beth's hair, clutched at her clothes, until finally her cousin let go and stumbled away with a shriek. Tara fell to the ground, trying to gather up all the pages, but they were ruined.

Her mother's spellbook was ruined.

Beth fixed her shiny hair, glowering at Tara like she was the monster. "When your father gets home, I will tell him *everything*. And I will make sure he sends you to that school. It served me well, and it will certainly fix you."

Fix her? Tara gathered the crumpled pages and pressed them against her chest. But she wasn't broken, not in a way that could be mended. She was just broken in the kind of way she had to endure, and she doubted that was something Beth could understand.

"Go to your room. You aren't getting dinner tonight," Beth snapped, jabbing a finger down the hall. "And don't you *think* about doing anything for Halloween tomorrow. It's the devil's night. Who knows what terrible things you could get up to?"

Tara let the pages fall to the ground again as she stood. The last bit of her mother was gone, and it felt like a bit of Tara was gone now, too.

It was a little funny that Beth was so scared of *her* when Tara had just faced a witch who could actually make life hell on earth. If Tara had been a different person, maybe she would have given the Red Witch's words a thought—maybe she might've given Beth a taste—but she wasn't that kind of witch.

All she could think about was the look Daphne had given her when she found out—as if she *was* that kind of witch. The kind who murdered. The kind who took, and took, and took, and drained the world around her of color and life and happiness. That broken, horrible look on Daphne's face twisted deep into Tara, so deep she could barely breathe.

She didn't know what kind she *was*, but she had no interest in finding out anymore, so she went quietly to her room, and closed the door.

CHAPTER THIRTY-EIGHT
THE LAST NIGHT ON EARTH

Halloween came as reds and oranges filled the dusk-colored sky, and Tara didn't care. She slept through the night and most of the day. She would sleep forever if she could. There were spells for that.

Maybe she could use one.

Whatever Adelaide was going to do, she might as well do it, and bring about whatever curse she saw fit. It couldn't be as bad of a hell as the one Tara was living in. She'd been in hell since they lowered her mother into the ground. A stranger everywhere she went. No one understood her. No one cared to.

And the one person who might have . . .

She'd lied to her. She'd ruined everything. Her father had warned her, didn't he? That she ruined everything she touched.

And this time, there was no one to blame but herself.

Distantly, she heard someone call her name from outside the house. "*Tara!* Hey! We've got a problem!"

She rolled over on her bed and closed her eyes and tried to ignore her name.

Someone pounded on the front door. Beth answered and snapped that there was no trick-or-treating here tonight and ordered them away. Tara pulled the covers up over her head and listened as they left.

Except they didn't.

A noise came from her window—a knock. She jumped, startled, and threw the covers off. A familiar face smooshed itself against the window. *"Baz?"*

"It's Elaine," he said in a panic. "She got the mark."

From the living room, she heard her cousin curse and start down the hall. "If it's that *boy* again, Tara—you aren't going anywhere!" Beth cried, her footsteps loud as she stormed toward Tara's room. The door locked from the outside, so she couldn't save herself from Beth's wrath even if she wanted to.

But she could stall her. So she grabbed her chair from her desk and propped it up against the door.

"Why should I care?" she asked, turning back to Baz, and he gave her the strangest heartbroken look. Like she was suddenly a stranger.

"Because it's getting worse. I burned the mark off her—but then Harris got it. Half the town's going to get it if we don't *do* something—"

Beth was at the door. She tried to open it and found it jammed. "Tara! Open this door! Open it *now!*" She slammed her fist against it.

Baz asked, "Who *is* that?"

"My cousin." One who would probably report this to Tara's

father, and she'd be shipped off to that finishing school before next week. She felt so tired with it all as she came back to the window. "And I'm sorry, I don't know how I can help. Clearly the witch is more powerful than I am."

"We gotta do something—"

"Why *me*?"

Beth rattled the door. The chair was cheap, and each time Beth pushed, it slid a bit farther on the floor. Soon, her cousin would be able to open the door enough to knock the chair away.

He gave her a level look and said, without hesitation, "Because you're *you*."

"Daphne can handle it."

"I don't think she can. Not alone. And besides"—he motioned to his car—"you're the Red Witch tonight."

A lump formed in her throat. "I don't want to be. Let Elaine."

"Please, Tara. I need your help—*we* need your help."

Even though she'd screwed everything up? Including the one thing that made her happiest?

"Tara!" Beth cried, wiggling her arm into the gap in the doorway and knocking the chair free. She threw open the door. The second she saw Baz on the other side, anger lit in her eyes. "*You!* I told you, Tara, you aren't going *anywhere*. Your father might not know what you're up to, but I *certainly* do!"

Tara turned back to Baz. "I'll try."

"That's what I like to hear!" He forced up the window from the outside, snapping the safety locks like they were weak plastic, and extended his hand. "C'mon."

Tara didn't hesitate.

"Don't you *dare* leave this house! You're never coming back if you do! You're a slut! A *demon*! A—"

Baz turned a hard gaze to her cousin, and his eyes became consumed with black. He bared his teeth, and his incisors were longer, pointed. "This is what a demon looks like, lady," he snarled.

Beth gasped, a hand on her heart. But then she doubled down as she shrieked, "I'll call the police! Your father! I'll—"

Tara was, very suddenly, tired of all this screaming. She turned back to face her cousin and summoned magic into her fingertips. "No, Beth, you won't do anything."

She waved her hand through the air. The lavender on her dresser was still good. Still a beacon.

"*Somnum,*" she commanded.

The magic took hold instantly. It swelled in the air, rushing to her instantly like a moth to a flame. It came because she was finally willing. It came because she knew who she was, even if she didn't want to be it. She was a witch. And maybe she wasn't nice.

But she didn't have to be.

Beth convulsed, trying to resist it, before she fell to the ground, so deeply asleep she was almost dead.

Then Tara turned back to Baz, and he helped her out of the window.

"Remind me not to piss you off," he said. His car was on the curb, as if he'd parked it in a hurry, barely missing the mailbox. She slid into the passenger seat and buckled up as he went around to the driver's side, got in, and slammed the door.

"Man, your cousin's a *bitch,*" he growled, his voice deeper than usual, full of gravel, and it scared her a little. Then he closed his eyes and took a deep breath. His features softened, like ice cream melting in the summer sun. He let out a tired breath, and when he opened his eyes again, they were the mint color that she knew. "Sorry. That just pissed me off a lot. How she treated you."

"Maybe I deserve it."

"You don't mean that."

"I mess everything up. Of course I do. My blood—"

"Her cruelty has nothing to do with whatever you think you have running through your veins," he replied adamantly, so much so, she almost believed it. Almost. He put the Mustang in gear and peeled off the sidewalk and down the street.

"What if I just make things worse than I already have?" she asked quietly.

He drummed his fingers on the steering wheel. "Maybe you will, but that doesn't mean you shouldn't keep trying."

"And fail again?"

"That's part of *trying*," he said, "and it has nothing to do with whatever demon blood you say you have going on."

"I *do* have going on," she clarified.

"What does it matter? It doesn't make you who you are. If it did, then what do you think I'd be?" he added. "I'm part incubus, part who the hell *knows* what. My parents didn't know what to do with me when I started growing horns. When I healed my broken bones by sucking up other people's good vibes. My maternal grandmother told my old man to give me back to whatever orphanage I came from. You know what they did instead?"

No, she didn't know, but she guessed they handed him off to someone else, to be *their* problem, because that was what her father would have done. Had done. *Would* do.

"They told the old woman to eff off and helped me figure

my shit out. I know who I am, Maclay, and I know the secrets I've got to hide, and I know that not everything will be sunshine and rainbows and I'm going to fail a hell of a lot. But you know what? We've got to keep trying."

"Why?"

"Because we deserve to be able to fail and try again. Because we're good."

It was something she could imagine her mother saying. That responsibility was just that—a mantle you took on not because you had to, but because you knew you should. What did she care if the town burned?

How could she *not*?

There wasn't a bone in her body that knew how to do anything else.

"We're good," she whispered.

"Exactly."

She had a bad feeling about this, but Baz deserved someone who could help. And she could help—though she might come to regret it in the morning.

If she survived.

CHAPTER THIRTY-NINE

HIGH STAKES

Tara raised the red hood over her head.

The reenactment started at the cottage, where a dozen or so townspeople would drag her out of the house and carry her along Main Street to an actual pyre that had been constructed at the Crossroads, where the old one had been. The same intersection with the bookstore and the café and the diner and hardware store.

It was a reenactment that was, in Tara's mind, a bit barbaric.

"Do they really light the pyre?" she found herself asking Baz as the townspeople began to gather with their literal torches and pitchforks.

"Oh, hell no," he dismissed. "Once you get tied to the stake, Principal Greaves usually reprises his role as Hot Cardinal and does his whole spiel—you got those lines memorized?" he added, pointing to the page in the binder Elaine had given her.

Tara glanced down at the words. "Mostly."

"Just ballpark it best you can." He gave her a look and then straightened her cloak. The costume the museum director had given didn't quite fit. The dress was tight around her, and it made breathing hard. The red sea of fabric, layers and layers of bloody red, shifted in the slightest breeze, which was beautiful to look at, but it kept tangling between her legs when she walked—never mind *running* in it.

And with just a spark, this entire dress would go up in flames.

"You look like a damn good witch, Maclay," he said with a wink, and she couldn't help but laugh. It eased the tension in her body a little. "Do you really think the witch will show up?"

"What kind of witch would miss her own Burning?" She chewed on her thumbnail, before she realized what she was doing and forced her hands by her sides. Things would be fine. This would be fine.

Baz put a comforting hand on her shoulder. Was she that easy to read? "Hey, if anything goes south, I'll be there, okay? You won't get burned alive on my watch."

"Thanks," she said, though at the mention of burning alive she wanted to crawl under the ancient bed and hide. If only she had the time.

Three sharp knocks rapped on the door. A pause. Then three more—louder this time, close-fisted.

Her heart leapt into her throat.

"Is that my c-cue?" she asked as he took the binder away.

He hugged her tightly. "Break a leg."

"I wish Daphne was here," she admitted.

"Me too."

Three more knocks rattled the door. "Come out, witch!" the man cried. "We're here to take you to the pyre!"

Ah, yes, the dialogue for this script was Pulitzer Prize–worthy.

Screw your courage to the sticking place, Maclay, Daphne would've said, so Tara said it to herself instead, steeled her backbone, and went to the door. This was the exact nightmare that every witch had. An angry mob. A pyre. A burning.

And here she was willingly going along with it.

"Let's go." She breathed in, bodice creaking. Breathed out.

And opened the door.

The next thing she knew, a hand had reached out and grabbed her by the cloak and dragged her out of the cottage. The evening had bled into night, and the brightest points in the darkness were the torches blazing liquid light.

Someone bound her hands; another person pushed her toward the front of the mob. She recognized their faces from school, but she didn't know their names. They weren't unkind, though, and someone muttered "Sorry" when they jabbed her in the arm painfully.

When she got to the front, Harris was the one who took the rope that bound her hands. "Baz told us you're gonna help with the marks," he murmured close to her ear. "I don't wanna die."

Neither did she.

She glanced behind her, and between the torches and the pitchfork, the shadow of Baz slipped out of the cottage to join the group. He nodded to her, and it eased her anxiety a little bit.

"Thanks," she told Harris, and he led her out of the museum parking lot.

The entire town came out, it seemed, watching from the sidewalks as if this was a parade and not a march to her proverbial death. There were kids eating sweet Halloween candy, dressed as witches and werewolves and zombies. Food stalls hawking hot chocolate and pretzels and pumpkin seeds. It was an execution dressed up as a festival.

At the Crossroads, there was a stage with a pyre on it. Tara had heard about crossroads. There were stories about them. Of magic. Of deals. Of tragedies. The fact that the pyre was built on one felt like it was too good to be chance. It felt purposeful.

She didn't like it.

Harris pushed her up the steps to the stage and told her that if the ropes were too tight then he'd loosen them as he tied her to the stake. There were bundles of sticks stacked up around her, a bit too real and too close for her to feel at ease.

"Uh—are they fake or . . . ?" she asked.

"No, they're real."

"Um."

"Only witches burn," he joked, and descended the steps to the mob again.

That didn't make her feel *any* better.

But honestly—this wasn't so bad. Or so she told herself.

She was tied up on a pyre, sure. Wearing a dress that pinched her around the waist, yes. But she looked very good in red, she decided, and a haunting October wind blew from the west, causing the torches to flicker and fleck into the night sky. Were those torches dangerously close to lighting the kindling surrounding the stage? Absolutely. But at any moment, the mayor would come up and call off the mob.

This was what people competed for? To be tied to a piece of wood and verbally berated? Great job, progress.

"Fiendish felon!" crowed a man from the edge of the stage. A man who could only be the Hot Cardinal. Principal Greaves. "We've finally caught you!"

He sauntered onto the stage. No longer in his trademark pin-striped suit, he looked very tall and imposing in a black cassock with a clergy collar tight around his throat, under a dark red cape. His gray hair was pushed back on his head, his eyes rimmed with black liner. He struck a well-practiced pose and glared at her, and a few wolf whistles rose up from the torch-and-pitchfork crowd.

Oh, dear. Tara guessed he *really* enjoyed his role as Hot Cardinal.

"Witch! How do you plead?"

This was her part.

"N-not guilty," she replied, her voice trembling.

Principal Greave's face was pinched. "Speak up, *witch!*"

"Not guilty," she said a little louder. "I am not guilty! A-are cows hated because they have milk? Are foxes shunned for their fur? Clouds denied rain? Wh-why should I hide my t-talent wh-when I can be of s-service?"

She could hardly believe that the monster lurking beneath Hailey's skin had ever said those words. They were ones that Tara could see herself saying. Because wasn't that what magic was for? Miracles and acts of love? To harness energy into something impossible?

Principal Greaves roared, "You brought famine to our town! You brought sickness!"

"You brought it yourself!"

The crowd gasped as they did in the script. But then something strange happened. The crowd shifted. A rotten tomato caught her in the face. Another one hit her leg. She hissed in pain. That wasn't in the script—was it?

The crowd grew louder. They began to jeer.

A bag of pumpkin seeds slammed into the wood in front of her and burst open, scattering seeds across the stage.

Then she felt it. *Magic.* The air shuddered like it had at the Conrads' home, like a siphon sucking the energy out of everything around her.

She looked out across the crowd.

The witch was here.

Principal Greaves sneered, and it looked much uglier than it should have. His eyes became a milky white. "You have been tried, and you have been found wanting." He grabbed a torch from one of the people in the crowd and thrust it into the air. "BURN THE WITCH!"

There was a shift in the air.

The night grew sharp.

The torches flared brighter, caught in a spell.

"BURN THE WITCH!" a man echoed, and another joined him. They held their torches higher, toward the pyre. All their eyes—they were all white.

"Kill her!"

"It's her fault!"

Onlookers began to rise from their places on the curb, tourists and townspeople alike, chanting with them—

"BURN THE WITCH!"

She tugged on her bindings. They held fast. Hadn't Harris tied them loosely? She glanced over the angering crowd, her heart hammering in her throat, trying to find a familiar face. But Harris had succumbed to the spell. He snarled, "BURN THE WITCH!" with the rest of them.

And Baz was—

He stood at the back of the growing mob and gave a thumbs-up. He'd done what she'd asked, put braids of dill and parsley at the four corners of the Crossroads, but she hadn't expected the crowd to be this . . . *angry*.

Out of the corner of her eye, she caught a glimpse of a head of blond hair. Then the crowd seemed to part, and there was Adelaide with Hailey's face. Tara inclined her head just a little, just enough for her hood to slip off her head so she could look her in the eyes.

"Shield and spear, parsley and dill," Tara said, her voice lost in the jeering of townsfolk, "protect the world from her ill will."

A biting wind howled through the trees. Adelaide's eyes narrowed.

She spoke again: "Shield and sp-spear, parsley and dill, pro-tect the world from her ill will. Shield and spear, parsley and dill, protect the world from her ill will." The wind grew louder, and creases furrowed Hailey's brow. She gritted her teeth. "Shield and spear, hear my words and still this wayward witch against her w—"

"Do you really think your silly little spell will stop me?" It was Hailey, but her words came from the air itself, quivering.

Tara had never felt an aura so angry before. So twisted and honed to a point.

There was rage in magic, just as there was relief. There was darkness that tempted, and darkness that pulled, and darkness that cajoled you into thinking that it wasn't so bad, the darkness, that it was purposeful. That it was yours.

Tara had never felt anything like it before in her entire life. And it suddenly, unequivocally, scared her to the bone.

Blackness flooded through Hailey's eyes like ink drops, until they were dark voids set into her face. She raised her hands—

And without so much as a word, the Red Witch's magic began to fracture her spell like it was spun sugar. She saw the cracks in the air, racing across the night sky from each corner of the Crossroads where Baz had hidden braided dill and parsley.

Hailey touched one of the reenactors, a man with a torch, and muttered something into his ear. His eyes grew glazed, and then he tossed his torch. It felt like it happened in slow motion, the way it arced through the night and landed on the bundles of firewood.

They lit like matches.

Honestly, she'd seen this coming.

Tara coughed, smoke flooding into her lungs, and turned her face away from the growing flames. She struggled, trying to jerk her hands out of the ropes. The fire roared higher and higher. Sweat prickled against her skin, hot and growing hotter. She could already feel her exposed skin beginning to burn. The moment the fire reached her skirt, she knew she would be done.

Think, she pleaded, trying to think back over all the books she'd read, all the magical incantations, the rituals, the spells. All the books upon books that had gone to ash and blown away in the wind—

Which was the way *she* was about to go if she didn't get out of this.

The flames inched higher, so high she could no longer see the crowd anymore, but she could still hear them over the roar of the fire.

"BURN THE WITCH."

"BURN THE WITCH."

"BURN TH—"

A shadow jumped through the flames. She winced against it, ready for whatever shadow had braved the flames to kill her. They went for her bindings instead. She cracked open an eye. Dark hair pulled back into a poofy bun, soft brown skin. She wore a zipped-up hoodie and black jeans. A crossbow on her back.

Daphne.

Tara stared at her like she was the Angel of Death. Was she?

"Stop looking at me like that," Daphne said, cutting through her bindings. "Are you okay?"

"I—I didn't think you'd come."

"Frosts don't give up the hunt halfway," Daphne replied, and took Tara by the hand. Together, they hurtled over the fire. The edges of Tara's dress caught in the flames, but Daphne tore it away, throwing the burning ends toward the pyre, and they made a break for it down the street.

"AFTER THE WITCH!" a man cried.

Daphne pointed down an alleyway. "Left—"

"Tara!" a shrill voice screeched above the roar of the crowd. Her heart jumped into her throat. A silver car had come to a stop in the road, and a redhead got out. Her face scrunched in anger. "Tara Maclay, you will be *punished* for your sins—"

Daphne asked, annoyed, "Who is *that*?"

"My cousin."

"You will *never* be welcomed again! You are just like your mother—worse than your mother! You are a *heathen*! An *ingrate*! Your soul will burn forever in the belly of—"

"Eff *this*," Daphne murmured, pulling out her crossbow, and shot a bolt straight through the windshield.

Beth screeched, one of the flyers Tara had seen at the bookstore crinkled in her hand. "You're one of *them*, too, aren't you?"

Daphne rolled her eyes, grabbing Tara by the hand, again, and pulled her into the alley, the sound of Beth urging her to repent echoing from brick wall to brick wall. Daphne's van had been backed into the shadows. They climbed in, and Daphne started the engine. The headlights flickered on, the radio blaring Nirvana. She jammed the van into drive—

Baz slid into the alley opening, hands up.

Daphne slammed on the brakes. The van screeched to a halt. "What's your damage?" she cried as he hurried around to the passenger seat and climbed in beside Tara. They barely squeezed into the cab, shoulder to shoulder.

"Go!" he cried.

Daphne didn't need to be told twice. She slammed on the gas and peeled out of the alley, right in front of the oncoming mob. Tires squealed as the van whipped around and rocketed away from the Crossroads, the mob growing smaller and smaller until they were a glow in the background.

"Thank you," Tara said softly, and Daphne's hands gripped the wheel tighter.

"I wasn't going to let you *burn*," she replied through gritted teeth. "I finally got to talk to Dad's Watcher friend Giles last night—and I know what the witch is going to do." She leaned forward, brushing Tara's leg and sending a chill racing across her skin, to open the glove compartment and take out a torn page—one, Tara realized, from *A Study of Demonic Arrays*.

"You didn't," Tara said, aghast.

"I wasn't going to lug around a nine-hundred-page book, cupcake," Daphne snapped. *Cupcake*—she still called her cupcake after everything. "Adelaide Grey made a spell with a hostile subterrestrial language that she learned from the teachings of Peronne Goguillon— You know, *whatever*. Doesn't matter right now. What matters is, is that the summoning circle you saw in Hailey's room?" she asked, pointing to the diagram on the page.

Tara nodded. "Yeah, I'm sure."

"Great, because change three words right there? Drawn at the right place on the right night, and she can open up a portal to hell and destroy the world as we know it. All she needs is enough blood and a place of power."

Baz asked, clearly dreading the answer, "How many is enough?"

"Five."

"But there have only been four sacrifices," Tara muttered, before she realized: "Unless *she's* the last sacrifice."

Baz gave a start. "What? No. *Why?*"

Tara replied, "She was summoned to avenge Hailey—destroying the town would fall under that. Besides, what's death to a witch who has already experienced it?"

Daphne agreed. "If I was going to bring hell to earth, I wouldn't want to stay for it. So, where's this place of power? It's gotta be a space big enough to draw a freakin' huge portal and also somewhere she has easy access—"

Baz and Tara exchanged a look before he said, "I mean, ain't it obvious? Good ole Hellborne A—"

They didn't see the deer until it crunched into the front of the van, and everything went dark.

CHAPTER FORTY
GHOSTS OF YOU

Tara came to when someone shook her shoulder.

She gasped, pushing herself to sit up. The world spun. In the distance, the light from the pyre turned the night orange. Glass and metal were scattered across the pavement. She blinked and tried to move, but everything hurt. The skin on her hands was almost ripped raw, and she felt a cut, open and bleeding, on her forehead. It stung when she touched it.

Crunched onto the front of the van was a stag, its antlers tangled in the windshield. Its beady eyes stared off into the distance, blood dripping from the fender onto the asphalt in soft ticks.

"Tara? Tara?" the person said, shaking her shoulder, the voice gradually growing louder. "Are you okay?"

It was Daphne. Her mouth was bloodied, a scrape across the right side of her face, but she didn't look much worse for wear.

"You're okay," Tara said in relief.

"Are you?"

"I . . . I think so."

"C'mon, let's get you up." Daphne helped her to her feet.

Tara held her side painfully. It ached. "Wh-where's Baz?"

"I don't know. He wasn't here when I woke up. I think he might've taken us out of the van, but then . . . I don't know where he went."

"He's going to go after Hailey," Tara replied. "He thinks he can still save her."

"He can't."

"Not alone," Tara replied.

Daphne grabbed her shoulders tightly. "Not at *all*! Tara, you can't still think she can be saved, can you? She killed *four people*."

"No, Hailey summoned *Adelaide*, who killed four—"

"Because of Hailey!"

Tara stood on her own. The pain in her side throbbed, but it wasn't anything unbearable. "I know," she replied, looking down at the asphalt, "but . . . there has be a way to save her. She made one mistake—and she asked for revenge. She didn't ask for their *deaths*. That was Adelaide."

Daphne opened her mouth. Closed it again. Looked away. "Then what do you suggest, cupcake?"

A flicker of hope ignited in Tara's chest. "I say we use the summoning circle to send Adelaide back, instead of bringing hell here."

"You can do that?"

"As you said, change two words and it's a different spell. We save Hailey, and you still complete your rite of passage."

Daphne thought about it for a moment, and then gave a nod. "Okay. But if things go south—"

"I know."

They looked back at the totaled van. Daphne said, "I guess we better start walking."

"Give me a moment." Closing her eyes, Tara listened to the night, quiet and creeping. There was a town—a world—to save. And even if it didn't like her in it, if it tried to pigeonhole her into a Tara Maclay that was soft and forgettable, she would still save it.

And prove them wrong.

"Please," she whispered, and waited. She didn't know what spell she was looking for; she wasn't sure what words to grab out of the ether to spin her needs to life.

She just stood in the road and pressed her call into the sky, her feelings into the world. The wind leafed through the trees. The sky broke wide, encrusted with eons of stars that shone from its every inch of every second of the universe, from its start until eternal end.

Daphne took her arm tightly. Squeezed it. "Oh my god."

Tara opened her eyes. The white mare stepped out of the dark line of firs. Her nostrils flared as she stomped her hoof against the road, impatiently. Like *Come on.*

Answering the call.

"Let's go," Tara said, moving toward the white mare. The horse came to meet her halfway, whinnying softly. She shook her mane. There were fall leaves caught in it that Tara picked away. Then she pulled herself up onto her back, and the horse shifted with the weight. She reached down to Daphne.

"I don't—I don't do horses," the hunter began. "I've been on a horse once and—"

"I won't let you fall off," Tara replied.

Daphne hesitated. Then she reached up. Their hands

intertwined, warm and familiar, and Tara pulled her up behind her. She took Daphne's arms and wrapped them around her waist.

"Hold on to me tightly," she advised, and Daphne nodded, pulling closer to Tara for safety.

Then Tara grabbed the reins and turned the white mare toward the school, pressing the horse forward. She started at a trot, then a prance, then a gallop, hooves beating against the pavement, sharp and sure against the wavering night. The rags of Tara's red dress billowed out behind her as Daphne held tight to her waist, and they raced through the darkness to save the world.

Together.

CHAPTER FORTY-ONE
DEVIL'S BARGAIN

Hailey stood at the front door to the Hellborne Academy, dwarfed by the massive arches and stone spirals rising behind her into the crystalline night sky, her spellbook in her arms. The moon was bright and full, flooding her face in silver, though her eyes were pitch black, veins spiderwebbing from her sockets like the branches of a tree. Her hand was outstretched to Baz as he writhed on the ground.

"Stop!" Tara cried to the witch, holding tight to the horse's mane. Daphne vaulted onto the ground, loading her crossbow, and leveled it at Hailey.

"N-no—please," Baz begged pathetically, his arm curled at a strange angle. His face was red with pain. "Don't hurt—don't hurt her."

"The hell I won't," the Red Witch spat. She laughed and eased off the spell. Baz broke free of it, gasping for breath. He was shivering, sweat clinging to his skin. "So, you managed to join us." She welcomed Tara and Daphne, extending her arms, palms facing up. There was a strange crackling red shimmer around the entire school. "Did you tell them how you wronged Hailey Conrad?" the witch asked, looking at Baz.

Tara slid off the horse. The mare nudged her on the shoulder, as if to tell her *Good luck*, or she was simply looking for a sugar cube. Either way, the witch hissed, and the horse pulled back with a startled neigh and darted away.

"He told us, yes," Tara replied calmly, "and we're sorry for what happened to Hailey—but this isn't right, and you know that—"

"Stop it, Tara," Baz interrupted, pushing himself up to his knees. He pulled his arms wide. "Use me instead," he begged. "Sacrifice me."

"What?" Daphne hissed.

"Baz, don't," Tara added, and just as they went to move beside him, red lighting struck between them and Baz, leaving a burnt spot on the cobblestones. She gritted her teeth. "Baz," she called, "this isn't how you fix things."

"Yeah, I think it might be," he replied, and gave her a sad look over his shoulder. "I could've stopped Brian and Chad from spreading those rumors. If I'd just—just stopped living so far up my own ass. I didn't think about any of it. I didn't care. I should've stopped Moss from threatening the others to keep quiet. I should've stopped Cory from covering all of it up. I should've . . ."

"But you *didn't*," the witch snarled. "I knew people like you when I was alive. People who just turned the other way. People who said it would be forgotten. People who chose *idleness* instead of integrity."

"But it isn't just *your* fault," Tara pointed out.

"No, but I should've done something. Because I . . ." He turned back to the witch, that horrid creature that possessed the body of his best friend, and said, "I love Hailey. I love her, and I let her down. We grew up together. She was my first friend. She stuck with me, and I—I wasn't there for her when she needed me. So, I'm—I'm here now. Take me instead. Take me and give Hailey back. She wouldn't want a portal opened. She wouldn't want that kind of revenge. This is good enough; I know it is. *Please*," he added, softer, more desperate. He forced himself to his feet and shuffled toward the witch atop the school steps. "I'm just as guilty—"

Suddenly, Daphne shot at Baz. The bolt scraped across his cheek. He whirled around to her, eyes wide, hand on his wound.

"What—"

"Look," Daphne snapped, reloading her crossbow, "don't be stupid. You might be guilty, but you can't just *die*, because if you do this entire *town* will die. And maybe even the world. Because you know this witch isn't just going to stop with you, right? So, like"—she popped another bolt into her crossbow and leveled it at him—"either suck it up and live with it, buttercup, or let me take you out if you're so intent on going."

He stared at her crossbow, hesitating to make his decision.

"What she means," Tara added, putting a hand on the tip of the crossbow to get Daphne to lower it, and she did after a moment, albeit reluctantly, "is that you dying isn't going to fix anything, and it won't bring Hailey back. Isn't that what you told me? That we should be able to make mistakes and try again?"

"But . . ." he said, his voice shaking. "Can't I do *anything*?"

"Afraid not," said the witch patiently from the top of the steps, looking more annoyed than angry now, "and while this has been a *delightful* revelation, I can't sacrifice you. You aren't human. So, Hailey—or at least this body—it will be." Then she pointed to the two stone mascots on either side of the great doors to the academy. "Athos, grant me soldiers of granite and stone, I beseech thee."

"Athos?" Daphne asked.

"Oh no," Tara replied.

The left stone lion gave a crack, and then another, before it moved its head. The lion on the right followed. They turned their stone gazes down to the three of them, ants in the eyes of the towering statues, and bared their stone teeth while the witch slipped inside the school.

Daphne fired her crossbow at the left statue, but the bolt plinked off the lion's shoulder. Barely even a chip. "Well, that's not good."

Tara shook her head. "Run."

Baz stood where he was, staring up at the moving lions as they stepped off their podiums and prowled toward him. He looked lost. Helpless. Ready to let the statues crush him.

She grabbed him by one arm, Daphne by the other, just as the two lions pounced. She pulled him toward the doors to the school. The statues landed exactly where the three of them had stood. They would've been pancakes. Maybe that had been Baz's new plan. But Tara had come this far without him dying; she wasn't *about* to have him die now.

If she was going to be disowned by her family, almost burned alive at the stake, called a *heathen* by her only cousin, and almost killed—twice already!—by the witch, she wasn't about to let Baz ruin the night by offering himself up as rock food.

She pulled open the heavy wooden doors and pushed Baz inside, Daphne closing it after them. The school was terrifying at night. The full moon cut through the darkness in blades of silver from the high windows. Shadows hugged the corners of the halls. The witch could be anywhere, but now—

The lions thudded against the door, cracking the wood.

"Let's go, let's go!" Daphne cried. "That's not going to hold!"

They rushed down the hall just as the stone lions burst through the front doors. Their claws scraped against the marble floor. The three of them turned left, and the sound of the lions followed them, thundering as they ran.

"We have to find the witch and stop her!" Daphne cried.

Tara replied, "She has to be somewhere with room enough to open a portal."

"The gym?"

Tara shook her head. "Not big enough."

"The library?" Baz supposed. "I mean, even with the books, it's the biggest space."

It was. And it was in the center of the school, too. If Tara was trying to open a portal from hell, that's where she would do it, too. "Okay, you two go there, and I'll try to distract those lions—"

"No way," Daphne snapped. "You'll get crushed and *die*. I'll—" As she was trying to load another bolt, even though the last one had done nothing, she tripped over her own feet. And landed face-first on the floor.

Her crossbow went skittering away from her, swallowed by the darkness.

Baz spun around. Decided, then. "I'll fight them. Go save Hailey—please. Please save her," he begged.

Daphne was shaking her head. Her nose was busted, stream-ing down her face, as she got to her feet again and wiped the blood away. "What are you doing? You can't fight those things!"

The stone beasts roared as they prowled around the corner of the hall. They sank their claws into the tiles, almost too large for the halls. They hunkered down, getting ready to pounce, like cats after a mouse.

"I'll be fine," he replied, shrugging out of his jacket. He handed it to Tara. "I won't die here. You're right. The best way to change things is to live to do it."

Tara hugged his jacket to her chest. "Baz . . ."

He winked. "I'll be fine, Maclay."

She wasn't sure if he would be, but she decided to trust him. Even though no matter what kind of demon he was, nothing could stand up to the force of those statues. They were two tons of granite in the shape of feral cats.

And she feared she'd regret this moment for the rest of her life.

Bastion Leto loosened his shoulders to ease his tension. "It's time to rock and roll, boys," he remarked, and pressed the palms of his hands against his forehead, combing his fingers through his hair. As he did, beautiful obsidian ram horns erupted from his forehead—the same ones she'd seen at his Halloween party—and curled into his brown hair. As his horns grew, his stance shifted and a long, thin black tail, tipped with a spade, flicked in delight. He cracked his knuckles, and when he grinned, his mouth looked too full—a jumble of pointed teeth. "Go—I've got these kittens."

Daphne, a bit afraid of Baz, quietly took Tara by the hand and pulled her down the hall toward the library. "Yeah, I think he's got this."

Tara glanced over her shoulder. She hoped Daphne was right. Could he really face those statues? Or was it simply a diversion? If he was only half incubus—what else was he? As the first statue pounced, Tara looked away because she couldn't watch. She didn't know a whole lot about demons, or a whole lot about herself, either.

But she definitely knew that whatever Baz was about to face was going to hurt.

CHAPTER FORTY-TWO
THE BEWITCHING HOUR

When Tara and Daphne pushed the door to the library open, they weren't sure what they were expecting.

Shelves had been knocked to the side, books scattered across the ground. A large ritual circle had already been drawn in chalk, crossed with lines, with Latin written around the outside. It looked exactly like the summoning circle Tara had seen in Hailey's bedroom, only on a massive scale; the chalk lines crackled with magic, shadows oozing out of them. The air felt loud and heavy—suffocating.

The witch stood in the middle of the circle, her arms outstretched, hands facing upward. She murmured softly, and with each repetition of the chant, another word in the gigantic circle glowed like fire, ash drifting up into the air, burning like stars. Her hair floated around her, as if she were submerged in a sea of darkness, and the Book of Blood levitated under her fingertips. She looked less and less like Hailey, and more like the portrait of the auburn-haired woman in the cottage at the museum.

"Daphne," Tara said, "keep her occupied?"

"For you to do what?"

It was too much to explain. "Trust me?"

Daphne hesitated. Then cursed. *"Fine."* She loaded a bolt into her crossbow. "Hey, *witch!*"

Adelaide Grey didn't pay any attention to them.

Daphne fired her crossbow.

The bolt slammed into the witch's shoulder, jolting her out of her chant. Stumbling back, she turned her red eyes to Daphne. "Meddling fool," she spat, grabbing the bolt and wrenching it out of her shoulder. Blood dripped out of the wound, but it didn't faze her.

"Come get me, you old hag!" Daphne taunted, going to load another bolt, when a book slammed into the side of her head. She went stumbling sideways, dropping her crossbow.

Then the witch appeared in front of her. "I think I won, witch hunter. *Animam agere.*"

Nothing happened.

She frowned.

"Animam agere," she ordered again, and then turned her suspicious gaze to Daphne, who was taking a stone out of her pocket. A charm.

"Surprise, *bitch*," Daphne sneered, tossing up her charm to dispel magic, catching it in her hand. Then she made a fist and slammed her knuckles into the side of Hailey's cheek. "Witch hunters have tricks, too."

Keep her occupied, Tara silently begged as she dragged herself to a point in the ritual circle. She scrubbed out the Latin chalk mark silently and wrote a new one in her own blood. There was enough of it to leave a smear as she went.

"You're no better than those men I brought to justice," the witch snapped. "You're just like them!"

"I absolutely am *not*," Daphne replied, offended, and slammed her fist into Hailey's face again. Blood ran out of Hailey's nose. "And even if I was, you had *no right* to kill them!"

"They were evil," the witch snarled, and with a pulse of kinetic energy, pushed Daphne back.

Daphne pinwheeled her arms to keep her balance and righted herself. "Yeah," she replied, "I didn't know them very well. Couldn't tell ya."

"Then why do you *care*? Do you think they could have changed?" Adelaide Grey laughed. "In two hundred years, nothing has! I left this world in fire and pain, witch hunter."

"Well, we don't want you back," Daphne replied, grabbing a dagger from her boot. She twirled and tried to strike the witch from the back, but the dagger stopped in midair—and then an invisible force flung Daphne backward.

She spun back and landed on her feet.

The witch cried, "As if I wanted that! But then that girl brought me back—and you know what I found? The same world I left behind. Hailey Conrad asked for vengeance against her ex-boyfriend. So I gave it to her—and I decided not to stop there. Those *men* deserved every nightmare that led to their execution."

Dragging herself to the next sigil, Tara erased the chalk mark and wrote down another word in Latin. She knew this circle. She'd ingrained it into her memory the moment she saw it on Hailey's bedroom floor.

If it could bring a spirit back from hell, then perhaps it could bring back Hailey, too.

"That's not the *point*," Daphne snapped. "The point is that *you* don't get to decide if they live or die! That's not how this works! You can't go—go dispensing *justice* according to your own feelings."

Was she talking about the witch, or perhaps herself? Tara paused, her fingers dripping with her blood at the end of the finished word, listening.

The witch laughed. It was high and shrill. "Ooh, is this about your little witch friend? The one you really like? Don't be bashful—everyone can tell!"

Daphne stood her ground. "Maybe a little, yeah," she replied quickly. "And maybe I was wrong, you know? About a little of it."

"But what if she turns dark? Hurts your family?" the witch went on. She hadn't left the ritual circle. The moment she did, the summoning and all the energy she'd already put into the lines would crumble. "If she does unspeakable things?"

"Like you?" Daphne quipped. "I don't know, I think Cupcake's a little sweeter—"

Suddenly, the north door—well, the entire wall—crumbled inward as Baz was thrown through the wall. He tumbled to a stop a few feet from the ritual circle and didn't move. The two lion statues prowled in through the gaping hole after him, seemingly as pleased with themselves as stone lions could. They looked terrible, though. One had its ears ripped clean off; another had large gouges in the side of its belly where Baz's horns had raked it deep. They were both also missing some parts of their extremities, but Baz was the one lying prone on the floor, scraped and bruised and bloodied.

Was he breathing? Tara couldn't tell, and she was too far to sense his aura. *Please be alive*, she thought, rubbing away the old incantation and wiping her fingers across the cut on her arm for the last word.

"Ah," said the witch, turning to her pets, "perfect timing. Take care of her, too." She pointed at Daphne.

Tara didn't have time to react. To throw up a shield for her. To even shout her name. She simply looked up, and Daphne met her gaze—then one of the stone lions grabbed her by the legs and slung her through the west entrance doors, and happily went to play fetch.

"*NO!*" The scream tore out of Tara's throat.

But Daphne didn't come back. And neither did the lions.

The witch turned her hate-filled gaze to Tara. Found her in an instant. Magic prickled from her eyes, from her mouth, like lightning. The witch bubbled with power, like a champagne bottle about to explode.

"Finally," the witch whispered, but her voice traveled across the library like a shout, "the last one left."

Tara clenched her fists, trying to wrest control of her motions. Her entire body quivered. She wasn't sure she could do the rest by herself. But she had to. Baz was motionless on the ground, and Daphne was—she was . . .

Tara gritted her teeth and told the witch, "You d-don't have to do this."

"I do, but *you* didn't have to. You could have been a good girl, like your father asked, but you are here. How curious." The witch made a motion with her hand, and a dozen books lifted themselves off the ground and began to swirl around her. She circled Tara like a predator, books churning around them as if they were in the eye of a tornado. "Sweet thing, no one will ever understand us. They want to destroy us—no matter how much you think they love you. They'll never accept you. *She* will never accept you."

No, Daphne probably wouldn't.

Tara had built Daphne a girlfriend who didn't exist. But it was because Tara had *lied*. Because she hadn't been authentic— because she had been scared and thought she knew how Daphne would react before she ever gave her the chance. Maybe if she had, things would have been different, if she'd held tight to what her mother had taught her.

About herself, and about magic. The best days of her life, in those quiet golden afternoons weaving charms and soft spells, her veins thrumming with good magic.

If she had shown Daphne that magic, that golden, light, beautiful magic, instead of this dark, heady storm, maybe then Daphne would have accepted her.

"I see a lot of myself in you. The way I once was," the witch went on, "before people began to fear what I did. Cure their boils, make their cows heavy with milk—seduce their husbands"—she added the last part sharply—"or so their husbands told them. I couldn't just be a *witch*. I had to be theirs—or I had to be evil. I had to be wrong. If I was not with them, I was nothing."

"I'm sorry that happened to you," Tara replied. "I'm sorry that they killed you. I'm sorry you experienced that. But—but this *isn't* the way. If you open this portal, if you summon these demons—"

"Why would I care? This girl, this *Hailey*," she added, pressing her hand to her chest, as if Hailey was still there, somewhere, still watching, "pleaded with me to take her pain away. To do the things that she was too nice and too good to do. To be a master of her own life for once. So I will. I am not nice. I am not good. Those traits were burned out of me hundreds of years ago. Now I use magic for what it was intended for—to *hurt*. To hone to a point. To injure."

But she was wrong.

Magic wasn't built on selfishness, and neither was Tara. It wasn't what her mother loved about magic. Her mother loved the life in it, the light.

"There is good in who we are, sweetheart," her mother had said. She had been in the hospital at that point, too weak to stand, but Tara remembered the way her hands were cold and frail but gripped hers strongly. "Tara, there is good and there is light and there is love in who we are."

Love.

And even without her mother's spellbook, she still had her memory. Something no one could ever take away.

"I wasn't sure, really, whether I should've killed you when you first began to meddle . . ." the witch mused, curling her fingers into the air, as if to grab on to it and split it wide with the last sacrifice. Tara. "But I decided to keep you around. After all, if your father thought you were useful enough to keep around, then I should, too."

"Leave him out of this."

"Would you rather me talk about your mother? She's doing great in hell, by the way. She burns every day, for eternity."

Tara's throat constricted. "Liar."

"Am I? She is a demon, isn't she? Just like you. Say hello to her in hell!"

Then Adelaide gathered the energy in her hands, to bring

the ritual to life, she tugged at air. She tried again, but the air stagnated like a spell gone awry.

"What?" Confused, Adelaide finally looked at her ritual circle. Her artfully crafted lines, her written incantations. They were altered, replaced by bloodied words smeared across the stone tiles. Enraged, the witch turned her red gaze back to Tara. "What the hell did you *do?*"

"Can't read curse-ive?" Tara retorted. "Let me help you. I made it myself."

Then, with purpose, she stepped on one of the ritual lines. A flurry of white burst from the line, igniting it, traveling across the rest of the circle like flaming gasoline. The witch watched in horror. She tried to step out of the middle but found that she couldn't. There was an invisible barrier.

She was trapped.

"No!" she cried, slamming her fist against the wall.

Tara smiled at her, raising her hands, presenting her palms to the sky and stars and heavens above. "I am no one's sacrifice," she said.

And activated her spell.

She wasn't looking to reverse what had been done. Whatever Hailey had gone through would change her forever.

That was irreparable.

Tara simply wanted another exchange—but without invoking the dark matter that lurked behind the curtain.

And she knew that only powerful witches made their own spells.

So, this was one of hers.

She accepted the light from the stars, the rays from the heavens, the soft twists of life that pulsed in the air. She gathered it, asking for the power from the world around her in gentle, pleading thoughts.

Let me, and I won't dabble.

Help me, and I will pay the price.

Even though she didn't know what the price was. Even though she wouldn't for years to come.

And the wonder of the world accepted it.

Light and hope and good pulsed through her fingertips, golden and bright. Magic her mother hummed in the garden. Golden afternoons with sunlight laced through her hair. Moments of happiness and heart. Moments there—then gone.

But never forgotten.

"Why am I *Tara*?" she had asked her mom once, long, long ago. "I hate Tara. Everyone says *Tah-ra*. I hate it."

"I love your name," her mother had replied, folding her into a hug. "Terra Mater is an Ancient Roman goddess of the earth, of flowers and fruits and trees. It's a good name. I hope someday, you will bloom with it."

"So, I'll be a flower?"

"If you want to be, but you're perfect the way you are— and I couldn't do this if you were a flower!" her mother cried and grabbed her sides and tickled her until she screamed for her to stop, and Tara remembered how they used to laugh and laugh, and how her mother always kissed her forehead goodnight, and told her she loved her.

Magic bloomed over blood-drenched fingers.

The spell spilled from her lips, loud and bright.

And it sounded like the first spell her mother gave her, a spell in no spellbook, on no page, in no one's knowledge.

The spell of her name.

Adelaide Grey screamed. She slammed her hands on the invisible barrier and begged for Tara to stop, but Tara couldn't hear her over the rush of magic. Or maybe it was because the witch's voice grew distant. Adelaide slid down to her knees, and then sat back, as if she was being pulled to the ground. And around her a tree grew up from beneath the marble floor, tall and gnarled and winding, pulling the witch out one thread at a time until an old and twisted oak cast a shadow over the body of Hailey Conrad, its limbs looking like a woman reaching toward the night sky.

As the last line of the incantation left her lips, Tara gasped for breath. The spell burst apart in glitters of starlight and left them in the dark, ruined library of Hellborne Academy, moonlight turning red and blue and green through the stained-glass windows.

In the middle of the circle, under the boughs of bloodred leaves, Hailey slept curled up on the ground.

And the witch was gone.

CHAPTER FORTY-THREE
DEATH OF A WITCH

Tara's knees gave out.

"Whoa!" Daphne caught her and looped her arm around her shoulder, holding her so tightly Tara couldn't have been imagining it. There was dirt caked on her face, and plaster stuck in her hair, but she was here. Alive. They sank to the ground together, fingers laced so tightly they'd be hard to pry apart.

"You're alive," Daphne said breathlessly.

"So are you," Tara replied, tears brimming in her eyes, and suddenly she leaned forward and they pressed their foreheads together.

In relief.

In happiness.

In safekeeping.

"I saw what you did," Daphne said, drinking in Tara's face, her matted hair, her bloodied lip, "and it was . . ." She glanced at the towering tree of crimson leaves, and then back to her with an awed look. "Tara, you were beautiful. It was beautiful. But how did you . . . ? Was that in one of the books you read?"

Tara laughed. "No, it was one of mine. I couldn't think of any spells on the spot, so I just . . . I made one myself. I didn't think I could or that I was strong enough, but I wanted to try."

"And the witch . . . ?"

"Trapped. Forever now." Then Tara said, "I'm glad you're alive. I'm sorry I lied. I was just afraid. . . ."

Daphne cupped her face and brought herself closer, because Tara was too tired to move. "I know," Daphne whispered.

And kissed her then, on the mouth, soft and hopeful and sweet. Their cut lips stung and their mouths tasted like iron, but it was so nice to be there and be alive, feeling each other's heartbeats underneath their fingertips. They were *alive*. Something neither of them figured they would be when they set foot in the high school. Tara wanted to cry. Maybe she was crying. Her skin still tingled from the magic, her heart flipping from the exertion—or was it the way Daphne nibbled at her lip? Pulling her hand through her hair?

Perhaps it was both. She wasn't going to complai—

Suddenly, Baz gave a jolt, gasping. Daphne and Tara shrieked, breaking apart, and turned toward their dead friend. Who wasn't dead. He rolled over with a cough, lying on his side. "Ooooh," he groaned, hoarse, "I feel like *shit*."

"*Baz!*" they cried.

"How?" Daphne asked.

"Why?" added Tara. "You were . . ."

He winced, pushing himself to sit up. "C'mon, New Girl, you know true love can do anything." Gingerly, he touched one of his horns and winced. His clothes were pretty much ruined, and he examined his rags before giving a long sigh. "Except save my favorite shirt. Damn. Wait—is that . . . ?" He quickly pushed himself to sit up, hope flickering across his bruised and bloodied face, and stumbled to his feet toward her. *"Hailey!"*

"Hailey," Tara confirmed in relief, and Daphne squeezed her hand tightly.

Gingerly, Baz pulled Hailey onto his lap. He ran his thumb across her cheek. "Hailey," he whispered. "Hey, Leelee? Wake up?" The moonlight reflected off his horns like oil on water. He looked more vulnerable than Tara had ever seen him, hopeful and afraid and—and relieved when Hailey began to stir.

Her eyelids fluttered open. "B-Bastion . . . ?" she whispered. Then she jerked upright, darting her gaze around. "Is this— Am I still . . . ? Is this . . . ?"

"You're back," he soothed, "you're okay—"

"But your horns—you're—you're one of *them*." She scrambled away from him, and Tara's heart fell. "You're a—"

"They're me," he interrupted softly. "I . . . I'm sorry. I'm sorry about everything. I'm sorry I wasn't there. I'm sorry. . . . I never wanted you to see me like this. With *these*." He motioned to his horns. "I know they're scary. I'm sorry, I'm sorry." He kept repeating it, staring at the ground, as if it would help things— sorry for his horns, sorry for his tail, sorry for his teeth, his claws. Sorry that he wasn't there, that he'd abandoned their friendship, sorry that he never told her, that he didn't know *how* to tell her. Sorry that he was a monster—

And that was when Hailey reached up and touched his horns.

His words caught in his throat.

"They're nice," she whispered, and he turned his gaze back

to her, tears in his eyes. Then she fell into his arms, and he hugged her tightly, resting his chin on the top of her head.

"You're okay," he muttered, holding her as though it was still the end of the world. "You're all right. I'll never leave your side."

Daphne curled her fingers through Tara's as dawn bled into the library, turning the ruined books and overturned shelves orange and pink. The lighter the morning grew, the worse the library looked. It was utterly ruined.

Daphne and Tara watched Baz cradle Hailey for a while longer as she whispered about where she'd been, about fire and demons and nightmares, her gaze a thousand miles away. Something that broke her, that would take a very long time to fix. But at least Hailey was *alive*, and present.

The Book of Blood lay facedown on the smeared ritual circle. Daphne picked it up and leafed through the pages. "I guess I'll never have what it takes," she muttered to Tara, who gave her a strange look. "This was my test, and I failed it. Even if I get another chance . . ."

"You'll have to kill a witch."

"An evil witch," Daphne clarified, but the longer she thought about it, the more lost she looked. She closed the book. "It's— it's what I do. It's what my family does. What we have to do."

Tara took her by the hand, rubbing her thumb over Daphne's. "It doesn't have to be."

"But then what else is there?"

Tara raised her free hand and waved it in front of Daphne's face, humming softly, just like Daphne had what felt like years ago. "I . . . see everything. There is everything."

"Everything," Daphne echoed, and kissed her again in the quiet library where anger once pulsed, dissipating away to light.

Tara wasn't all that sure if magic was only good or only bad. She felt a little bit of both sometimes because she was only human. But in that instant, she was filled with light and love, and for the moment, everything was okay.

"What happened to the, um, lions?" Tara asked.

"Oh, I locked them in the gym. Though I'm *guessing* they're statues again. . . . That's going to be hard to explain."

"And the rest of this isn't?"

Daphne looked at the spellbook, then at the ritual circle and the downed bookshelves, and the blood smeared on the floor, and the blooming tree. "We should probably get out of here before the police come."

"I feel like I've heard that before," Tara teased, and tried to get to her feet, but she needed Daphne's help. The world spun. She'd spent so much energy on the ritual, she had no energy left. Baz picked Hailey up, and she clung to him like he was her last lifeline.

As they left, hobbling as fast as they could, Daphne said, "I never told you I thought you looked really sexy in that dress."

"Is red my color?"

"It'd be better coated in the blood of our enemies."

Tara laughed. "Of course it would."

CHAPTER FORTY-FOUR
UNTIL NEXT TIME

Hellborne Academy didn't open for the next week as the community scrambled to cope with the aftermath of Halloween.

When the pyre went up in flames, it burned down half of Main Street. No one was hurt, and what was curiouser was that no one remembered it burning until they came to around midnight and half the street was on fire. Somehow, only the bookstore remained unscathed.

As for the school itself, Principal Greaves said there had been a freak tornado in the area, but no one believed that. They weren't sure what to believe, really. All they knew was that when the police arrived, there was just the white mare that had escaped from the school barn, Q, nibbling on a copy of *The Crucible* in the library.

But by the time school *did* open again, Daphne's house was packed up, her entire life squeezed into cardboard boxes. Tara sat on Daphne's bed as she finished cleaning off her desk. The moving truck was outside, and almost everything had been loaded away. Then the movers took away Daphne's last box of desk items and the bed Tara was sitting on and left them in the empty room. Daphne's family were outside bickering over who would drive first and who'd ride shotgun.

"So . . ." Tara hesitated. "You . . . never told them?"

Daphne shrugged, watching her brothers rock-paper-scissors for the front seat. "I told them I was knocked out for most of it, and when I came to, it was all over."

"And they believed you?"

Daphne barked a laugh. "Absolutely not. But they're not prying. They figured I'll tell them when I'm ready." She crossed her arms over her chest. "How about your family? The whole Beth thing . . ."

Tara hesitated. "I . . . am grounded for the rest of forever. I'm currently on a 'grocery shopping trip,'" she added with air quotes.

Daphne's eyebrows shot up, and she gave a low whistle. "Cupcake, you lied for me?"

"I couldn't miss saying good-bye." Besides, she wasn't quite sure if she'd ever see Daphne again. Tara made sure to stay on her best behavior, and she cooked dinner for them every evening and she said *Yes, sir* and *No, sir*, and she kept her eyes trained on the ground.

And quietly, while no one was looking, she researched colleges that could take her far away from Hellborne, Vermont. She might not have wanted the Red Witch scholarship, but she had it now, and it opened up a lot more doors for her.

"Daphne! You got some friends here!" Fred shouted from the front yard.

They gave each other the same puzzled look. "Friends?" Daphne asked, perplexed.

Tara shrugged. "Maybe you're more popular than you thought."

"I doubt that." Daphne started to leave the room, but then paused, as if something was missing, and reached back to Tara, who accepted her hand for the last time. Tara committed the feeling to memory, their fingers together.

She still wasn't sure what love was. She wasn't sure if this was it, but perhaps this was a kind of love. The soft kind that lingered, that changed you for the rest of your life, that left echoes, like the refrain of a song you almost remember.

When they walked outside and closed the door for the last time, Daphne's parents decided to take the moving truck while her brothers fought for the rental van keys. The afternoon was crisp and golden, perfect for heavy coats and warm cocoa. Winter was on the tip of autumn's tongue, and the smell of old leaves and coming snow seared into Tara's memory like a brand. She wanted to capture this moment like a photo.

Maybe she'd revisit it in her dreams.

On the sidewalk, waiting for them, was Baz in his signature letterman jacket, looking as fresh and peppy as he always had, though there was a cut on his cheek that was still healing. He looked worlds better than either Tara or Daphne, with their bruises and bandages. Demons and their unnatural healing. Beside him was Hailey. She'd cut her hair a bit shorter, ear-length now, because the ends had been singed in the ritual spell, but her clothes were as immaculate as ever, a dark button-down and a plain denim skirt with black tights and sensible black flats.

She held out a gift bag as Tara and Daphne came to greet them. "It's sad to see you go," Hailey began. Her voice was a lot softer than the witch's and tinged with a Canadian drawl. It had surprised Tara, when she first heard her last week, how *anyone* could think that the witch had been Hailey, even if they wore the same skinsuit. "Admittedly, I don't really know either of you, but you saved me anyway. Bastion told me everything that happened. So, I just wanted to say . . . thank you."

Daphne took the gift and peeked inside. "Yeah, you're welcome, as long as you don't go meddling in—you know—the occult again."

"*Daphne,*" Tara hissed.

"What? It's true. I don't want to have to come back and find you having—I don't know—summoned Baphomet or some shit."

Baz gave a soft laugh. "She's like that," he said to Hailey.

But Hailey only smiled. It didn't reach her eyes. "I won't. But what happened to the spellbook?"

Daphne said, "We sent it to a family friend in Sunnydale, California, who has a very expansive library. He'll keep it in case someone in the future needs a spell to open hell or something."

"Oh." Hailey sighed, though Tara couldn't tell whether it was in relief or disappointment.

"It'll suck at school without you, Icy Hot," Baz went on happier. "I mean, once we *get* back to school. The principal said this week, but there's still a wall missing in the library. At least football's still on!"

"Yeah, so you all can keep losing," Daphne remarked.

"I don't play football to win; I play to look hot in spandex pants. They don't call me a tight end for nothing."

Hailey said, "I thought you were a tight end because you couldn't catch or throw a ball?"

"Shhh," he replied, placing a finger over her mouth, and she laughed, batting his hand away. They grinned at each other.

"Baz, so you're an incubus?" Daphne asked, earning an elbow in the side from Tara. "Ow! What? It's been bugging me and I've never seen him, you know, do *incubus* things."

"Well, that's because I'm asexual."

"*Huh.* An asexual incubus. That's a twist."

"Not everyone is who you think they are, Icy Hot," he nobly replied with a wink. Then he nudged his chin toward the moving truck behind them and said, "I think your dad's signaling us to wrap it up. Take care, okay?" He held up a hand, and Daphne high-fived it.

"Absolutely. You too? And I mean it—no occult business that gets on the news or whatever, okay?" she added, making an *I'm watching you* motion with her hands to Hailey, who simply smiled and gave an innocent shrug.

"I'll see you at school, Tara," Hailey added. "You'll sit with us, right?"

"I'd like that," Tara replied, and this time she was sure she would. She and Daphne waved as Baz and Hailey left for his Mustang and pulled off onto the road. Maybe Hailey would dabble in magic again, maybe she wouldn't, but at least Tara would be there to make sure she kept on the light path. And it'd be a little refreshing, honestly, to have someone to practice magic with. She didn't know Hailey—the entire time Tara had known her, she'd been possessed by Adelaide Grey—but that was half the fun in making friends.

And any friend of Baz's was a friend of hers.

Or maybe if Hailey didn't want to practice anymore, then Tara would find someone else. Someone who understood the ebb and flow of magic, who wanted to learn, to absorb the knowledge and still desired more. Like Tara did. When she first came to Hellborne, she wasn't sure whether her magic was good or bad, but now she knew that wasn't really the question she should have been asking herself.

The question that she needed to ask was a lot harder—

What will you do with it?

And while Tara didn't know, she wasn't going to hide anymore. Even if her father didn't like it. Even if he called her wicked and terrible. She knew she wasn't, and his words—while they always stung—were just that.

They only held the power that she gave them.

When the Mustang was gone, Daphne turned back to her and pulled a piece of paper out of her back pocket. "Before I forget, it's my email," she explained. "It's the same for AIM, too."

"Oh. I guess I'll have to make one," Tara replied. "My brother just got a computer, but I don't think I'll be able to use it."

"Life finds a way," Daphne replied with a wink, and then she asked—a little hesitantly, "What are you thinking about for college?"

"I don't think my dad will . . ." But then she stopped herself. Frowned. Her life wasn't her father's to control, and after this year, she would be done with high school and free to do whatever she wanted. And that included college. Travel. Everything her mother hadn't been able to do. She had a scholarship to spend, anyway. "I've been looking at a few colleges, but I haven't decided yet."

"Really? Maybe I'll see you at UC Sunnydale," Daphne said. "Heard there's a lot of weird shit going on there. Lots of demons and witches and vampires. Maybe I'll get into the vamp-hunting business instead. Really raise the stakes."

"Sunnydale? Maybe I'll look into it, too."

"Could you imagine us at college together?"

"I can," Tara replied. Truth be told, she didn't want Daphne to go. "I wish you could stay. I was happy for a minute."

Daphne wiggled her fingers over Tara's face and hummed in that soft, soothing way of hers. "There. So you can be happy forever."

Tara snorted. "You know, if you keep doing that to people, they'll start to think you're a witch."

"That might not be so bad," Daphne replied. "I know a good one."

"She's not that good."

"I think she underestimates herself a lot, but she's very good, and she's bold, and she's surprising, and has a great laugh," Daphne replied, and squeezed Tara's hand tightly. "You'll be happy again, Tara Maclay. I know it."

Then Daphne kissed her on the cheek, a kiss good-bye, a kiss to go, and climbed into the back of the van and closed the door. Tara pulled her cardigan around herself to fight off the biting chill of autumn as the van pulled away and the moving truck followed.

Daphne stuck her head out of the passenger window and

waved good-bye. She shouted something, but she was already so far away that Tara couldn't hear it. She waved anyway, and found that she was smiling, because for the first time in her life—

She believed it.

That someday, far from the autumn cold of Hellborne, she would be happy.

If only for a little while.

THE END

ACKNOWLEDGMENTS

To say it's an honor to be able to contribute to Tara Maclay's canon is an understatement—I'm over the moon. *Buffy the Vampire Slayer* was the first place outside of fanfiction where I saw myself reflected, and it left a lasting impression.

I like the idea that we, as fans, can take a story and turn it into something new. Something that reflects us, the viewers. Us, the fandom. Us, the queer community who watched *Buffy* and saw a little bit of ourselves in Tara and Willow.

And (spoiler!) while Tara's story ends tragically (Of course it does, the LGBTQIA+ community in the early '00s couldn't have nice things. Sometimes we still can't.), I think it's important to note that it doesn't have to anymore. That future stories we create, stories that we give to others to find themselves in (like I found myself in *Buffy*), can have happy endings. That happy endings don't take away from a story—don't diminish the gravity of the characters' fight. Happy endings are yawps into the void screaming, "We deserve this, too."

Tara does not get a happy ending in the TV show, and that I can't change, but . . . death has never been the end in the Buffyverse, and I'd like to think that there's a fanfiction out there just waiting for you to find it.

I'd like to thank my agent, Holly Root, and my fantastic editors on this project—Brittany Rubiano, Cassidy Leyendecker, and Elanna Heda—for this amazing experience, as well as my copyediting team, Guy Cunningham, Jacqueline Hornberger, Meredith Jones, and Jenny Langsam; managing editor, Sara Liebling; and everyone else who has worked on this project: Matt Schweitzer, Holly Nagel, Danielle DiMartino, Scott Sosebee, Ian Byrne, Maureen Graham, Dina Sherman, Maddie Hughes, Bekka Mills, Crystal McCoy, Ann Day, Julie Leung, Monique Diman, Michael Freeman, Loren Godfrey, Kim Knueppel, Vicki Korlishin, Meredith Lisbin, Samantha Voorhees, Amanda Schlesier, Mili Nguyen, Lia Murphy, Phil Buchanan, Sam Shechter, Marybeth Tregarthen, Anne Peters, Chip Poakeart, Jerry Gonzalez, Jeremy Burton, Troy Wallace, and Rob Celauro.

It takes a village to raise a book. Thank you for being a part of this one.